MOGHUL BUFFET

MOGHUL BUFFET

CHERYL BENARD

FARRAR · STRAUS · GIROUX

NEW YORK

Farrar, Straus and Giroux
19 Union Square West, New York 10003

Distributed in Canada by Douglas & McIntyre Ltd.
Printed in the United States of America
Designed by Peter Buchanan-Smith
First edition, 1998

Library of Congress Cataloging-in-Publication Data
Benard, Cheryl, 1953–
    Moghul buffet / Cheryl Benard. — 1st ed.
        p.   cm.
    ISBN 0-374-21179-5 (alk. paper)
    I. Title.
    PS3552.E5363M64   1998
    813'.54—dc21   97-49954

ACKNOWLEDGMENTS

I would like to thank my editor, Elisabeth Kallick Dyssegaard, whose sense of humor, calm aura, and steady nerves make her wonderful to work with;

my agent, Joe Regal, who went beyond the call of duty and put an enormous amount of thought, heart, and effort into this book;

my brother, Charles Etienne, for providing amusing insights into contemporary life, and of course for fixing my computer, solving all my problems, and always liking everything I write,

my friend Lala Rukh, who is the real and better Lilly and an artist in Lahore, for showing me how to love Pakistan in spite of it all;

my mother, Charlotte, for all those good stories she told and all those great books she read to me, and for being the best kind of critic—harsh, relentless, loyal;

and of course Zal, Alex, and Max, my thorny companions on the road of life, my heart, my soul, my perfect men.

MOGHUL BUFFET

INTRODUCTION

August. We are in the Khyber Inter-Continental Hotel, on the perimeter of Peshawar. The downstairs dining room is serving its Moghul Buffet, all-you-can-eat of a variety of Oriental kebabs and curries and silver-sprinkled sugary desserts presented in huge copper vats, but on the third floor room-service waiter Yussuf is awaiting the nightly order from Room 307. A hamburger, and french fries, every night without fail. Lounging near the telephone in his cubbyhole off the hallway, Yussuf hears a noise and turns to see a woman in a green pleated chador rushing around the corner and down the staircase. This is unusual; the female guests of this establishment are, on frequent and delightful occasions, seen wearing bathing suits on their way down to the hotel swimming pool, but very rarely are they to be found wrapped in chadors. Yussuf concludes that it was the relative of one of the hotel staff and forgets all about it to ponder, once more, what has disrupted the predictable American in 307.

Won't he starve to death without his nightly hamburger fix, Yussuf irreverently wonders.

Later, he will regret the sentiment. The big, friendly American will not be calling him tonight or any other night. He is gone, nothing left of him but a cryptic message smeared in blood on an ice machine. Boring, nondescript Malone is about to become a headache for state-to-state relations, a three-minute report on the Maryland news, a pain in the neck for Detective Iqbal —and a story for me to tell you.

The events I will recount took place in Peshawar, an unpleasant border town in the most troubled part of the troubled country of Pakistan. Unpleasant but, for those of us who do not have to live there, scenic, too, and utterly unique. There is absolutely no other place on this planet quite like Peshawar. There is something extraterrestrial about Peshawar, something disorienting, but that may just be the effect of the adrenaline that courses through you here, as your body and your reflexes yell at you to look out, to stay alert—indeed, if you have very intelligent reflexes, they will probably be telling you to leave, right this minute. Peshawar is like no other place, like no other time either. Just a short walk down the street will hurl you between the centuries like a time-machine roller coaster. Peshawar—but no. I'm not doing it justice. I want you to be able to picture it, to really see it in front of you, and for that we have to back up. We have to go out a few miles, into the drab, dusty plains around it, so that we will first realize where it is: in the middle of nothing. Suspended in a yellow haze of dust and cheap gasoline, the city hangs between desert and mountains, between God-fearing ascetics and lawless warlords. Genghis Khan would feel at home here. So would Karl Marx.

But I'm getting ahead of myself. At the moment, we are still a few miles outside of Peshawar. Let's approach it slowly. Let's say it's dusk, let's say we're driving. There is nothing to be seen yet but a dusty, barren plain, cut now and then by a ridge of rock or the slice of a river.

Let's have some music; perhaps a ghazal sung by Malika Pukhraj. *Ghazal*, which is a type of ballad, literally means "gazelle." This type of song is supposed to be sad, more than sad; it is supposed to capture the poignant sadness of the instant when the gazelle, trapped by the hunter, knows the imminence of its death and the hunter, paralyzed by the beauty of the gazelle, knows that his paralysis will lift and he will kill it, anyway. The ghazal is a song about that frozen second in time when their eyes lock. Crippled by terror, the gazelle cannot flee; moved by its grace, the hunter cannot shoot. They are caught in each other's gaze, but they both know that this will last for only a moment; at its conclusion, remorselessness will take grace and turn it into carrion. The development of the ghazal genre is based on the premise that this fateful moment is the perfect analogy for love. Which tells us one thing straight off: this is not a country of incurable romantics. A good ghazal can make you feel wonderfully melancholy. There is often some confusion of gender in these songs, which makes them peculiarly appropriate to our story. But no one is misled. No matter what the voice or the text may imply, the audience knows perfectly well that it is always the woman who stands for the gazelle, the man who is the hunter.

As we linger over the barren landscape of this border province, we can let Malika Pukhraj sing about unrequited love, her voice as bleak and beautiful as the horizon. She will have to sing quickly, though; already other, more mundane noises are threatening to drown her out. Shouts and curses, screeching tires, horns honking incessantly under aggressive fists and elbows. Our drab little side road is merging into a narrow, busy highway. On this road, processions of apparently lunatic drivers are piloting their vehicles at breakneck speeds through the desert. And the vehicles are no less astounding than their masters. Vans painted in neon colors with garish fantasy scenes, buses strung top to bottom with green and red blinking Christmas-tree lights zoom through the night, hurtling maniacally toward Peshawar. The roadside is seamed with the upturned remains of those who will never arrive at their destination, but they are no warning to others. Passing on hairpin curves, screeching into the sand to the right and left of the road: this is the panache with which you are expected to approach the city of Peshawar.

Poor Malika Pukhraj, gently wailing the story of her betrayal into the settling darkness; this is no place for gazelles, this is the home of the hunters.

1

The West-Fab prefabricated housing company is located in Langley, Virginia. Micky Malone lives in Bethesda, Maryland, which makes it a tolerable commute. On his vacations, Micky visits friends in Cape Cod; sometimes he goes fishing in Florida, and one summer he went to Hawaii. But on the whole, Micky hates to travel. Joshua was supposed to go to Pakistan, that first time, but at the very last minute he crashed his car into a truck stalled on the off ramp of the Beltway and ended up with his neck in a brace. And that left Micky, the only other person familiar with all the paperwork on the Pakistan deal. Since he had gone there the first time, it only made sense for him to follow up and go on the second trip, too, although he tried his best to dispute that logic. "Come on, Micky, you did a great job there," his boss said. "And the cannibals didn't eat you, did they?" "Yeah, yeah," Micky said, bowing to the inevitable. "But after this, don't even ask me again. This is positively my last trip."

But actually, as he will admit only to himself, it hadn't been that bad. Islamabad was fairly clean, a nice hotel, and they asked you which menu you wanted and then brought you one with familiar things on it, none of that exotic stuff. Most of the meetings were in the hotel, and aside from the fancy dressed-like-a-dervish doorman, everybody looked normal, business suits, neckties, English spoken and spoken very well. So Peshawar, he guesses, will be more of the same. He knows just about everybody he'll be dealing with, by now, and that helps, too. In Peshawar, it'll be that Walid Khan fellow, who's no backwoods wild man. Quite a man of the world, in fact, a little sleazy with his fancy suits and his British accent, a little scary with that smile that says "I know all about you and I can buy you and have plenty left over," but heck, it's only three days. Have a look at the warehouse, clear up a few points, and that's that.

Poor Micky. Islamabad is to Peshawar . . . well, words fail me, and I'm certain they fail Micky when the chauffeured car sent by his Pakistani hosts leaves the neat suburbs of Islamabad behind and the mad silhouette of Peshawar appears on the horizon two nerve-shattering hours later.

The Khyber Inter-Continental—Micky pins all his hopes on it, during that drive. There will be a lobby and a coffee shop where one can hold one's meetings without seeking out any forbidding addresses. There will be a room with a telephone, and that telephone will be connected to a polite person who will locate all one's numbers and shout his way through all the wrong connections and non-English-speaking houseboys until the person one wants is on the line. There will be a television, a shower, a room-service menu, a laundry service. One will never have to haggle over any prices or figure things out in rupees; one will simply hand over one's American Express card at the end . . . and in three days one will go home!

The Khyber Inter-Continental . . . it has everything Micky expected. There is a lobby, a dining room, a telephone; there is room service and in-room video. And yet, and yet . . . something is not quite right. Malone, feeling edgy, tries to puzzle it out. Why is this hotel different from the one in Islamabad, while seeming to be the same? What makes this place, so apparently an Inter-Continental like any other, nothing missing, what makes it seem so clearly not quite right? Maybe it's a certain shabbiness, as if this had been an Inter-Continental years ago and had now slipped into a kind of Twilight Zone of Hotels Past. Malone studies his surroundings with a frown; subtleties are not what he excels at. The carpet: it's thin and worn. The light bulbs are missing perhaps twenty watts each. Every face in the lobby is brown, and most guests are wearing that baggy native pajama outfit. The elevator that takes him to his floor is slow and jolty and smells distinctly of curry. Nor does his room offer a respite to his frowning survey. The little pamphlets welcoming him to the hotel contain numerous misspelled words, which Malone hopes to find comical a bit later, when he has regained his balance . . . or, at the very latest, when he is back in Langley, next to the coffee machine, narrating all of this to his co-workers. Sighing, Malone checks out the bathroom. The soap lies neatly packaged on the side of the sink but smells reekingly of jasmine, and the fine print reads "Juneko Brothers, Rawalpindi" instead of Pond's. Malone clicks on the in-house video. Omar Sharif, *The Horsemen*; Malone has seen it before, years ago, but not like this. In this version, whenever Omar Sharif bends forward for a kiss, the screen goes blank and static hisses obscenely for the duration of the scene. Censorship, Micky remembers; Jesus, if these guys can tinker around with atomic bombs, why can't they splice their videotapes instead of just blanking out the parts they don't like.

Jet lag, Micky mumbles to himself; otherwise, such small things would not make him nervous.

Hanging up his suit jacket in the closet, he peruses the laundry list and discovers that he can have his shalwar kamees cleaned and his dupatta, whatever the hell that may be, washed and ironed within twelve hours for thirty rupees. Shirts do not figure on the list, and boxer shorts have probably been censored off. A cold drink, that's what he needs: grabbing the room-service menu, Micky scans it for a Coke and finds instead that he may order a "Lassi salt-ish" or a "Lassi sweat-ish." Micky's head is throbbing. "Three days," he says, loudly, clicks the television off, and drops onto the bed for an hour of blessed oblivion.

Even Walid Khan seems slightly off when Malone sees him that evening. He seems to have grown in size, compared to the way he looked in Washington; he seems taller, heavier, darker. He has brought three men with him, and they follow behind him at one and a half paces. They seem much more foreign than Khan, more ill at ease with Malone; they are too polite, too nervous, and despite complicated introductions Malone cannot figure out quite who they are in relation to the business at hand. A lot of questions are asked: about the routing of shipments, the weight, the type of containers, the experiences with customs officials. Malone cannot say the questions are irrelevant, exactly, but they, too, seem a bit off. Are the men exchanging glances as they select the farthest corner of the lobby for this conversation? Malone assures them about delivery dates and liabilities, assures them that they will receive what they want when they want it, and in good condition. Still they persist in their questions about volume, routes, whether there are any especially cooperative officials in Baltimore who can "expedite matters," and their sentences wind around and around only to dangle, at the end, with the sense of something left unsaid. Finally Khan rescues him. How rude they are all being, Khan exclaims. Here is their friend, who has just completed a long trip and doubtless wants only to rest, and they are leaping right into the middle of business! Well, not to be offended; it's only a sign of the closeness and friendship between them, and of course between their respective companies, too, that they dispense with formalities in such a fashion. But enough! Now he really must rest! Or perhaps dinner first? May they take him to dinner? A little local place, really good food, no tourist would ever find it? Malone flounders about in search of a means of escape, but again Khan rescues him. Of course, of course, perfectly understandable, he is too tired. He shall rest now, and tomorrow, tomorrow there will be ample time to show him the attractions of the Frontier, time to see Peshawar, time for all this talk about business, too.

The profound relief at having escaped dinner at a "local place" makes Micky's room seem almost welcoming. After a short rest he even feels bold enough to explore the hotel in search of real food. Passing the bar—FOR NON-MUSLIM FOREIGN PASSPORT HOLDERS ONLY, a large placard in front of the door warns, and tinkling Oriental music emerges uninvitingly from within—he arrives at the dining hall. A "Moghul Buffet" is announced on a large sign at the entrance, stopping Malone in his tracks. "Very good," a young man in gray pajamas says to him, encouragingly. "Very delicious, sir." "You work here?" Malone asks. "Isn't there, you know, a snack bar?" "Tsss," says the young man, throwing his head up in what looks like the beginning of a nod but apparently means the opposite, a negation. And then he introduces himself officiously, Yussuf, room service, and flourishingly produces a finger-smudged menu decorated with Oriental curlicues but bearing the welcome heading: "Continental Dishes." Grilled cheese sandwiches! Hamburgers! Iced tea! Micky places his order and returns becalmed to his room. Three days. He can certainly survive three days.

The following morning finds Malone in much better spirits. A staffer from the American consulate stops by to "brief" him over breakfast. The man's warnings about Peshawar—recent car bombings, don't linger if you hear an explosion because there is almost always a second one to follow, avoid bus terminals and the bazaar—might be alarming but seem reassuring to Malone, since they confirm to him that he is not a fool, not a coward, and not paranoid, but merely an enterprising American abroad in a mad world. Jim, from the consulate, is a pleasant fellow, confiding that Peshawar is not exactly his dream assignment, either. A good career move, though. You have to take assignments like these while you're still a bachelor, can't expect a wife to live here. Though there are a few American women here who seem to get along just splendidly, God knows how. Even worse here for a woman, you would think, can't go anywhere, can't do anything, but some claim to do well, to like it just fine. Let's see . . . there's Hailey, a journalist. She doesn't even bother with any restrictions, just does as she pleases and seems to get away with it. Rumors have it she's been inside Afghanistan, rumors have it one of the rebel commanders is her lover, but please don't quote Jim on that! Let's see, then there's Monica, a nurse, but she's miserable, poor woman, just waiting for her assignment to end. And Mara, a New Yorker, a good-looking woman. She's tough to figure out, doesn't like to talk about her failed marriage to a Paki, a rich Paki, too. At least he let her go without any drama, so often they don't. Everybody thought she would go home then, but no, she just stayed on, still is working in the camps. Mara? A pretty woman, married to a Pakistani? A faint memory stirs in Malone. Mara, New York, Pakistan. "Mara what?" he asks. "Blake," Jim says. "You know her? Mara Blake."

My God, Mara Blake. He didn't know her very well, at NYU, but they shared a couple of classes, and then later she and the guy, Micky forgets his name, the loudmouth foreign flashy lady-killer one, they made a striking couple. And she married him, Micky remembers that now, and went off with him to Pakistan. So now here she is, in Peshawar, unbelievable. "Give her a call," Jim urges, amused at the prospect of this unlikely NYU reunion, and promises to find her number for him as soon as he's back at the office. In fact, wait a minute, he has her number right here, in his briefcase, on the invitation list for a consulate party.

Buoyed by his whiff of America, Malone is ready to meet with Khan. Malone chides himself for his nervousness of the previous day. Jet lag, obviously.

So he is quite unprepared when Khan sits him down in his office and, with a determinedly patient voice, spells out for him what the three underlings had apparently been alluding to, and what he has apparently failed to understand. That shipments from West-Fab Industries, consisting as they do of large objects containing inviting hollow spaces, never arrive in Peshawar without profitable undeclared content. That the deal is contingent on their taking a cooperative, mature—he actually says "mature"—position on this. Micky's role is a simple one, really, Khan explains. It is a simple matter of invoices that are to be filled out in duplicate versions, with a different weight on each one.

Malone is surprised to discover that he is not really surprised. Does he feel just a little bit glamorous, Malone the gunrunner, as he imagines himself telling this story to friends and colleagues back home? Maybe; his face, though, registers shock. So much shock that Khan laughs in spite of himself, and concludes that he will have to keep this poor fellow here for at least ten days, to allow for acclimatization, before business can satisfactorily be done. "Michael," he says, almost fondly, handing him into the car and sending him to his hotel to recuperate. "It is time for you to grow up, my friend. We're not in America here, Michael, and even if we were—what kinds of things do you suppose go on every day in your own city of Washington? And we are not in Washington, Michael. We are in Peshawar, where the rules do not apply. But don't be worried, Michael. We will work this out, before you leave, and you will be quite happy and satisfied. And not such a virgin anymore, my dear boy."

What the hell does that mean, Malone wonders, bristling. Is there contempt in that? Is it a threat? Malone doesn't really care. All he wants is his room, and his dinner, and then he will think this whole thing through, and decide what to do.

Khan is worried. He has told Malone not to worry, but is worried himself. Who is the fool here? Malone, as seems so utterly apparent? Or is he himself a fool, by too easily taking Malone for one? Surely Malone is too much of a cliché to be true. What if this is a trap, and Malone the clever decoy, playing the fool to entrap him? But why should he want to do that? West-Fab Industries, Langley, Virginia . . . Langley, Virginia, an address resonant with meaning, to any knowledgeable Pakistani. What if this whole West-Fab outfit is just part of the American scheme to discredit and disgrace Pakistan, to make it seem like a country of nuclear thieves and technological smugglers, to toss it on the rubbage heap of their New World Order? What if Malone is just waiting to hear what it is, precisely, that Khan proposes to tuck away into those alluring crates and containers? In order to serve Khan up to some U.S. Senate committee, ruining him for good in both countries? The CIA, never far from Third World minds; suddenly it seems eminently plausible to Khan that Malone is an agent for the CIA.

On the other hand, what if Malone is precisely what he appears to be: an overweight, uncouth, timid American idiot? Shall someone like that be allowed to spoil a potentially marvelous deal? And the most galling thing about this whole affair is that the overweight, uncouth, timid American—if that is what he is—now has the advantage over Khan. Malone knows, now, something about Khan. But Khan does not know anything about Malone . . . not even his real identity.

Something must be done to restore the balance. Khan decides to let Malone stew a bit. For forty-eight hours, he ignores him: does not send a car for him at the designated time, does not call, is not in when Malone calls. If there is indeed more to Malone than meets the eye, then perhaps he will do something to reveal himself.

Poor Micky. Khan gave him forty-eight hours to be miserable in, and miserable he is. With a little encouragement, he could out-moan the best of the ghazal singers. What shall he do? Refuse, and return to his office as the man who screwed up a 99-percent-certain deal? Well, for the best of reasons, of course . . . Only: what if he is being hopelessly stupid and naïve? What if his boss knows all about this deal and approves, tacitly? Or if he doesn't know, but wouldn't care?

Forty-eight hours. When you are in the Khyber Inter-Continental, afraid to stray too far from it because of bombs, afraid to go to the U.S. consulate for fear your guilt will show up on your face, with only *The Horsemen* (censored) for entertainment, forty-eight hours can be very long. If such were not the case, Malone might never have gotten up the nerve to call Mara Blake, a woman he does not know very well and has not seen for many years. After that, he picks up the phone again to contact his only other friend in Peshawar, the room-service waiter Yussuf.

Khan has exiled Malone, but he has not forgotten him. Nor does his anger cool with the passing hours. On the contrary; he is becoming more and more annoyed with this stupid, obstructionist, slow-witted individual. And he must be stupid, and slow-witted, it cannot be a trick. Still, it just doesn't make sense. He hasn't even asked about the size of his reward, for cooperating. But he hasn't indignantly refused, either, as he should have if he were really as provincially moral as all that. Khan trusts his instincts; no way he could have gotten as far as he has if he didn't have first-rate instincts. And his instincts tell him that Malone is a silly person, an unimaginative fool. A fool who stands between him and his goals, and must therefore be moved, or educated, or bought, or intimidated . . . but actually, Khan prefers the benign view. A deprived person, in a way, this Malone. One who knows nothing about the real world, one who is frightened even of his own shadow. First, he needs to stew a bit.

Micky is, indeed, satisfactorily miserable. He is asking himself how he got into this mess, he is asking himself what he should do, but there are other questions he fails to ask. His total ineptitude in the face of international intrigue is evident from his blind panic. It leaves no room for substantive curiosity. Wouldn't it be useful to know just what it is that Khan wants to move from point A to point B with the aid of West-Fab? Is it guns? Microchips? Liquor? Uncut copies of *The Horsemen*? "Contraband" just may not be enough to know, if you really want to make an informed decision. Or even if you just want to accomplish an elegant escape.

Two endless days, and no word from Khan. There is nothing on television, and every time his restless flicking through the pitifully few channels summons up *The Horsemen*, Micky shudders. He is starting to feel like the trampled dusty goatskin flung about between the riders as they play buzkashi. Maybe he should take the chance and call his boss. Could George really be a smuggler? It's hard to believe; on the other hand, it's increasingly hard for Malone even to conjure up a contoured image of George. Instead, images of remembered *Newsweek* cover stories fill his brain. Western businessmen, gunned down in the streets of Moscow by the Russian Mafia, blood and brains spilling out onto the alien pavement . . . That could happen here, too, he surmises.

Micky overcomes his fear of bugged telephones and

17

decides to call his sister. She's constantly hanging out in weird places like this, maybe she'll know what to do. Besides, they learned as children to converse in cryptic sentences incomprehensible to outsiders and parents— she'll understand what he wants to say without his having to spell it out, which would not be the case with George. Assuming he is innocent, George would chew this problem over in his usual blunt, clumsy way. "Smuggle? What's that you're saying, Micky, speak up! They want us to smuggle?"

No no, it's far safer to call Julia. He studies the instructions on the little plastic card beside the telephone. Long-distance calls . . . He follows the enumerated steps, one by one. Quite easily, he gets a dial tone; soon, a phone is ringing. Three times, then he hears Julia's voice: "I'm not available to take your call right now. Please leave a message after the beep. Ciao."

That avenue closed, Malone makes a decision. He will confide in the U.S. consul. The decision once made, this course of action seems obvious. What has he been thinking of? He hasn't done anything wrong. He doesn't plan to do anything wrong. He is a fine, upstanding, law-abiding U.S. citizen, exactly the kind of citizen U.S. consulates were created for. So let them take care of him.

Malone calls the consulate. An operator informs him in good English, but with an obvious Pakistani intonation, that Jim is not there. The consul is not in either. They are traveling in the region with a Senate delegation and will not be back until next week, at the earliest. But perhaps someone else can help him, if Malone would like to explain what his problem is? No! No! He would not! No! After he has hung up, Malone's heart is beating wildly. It is pounding like the hooves of the horses in Omar Sharif's movie, when they thunder across the ground, trampling the goat corpse.

He'll have to let his office know something, too, eventually, but what should he tell them? Well, maybe it won't be that long. Maybe Jim will return much sooner. And Julia should be calling him back . . .

Malone is very tense, very nervous. Still, his call to Julia has cheered him up a bit, unaccountably. Julia; won't she be surprised to learn of his adventure, his dip into international intrigue!

2

————

I like Pakistan. I want to say that right at the outset, to avoid any misunderstandings. Its cities are distinctive and alluring, smelling still of ancient travel routes and splendid dynasties. I like what the British left behind: a widespread command of good English, a dry sense of humor, and, as their final gift, the uppityness that comes of having rousted them. Even the dreadful Peshawar has its unique, dusty attractions. So let's return to the crazy highway below, and see if we can find our protagonist.

Why yes, there's our group right now, rumbling along in a small green Suzuki, one of many, for Suzuki manufactures under license in Pakistan. Behind the wheel we have Iqbal, the handsome and promising young Islamabad detective. There is his wife, Gul, right beside him, body contorted so that she may better chat with her friend Lilly, who occupies the backseat. Iqbal is on his way to Peshawar because he has been detailed to discover what has happened to the missing, presumed dead American businessman Michael Malone. Gul is there because her Aunt Sonia lives in Peshawar, and they haven't visited for a while. Lilly is there because she managed to charm her way into this assignment, to cover the murder for her newspaper. And she is there for her American friend Julia, because the instant she read the APA bulletin about an American from Bethesda named Michael Malone she suspected that it could only be the brother of Julia Malone, a journalist who frequently covers Pakistan. Julia Malone, of *The Washington Post*, whose answering machine is on because she is far, far away from home, trudging through Croatia for a story about refugees. Whom we will meet just as soon as she gets close enough to civilization to retrieve her messages, and discover that Asia has swallowed up her brother.

Malone's most significant characteristic in the eyes of the homicide unit is his passport. Were he not an American citizen, the machinery of investigation would concern itself about him in a far more desultory fashion. To be shot, decapitated, stabbed, or otherwise meet a hideous fate, is commonplace in Peshawar. Afghans of opposing factions routinely behead one another, leaving insulting notes pinned to the shirt collar of the headless torso; women are summarily executed by whichever male relative detects a note of impropriety in their behavior and feels his honor besmirched by it; young would be Pulitzer Prize–winners from various Western capitals vanish without a trace and are presumed, until found robbed and stabbed in an alleyway, to be making their way to Kabul for a scoop.

As I said earlier, Peshawar holds its own peculiar fascination, but Iqbal for one has never discovered it. Along with most other Pakistanis of the urban educated class, he finds Peshawar neither scenic nor intriguing. Modern Pakistanis regard a trip to the North-West Frontier Province with about as much pleasure as your average white-collar New Yorker views a late-night stroll through Central Park or an evening drive through Harlem in a convertible. And yet the mood in Iqbal's little green car, as he pilots it through the homicidal traffic, is quite festive. Gul looks forward to seeing her Aunt Sonia. Despite a twinge of a guilty conscience, Lilly cannot help being in good spirits, too, because Islamabad can get quite boring, and to be sent off on nearly any kind of trip by her editor makes a welcome break. And she's never met Micky, so her grief is abstract. Iqbal is not happy, exactly, but there's always something exhilarating about starting a new investigation.

"So tell me, Lilly," he says, addressing the backseat, "does your newspaper issue chadors to lady journalists when they go to Peshawar, or just the standard tape recorder?"

"Oh, shut up," says Lilly, good-naturedly. "Let's just wait and see how you get along there, city boy." Iqbal's mood is dampened slightly by this retort. It's true; you never know how your local colleagues will receive you.

"YOU ARE," his local colleague says, the following morning at 9 a.m., when Iqbal arrives at the office for his briefing. The man's name is Toufiq; he is small and round, has a mustache, and reminds Iqbal of Hercule Poirot. "YOU ARE," Toufiq repeats with great earnestness, looking into Iqbal's eyes with an exaggeratedly efficient gaze and slapping the case file onto the desk repeatedly as if truth could be pounded from it like dust from a rug. The words are simple enough, though they look ghoulish on the crime scene Polaroid Iqbal has before him, which shows them smeared across the pebbled white plastic surface of the hotel ice machine in a brown substance that Iqbal knows, even without the lab report, to be blood.

"YOU ARE," Toufiq repeats. "That's not a threat. That's not a confession. That's not a message. So, we conclude that the killer is interrupted. He is writing us a letter, but something happens, and he flees. What did he want to say? YOU ARE . . . what?" he asks, interrogatory sternness suddenly clouding his good-natured, mustachioed face. Iqbal could be his son; fortunately, he is polite and smart enough to behave like a son, not like Mr. Know-It-All from the Nation's Capital. His face reflects just the right shade of respectful anticipation as he waits for Toufiq to finish. Tentatively, Toufiq approves of him, so he goes on with his musings. "YOU ARE . . . an imperialist pig, sent by the Great Satan America? YOU ARE . . . building secret bases in Baluchistan? YOU ARE . . . a miserable opium dealer? A cheat? A CIA agent? If only the murderer had had the time to complete his sentence, we would know where to begin looking for him. But, no. YOU ARE . . . what can one do with that?"

"Murderer?" Iqbal asks hesitantly. "Any chance this Malone is still alive?"

Toufiq studies his young colleague gravely. "A chance? There is always a chance. Until we have the dead body, of course there is a chance. But where is the ransom note?" he asks. "Of what use is a secret hostage? We have received no demands, and there's no trace of him, just the unfinished message in blood. In my professional opinion, the fellow is dead. What we've got to do, we've got to deliver the perpetrator double quick, neatly tied up and gift-wrapped for the Americans."

In pantomime, Toufiq wraps an imaginary rope around his neck and hangs himself, head lolling, tongue out, to illustrate the appeasement of the Americans through rapid dispatchment of the killer.

Good son Iqbal smiles dutifully. "Malone was a businessman, on his second visit to Pakistan?"

"But first time in Peshawar," Toufiq agrees. "No evidence of any involvement in drugs, guns, anything of the sort. No record of his company here. The Americans may have something on him, but they're not saying."

"His local partner?" Iqbal asks.

Toufiq sighs. "Walid Khan. He has been very helpful. He came forth immediately the disappearance was noted, and has sketched for us the timetable of the American, during his days here. He has provided copies of the contracts, almost complete, just missing the signatures. A simple transaction. All the information is here. We can visit Khan again, if you like, but I think it isn't necessary. He will not be having anything to do with this. Khan is, how shall I explain this? A powerful man. He may break the law, but he doesn't break the rules. There is an arrangement. Here are we, the police, with our work, and there is Khan, running his local empire, and between us, we have rules."

Iqbal nods. Every Pakistani city has its Khans, Islamabad included. The rules are different for them, but they are rules nonetheless, and more often than not, they work.

"What about the woman leaving by the emergency staircase?" says Iqbal, moving on to the next point in his notes.

"Seen by the room-service clerk." Toufiq nods. "Especially noted by him for two reasons. One, wearing a chador in a hotel for Westerners. Two, in a great hurry.

This is of no value, I am sure. Of no meaning. The wife of one of the staff, without doubt, bringing her husband his uniform or his dinner, which he has forgotten, or helping him steal some hotel supplies."

"Maybe a maid, going home in her chador?" Iqbal supposes. Toufiq is truly delighted.

"My friend," he says jovially, warming to his colleague without any further reservation. "I can see that you are truly an Islamabad man. In Islamabad you have the ladies serving in the hotel restaurants, you have the ladies cleaning the rooms. In Peshawar, no. In Peshawar, our ladies are staying at home. In Islamabad, you are thinking like the Americans. But this is a Peshawar murder, so now you must think like a Pathan."

"I must think like a Pathan," Iqbal repeats, some hours later, for the benefit of Sonia, Lilly, and his wife over lunch in the garden of Aunt Sonia's house. "Eventually," Iqbal continues, seeing that he has the bemused attention of all three ladies, "I will succeed so well that I will actually have become a Pathan." He scowls ferociously at Lilly in preview of that moment. "Gul will be locked away in strict purdah to protect her from bad influences like you. Not to mention you," he adds, fixing a menacing look on Sonia, who shakes her elegant, well-groomed head and sighs.

"At heart," she says, "every man is a Pathan."

Iqbal may be polite, but he isn't lazy. He throws himself into the investigation with vigor, and in short order has made an important discovery. Toufiq believes that the motive for the crime will turn out to be political. Iqbal, educated with Western textbooks at the modern university in Islamabad, has ingested a different philosophy.

25

Statistically speaking, he knows, almost all murders can be traced to personal involvement. There is nearly always a link between the killer and the killed; unearth it, and you're on your way to a solution. Sure enough, persistent inquiries quickly turn up something personal about Malone. A woman, an American woman, called the hotel repeatedly to ask for his room. And the waiter in the Non-Muslim-Foreigners-Only bar distinctly remembers a heavyset American man who ordered a bottle of wine and consumed it in the company of a blond Western woman. And finally, room-service records show that Room 307 ordered two breakfasts. Aha! A tryst! Maybe a love triangle. A jealous husband. A woman scorned.

There are limits to Iqbal's euphoria. A blond American woman, between twenty-five and thirty-five years old; that's the best his newfound witnesses can do. At this point, the investigation hits a brief snag, which is not untangled until the unraveling begins at quite another point. The contents of the wastebasket in Malone's room included a crumpled telephone message from a certain "Murrie."

The desk clerks, queried once again about a man named Murrie, shake their heads and shrug their shoulders until one of them, comprehension dawning, informs Iqbal that yes, this Murrie phoned and he took the message, but Murrie was a woman, not a man; and why did Iqbal suppose it should be a man? Murrie. Mary? Marie? The desk clerk, who did his phonetic best with the message in the first place, cannot do any better now. It was a woman, and she had almost the same name as Murree, the resort area outside of Islamabad, that's all he knows. But it's good enough for Iqbal, who traces this information back to a certain blond American woman named Mara Blake, and in less than twenty-four hours, too.

If he expected praise from his local colleague, he is disappointed. Toufiq handles the dossier of Mara Blake with uncustomary kindness, placing it gently on his desk, touching it gingerly. Iqbal is annoyed.

"I'm not saying she's the killer, for God's sake," he says. "But she's right in the middle of this, isn't that clear? How can you doubt it?

" 'Mara Blake,' " he reads out, having roughly snatched the file from the protective clasp of Toufiq's fingers. " 'Twenty-nine years old. Born in Long Island. M.A. degree from New York University. Married to Farid Tariqi, heir of a prominent Pakistani family. Separated from him seven months ago, she is working for a refugee aid organization as a "health services consultant." ' " This last comes with a heavy note of sarcasm, Iqbal being highly skeptical of well-intentioned foreign experts ever since Italian geologists hired to build a dam nearly washed away most of his native province.

He smiles malignantly as he prepares to read out the climactic grand finale of his file. " 'Engaged in a sexual liaison with our deceased friend Michael "Micky" Malone, consummated on the premises of the Khyber Inter-Continental Hotel!' " Toufiq sighs heavily. "YOU ARE . . . an adulterer!" Iqbal concludes, in triumph, completing the fill-in-the-blank murderer's message with his own solution, and smashes the file shut on the desk of Toufiq, who winces. They sit for a moment in disharmonious silence. Iqbal wants his colleague to agree with him. "Two men, one woman," he insists, almost imploringly, after a few moments. "That's trouble, friend, anywhere on this earth. An American man, a Muslim man, and an American woman who is the wife of one

27

and sleeping with the other; in Peshawar, that's trouble for sure. I'm not naming names, yet. I'm only saying, this is a triangle to look at." Toufiq grunts noncommittally.

"You still think it's political, don't you," Iqbal sighs. Toufiq holds his hands out, palms up.

"And I wish we knew which kind of political," he admits. "Inshallah it will turn out that Malone was involved in some kind of shady business dealings here. Because if not, if we've just got somebody out to get Americans, then we're really in trouble, my friend."

"No, no," says Iqbal. "This is an isolated event, you'll see. Nobody has claimed responsibility. Aside from those two words, there have been no messages. And besides," he goes on, dispensing as an arrogant urbanite with even a cautious religious disclaimer, "no threats have been received, no one else has vanished."

If Toufiq were Catholic, he would cross himself; "Don't paint the Devil on the wall," my European grandmother used to say. As it is, he mumbles something that may well be a propitiatory Islamic formula.

Iqbal goes home. He is, despite the efforts of the annoying Toufiq to pour cold water on his accomplishments, in good spirits. Such progress in only two days! He is showing these Frontier folk what's what. It is in this spirit that he disdains the taxis and instead hails a rickshaw cab to take him home in local style.

His cab is distinguished by three unusual female decorations; as he hangs on to the hard plastic seat with one hand and to the metal frame of the cab with the other to avoid being dislodged, they bounce along above him, affixed to the cab's plastic canopy. Directly above him, molded from blue plastic, is a hand, the Hand of

Fatima, guaranteeing safety on this bumpy, uncomfortable ride. On his right, an improbably bosomy Indian woman, hair fluffed into a 1960s beehive, chest squashed into a size 38D sari top, leers down at him; a pinup from one of the ever-popular Indian film magazines, Iqbal supposes. On his left, grim and commanding under a deceptively feminine frame of silver ringlets, none other than Her Hapsburg Majesty the Empress Maria Theresa, who by God knows what route has found her way to Peshawar and entered the paper harem of Hassan the rickshaw man. Jolting along, Iqbal finds them first funny, then eerie; "Aspects of Kali," he mumbles to himself, and shakes his head to find them funny again. Pantheistic superstition, monotheistic superstition, matriarchal deities—Iqbal is offending too much and too rashly.

The next morning, punishment is served up just before breakfast, in the form of a telephone call from Toufiq, informing him that a body has been found. No, it's not Malone. But yes, it's a murder. And there's a message. This time, it's written in ink, on a piece of the victim's monogrammed stationery, and left beside the body. The message is a little longer this time; it says: YOU ARE THE DUST. The victim is Ali Hakim, an Afghan émigré, now an important local lawyer. And the partner of Farid Tariqi, the deserted, betrayed, and presumably irate husband of Mara Blake.

Toufiq refrains from any sort of comment. Iqbal looks grim and begins immediately to chart the best course of investigation. Not enough is known yet about Farid, about the victim, and about the relationship between them. However, it is high time to have a very close look at this Pakistani gentleman and his unruly American wife.

The husband is easy; one can consult with him, quite legitimately, concerning the habits, activities, and personal circumstances of his deceased partner. In the case of Mara, a slightly more circumspect approach recommends itself. A nymphomaniac, seducing her husband's business partners, driving him to homicidal insanity? If so, the nymphomaniac nonetheless carries an American passport, and it behooves Iqbal to tread lightly. For Toufiq's amusement, Iqbal repeats the instructions he received, before departing, from his superiors.

"Before interrogating or accusing an American, Iqbal, ask yourself one thing: is this person worth an F-14 fighter jet?"

More important, Iqbal does not want to formally investigate this Mara. He wants information, real information about her. He wants to approach this circuitously. And he has a plan. The American woman has a job working with the refugees. Lilly, as a journalist, can go to see her at the camp, gain a first impression of her; she has mentioned, anyway, that her newspaper wants an article about the situation of Afghan refugees. Then, when Iqbal goes to see her—or has her brought in for questioning—he will already have some kind of an idea whom he is dealing with.

"You will be my eyes and my ears," he whispers seductively to Lilly. "No, you will be the eyes and ears of your country. The future of Pakistan lies in your hands. Will mighty fighter jets roar through our airspace, guarding us against all enemies, or not? It's up to you."

"You're ridiculous, Iqbal," Lilly replies in irritation. Her reluctance is all for show. Of course she will do what he wants. Not for him and not for Pakistan, but for the sheer thrill of meeting a possible murderess.

Lilly, and Mara. Two citizens of the Nation of Cultural Limbo, but from its two far corners; will they get along? Lilly: a well-dressed, sophisticated, leftist feminist journalist daughter of Pakistan's upper middle class. Mara: a puritanical, serious-minded, liberal feminist American.

Didn't I read somewhere that sisterhood is global? Well, on this particular morning the fact is not very much in evidence.

Mara, standing behind a wobbly wooden table in a dispensary tent in the middle of a silent, black-shrouded crowd of women, looks up and sees a sleek, well-groomed, confident young Pakistani woman teetering toward her in heels unsuitable to the terrain and, in Mara's opinion, unsuitable to any self-respecting member of her gender, on any kind of ground at all. Lilly, lemon-yellow Filofax in hand, walks on wobbly feet toward a disheveled, annoyed young American woman whose green-gray eyes seem barely less distrustful than those of the refugees. Mara has the arm of a dirt-encrusted refugee child in one hand and a sheaf of well-worn and mud-spattered patient registration cards in the other, and is dressed in the Western compromise version of the chador: baggy pants and loose shirt of the shalwar kamees, head covered by a long scarf knotted severely under the chin. In her elegant career-woman outfit, Lilly looks like the foreigner, Mara like the native.

Nor is this a good day for Mara. The events with Micky have shaken her badly. How did she get into this, how did she end up having a one-night stand that has turned into this kind of a major headache?

And that's not the only thing wrong with this day. The weather is nightmarish. Mara's face is covered with an inch of dust, stuck to her skin like a makeup base by the adhesive of her sweat. She hates the scarf. It makes her feel ugly, and it makes her feel humiliated. And the fact that her objections come to her in that order fills her with self-contempt. The scarf, a symbol of female subjugation; when worn by herself, a symbol of Western kowtowing to Eastern sexism. How can she be vain enough to even consider its effect on her appearance, when she should be exclusively enraged about the principle of it all?

I could have told Mara what her problem was. Like so many people, Mara just doesn't know how to pack. She forgot her insect repellent, her shampoo, and her raincoat; instead, she stuffed her luggage with far too much principle.

Mara's task, on this inhospitable morning, is to distribute supplemental food rations to refugees with special needs: pregnant women, nursing mothers, and underweight girls. So is she passing around vitamin tablets, milk powder, and oranges? Oh no. That would be unthinkable, impossible. Face pinched, jaw tightened against anger, Mara is distributing sawdust-flavored crackers while questions of principle buzz around in her head, annoying as mosquitoes, itchy as sand flies. I sympathize with her, I really do. It's hard to abandon your principles; we all have them, we all love our own the most. The refugees, for instance. They've lost nearly everything, but they managed to pack their principles when they fled. They left behind their houses, their fields, their goats, their rugs, and most of their clothes, but they brought their principles. How much easier for all concerned if they could have done it the other way around!

Their principles include a very definite image of the Order of Creation. In their Order of Creation, Afghan men are at the very top, right above the fierce lion and the deadly cobra. And women are at the very bottom, somewhere between the crawly earthworm and the creeping snail.

Where is this information leading us? It is leading us to the apples, the oranges, the sawdust-flavored crackers, and the pinched look on Mara's face. Apples, oranges, eggs, and meat are too precious to waste on women, in the Afghan Order of Creation; as soon as they are distributed, they are gobbled up by the men. Well, that makes sense, doesn't it? Would you feed vitamins to snails?

Westerners, with their disdain for the principles of others, have not been content to accept this. The crafty Australians have devised protein biscuits, crackers with the flavor of sawdust and the consistency of bricks, but each one a highly caloric bombshell of vitamins, minerals, and health. You don't need to fight, you don't need to argue, and you don't need to get into the matter of principle at all. You merely hand out the biscuits. The men take one look and one disgusted bite, and throw them aside in revulsion for the women and the girls. The women and girls get their vitamins, the Afghan men get to keep their principles, and the Australians get the last laugh. If that's not a cross-cultural happy ending right out of diversity school, I don't know what is.

Mara is learning, slowly, painfully, unwillingly, to take her victories as they come and kiss sweet principle goodbye. She needs some time to figure out why she is here, in the middle of a godforsaken desert, with a scarf on her head, with a one-night-stand boyfriend who has become an international incident. She does not need yet another city-slick, snazzy Pakistani journalist "interviewing" her, with all of the usual insinuations: that she

33

is a busybody, possibly in the pay of the CIA, a neocolonialist meddler, and that Islamic women were perfectly happy before she, the Western know-it-all, came along.

Lilly, recognizing a kindred spirit even under these inauspicious circumstances, feels a blast of anger heading her way and cannot think how to turn it aside. She tries. "So," she says, smiling her most disarming, feminist, we-are-all-sisters-together smile, "these are your patients?"

"Not really," Mara drawls, pulling her scarf an inch farther over her forehead in order to look, or so she believes, even more repellent and witchlike. "Actually, what you see here is the enlightened minority, the daring avant-garde of the camp." Her hand sweeps generously across the mass of female figures, huddled nearly immobile on the dirt floor of the tent, barefoot, wrapped in layers of torn cotton, with infants peeping out here and there like raisins from the layers of baklava.

"Actually," she says, "those who are really sick, who are really badly off, rarely come to our clinic. A good Muslim man prefers his women to die modestly, in his tent. And a good Muslim woman," Mara lectures, in the hopes of grinding on the nerves of the Muslim woman who stands before her, "if she has any decency at all, will prefer to be shoveled straight into her grave rather than display her body to one of the leering, depraved foreign doctors who staff our clinics.

"Oh, listen," Mara continues, sweetly, insincerely. "You're not a psychologist, are you? Because we've just had mobs of them passing through. They're intrigued by this problem we're having called 'hysterical paralysis.' Yes, we've got dozens of women who are paralyzed, crippled, without any organic cause, just from the

34

trauma of never being allowed to leave their tents at all for two, three, four years. The last time this disease surfaced in any major way was in the Dark Ages."

Mara pauses, but only to take a small breath before winding up for her grand finale. "In the Dark Ages, and among the wives of your Islamic freedom fighters, whose wives aren't allowed the freedom to visit the nearest toilet."

A little frightened by her own impetuousness, Mara glares at Lilly.

"I have a friend," Lilly says at last, "who says every man is a Pathan at heart. Come on," Lilly pleads, "give me a chance, I'm on your side."

"That was my trial by fire," Lilly will say, later, with a laugh, whenever she introduces Mara to someone new. And Mara, blushing just a little, will say defensively, "Well, it was nothing but the truth."

Iqbal, who receives a glowing and detailed account of the American woman that evening, fails to see what Lilly or anyone else could possibly like about her. She sounds thoroughly unpleasant.

"I'm sure she's the killer," he announces, to annoy Lilly. "The way you describe her, she has clearly lost her mind."

"If you don't lose your reason over some things, then you have no reason to lose," Lilly counters primly. "Heinrich von Kleist," she adds, German literature having been her unlikely minor in college.

"Hysterical Americans and philosophizing Germans —how am I supposed to concentrate on solving this case?" Iqbal complains. He doesn't seriously think the American woman is the killer. If anything, his money was on her jealous husband. But he has already ascertained that the man is abroad, has been abroad for nearly a month.

Nonetheless, he will pay her a call. Ostensibly, he will merely be visiting everyone who knew Ali Hakim. So sorry to bother her. But her husband, her still-husband, is out of town, and she may have met his murdered partner informally at some point? And have noticed something, been told something by him? Or did her husband ever mention enemies his partner may have had?

Returning from the interview, Iqbal looks so smug that Lilly thinks she had better check up on the canary. She phones Mara, but the combative, chipper person she remembers sounds so nervous that she decides a personal visit is called for. Arriving at the American woman's house, she finds her looking as bad as she sounded. Her face is drawn and narrow, and when she moves around the kitchen, getting them drinks, her movements are jolty and distracted.

"Your friend hated me," she says. "You know, Iqbal, that detective friend of yours. Well," she says, "no wonder. I hate myself."

Lilly clucks with journalistically professional sympathy.

"He's funny, though." Mara laughs bitterly. "He's good. Very good, and very mean, oh God. 'And now if you will be so kind, Ms. Blake, is that how I may call you? And thank you for your cooperation, by the way, this really is most forthcoming of you. So, you didn't really know your husband's business partner? Then, so long as I'm already here, I wonder if we could spend a few moments on the first victim, whom I believe you *did* know? There are just a few little points you could help me with, perhaps. For instance, if you would just tell me, please, did you know the dead man at all before, ah, joining him for the night?' " she mimics. " 'And was he expecting you to do that, do you think, Ms. Blake? You see, we are trying to ascertain if he was perhaps expecting a Murrie or Murray, as well, or if you are the desk clerk's idea of a Murray. So we need to know if he was counting on you to, umm, you know, and whether the idea came from him, you see, Ms. Blake, or from yourself, and if he seemed at all hesitant about your spending the, mmm, the night.' And his sidekick, the fat guy, was blushing, was actually blushing. Oh God," Mara says again. "Well, I deserve it."

Lilly murmurs something and silently resolves to punish Iqbal for this.

" 'Did you know the dead man before you spent the night with him,' can you imagine," Mara repeats. "How that sounds! And he insisted on calling Farid my 'husband,' just to make me look really bad; well, he's still my husband legally, but we've been separated for over half a year."

Mara pauses. "The dead man . . ." she repeats, thoughtfully, and if Lilly were not so busy planning ways to make Iqbal pay for his cheap detective bully act, she might notice that the American woman almost says something, before stopping herself.

When she drives home, much later, Lilly will feel that they have had a long heart-to-heart, that Mara has unburdened herself on the topic of her marriage and other intimate matters, and she will not realize that, even after three glasses of wine, Mara was very much in command of what she chose to tell her, and what not.

A s she explained to Lilly, Mara met Farid at NYU. It was his second year, which in a way was fateful. "If I had met him during his first year, I wouldn't have given him the time of day," Mara said. His first year in

New York was for Farid as much of an Altered State as the East can sometimes be for Western newcomers. Everything was a shock: the city, the subways, the classes, the morals, the clothes . . . But the most disorienting aspect was the sexual anarchy that loomed frighteningly, enticingly over it all. It was not unusual for Farid to go to a party and be accosted by a young woman with the observation that he looked as though he might be a rough lover, and was he? Because that was how she liked it. I am the last person in the world to make excuses for Farid or any other Muslim man, or any other man at all for that matter. But nevertheless, I can imagine that in those first weeks it was difficult for Farid to comprehend that these self-confident, aggressive creatures were really women, the same gender familiar (or, rather, totally unfamiliar) to him from back home, and not some bizarre apparitions, female jinn, visitations from mythology, from hell, or from deep space.

Once he became convinced of their mortality, though, culture and upbringing rapidly took over again, and he felt free to despise them. If these were indeed women, and not jinn, then they were whores; dreadful, probably diseased, slightly insane creatures who at home would have been kept locked away by their distressed families. But here no one seemed to find their behavior dismaying . . . although, and this struck a resonant chord in Farid, the American men's attitudes to these creatures were not as casual and fraternal as it had seemed initially. Chicks, broads, cunts even; at first Farid was shocked at the familiarity with which women were discussed, but soon he recognized that this was merely a Western variant of the way he himself was accustomed, at home, to viewing women: as beings composed of 90 percent sex and 10 percent humanity, to whom one felt attracted but with whom one otherwise shared very little. You could not trust them, and it was best to keep them out of the company of men, or who knew what chaos might result.

Well, actually, Farid now knew exactly what chaos would result: the kind reigning in America, where girls you had never seen before walked up to you and stated their copulatory preferences, right out, as though talking about the weather. And the men, the men might act cool and debonair, as if they thought all of this was perfectly fine and natural, but after a few months in the men's dorm, Farid knew better. At heart they despised these terrifying women, and were nearly as frightened of them as he himself.

Once he thought he had it all figured out, Farid went on what Mara termed the "dislocated Muslim's sex spree." This, she explained, was part of the "Islamic erotic binge and purge syndrome," in which phases of excess are followed by periods of purification, abstinence, and hatred for yourself and your partner. The partner, most of all, who as a woman is considered to be acting far more against God, morality, and nature than the man, who in some strange and wonderful way is only loosely connected to his sexual organs and any activities thereof. Anyway, it seems that Farid's first seven months in America were one extended binge. To nourish his contempt, he avoided the brash girls who signaled their interest unambiguously, and instead pursued the quiet, the reluctant, the seemingly virtuous. A number of girls fell hopelessly in love with him that year, or believed that they had—so quickly! So easily, so automatically. In love! With him, who cared about them not a bit, made no promises, was a stranger! An absurd culture, where girls fell in love just like that.

Through the field of fair-haired young East Coast girls, Farid cut a remorseless swath, Genghis Khan on a sexual rampage against Western civilization. Romantic girls would succumb to Farid, hearts aflutter at his dark good looks and stern demeanor; Farid pursued a scorched-earth policy with them, trampling every last little fragile sentiment mercilessly into the ground. Rarely did he receive a woman in his chambers more than once; never was one permitted to spend the night, and most were dismissed without being allowed to take a shower. "I have this thing about my towels," he would say, teeth bared in a shark's smile. "I don't like anyone to use them. It's related to my religion," he would say. "If a non-Muslim used them, they wouldn't be clean anymore, in the religious sense." The girls would leave, thunderstruck at so much cruelty, and Farid would go to sleep, unsure whom he hated more, them or himself. Few girls ever confided the full extent of this treatment to even their closest friends; the little that leaked out only served to enhance the legend.

"There is a strain in the female personality," Mara says, "that finds male cruelty just as irresistible as a baby's cry." She considers this one of the crucial elements in the female personality. "Only a woman," she says, "could look at the man who has just kicked her in the face and think, poor thing, he must be so unhappy. If only he were mine; what couldn't I make out of him."

During those months, Farid's nastiness had dozens of women flocking to him. An endless stream of blond co-eds paraded through his life, led by his appalling viciousness to believe there must be a rich lode of vulnerability just below the surface; they swarmed through his room like destitute forty-niners heading West to pan for gold in the muddy sludge of a barren

40

river. The distinction of breaking Farid fell to a girl named Alexandra. Alexandra was one of Farid's triumphs, so it was fitting that she became his Waterloo. There was nothing of the Venus flytrap about Alexandra. She was not seen at campus parties, she did not accost men, in her bearing there was even something of the modesty and reticence of a nice Islamic girl. She worked on the staff of the campus newspaper and was assigned to do a story on Farid, who at this point had become active in campus politics. Farid, who enjoyed having his victims bait their own traps, was not slow to respond to this opportunity. He listened to her request for an interview with arrogant indifference. He did not have time to meet her for coffee in the cafeteria. He could not give her an appointment during the lunch break. He was unavailable after class, and could not see her in the library. She wanted to see him? She had a deadline for the story? Very well, she could come to his room at precisely ten-thirty the following night. When she hesitated, he said in the heavily sarcastic tone in which he had so often heard this line delivered by his American male friends and mentors, "I promise not to rape you. You're a journalist, aren't you? I thought American women were more professional than this."

Alexandra came, shoulders squared for battle. Instead of the loathsome, conceited individual who had spoken to her the day before, she found an entirely different Farid, cordial, expansive, somewhat shy, speaking enthusiastically about his interest in America, in campus politics, and in the affairs of the Middle East. He gave her tea, a green tea which he brewed with some ceremony; much later, they had brandy and talked about Nicaragua. Farid put his hand under her skirt. Alexandra drew away, surprised. Farid paid no attention; it was common knowledge, among male students, that girls always said no, and never meant it. Alexandra was a quiet and polite girl; the resistance she offered was quiet and polite. It was not in her to scream for help in a student apartment complex, though she certainly would have in a deserted parking lot or a dark alley. Afterward she jumped up, grabbed her things, and ran away, an unheard-of response in Farid's experience; her eyes were smeary, from what Farid wanted to think was passion but feared, for one short sinking moment, was tears. The experience made him feel very odd; the memory of it was quite unpleasant. Well, the girl really hadn't fought him, had she? The interview never appeared. When he ran into Alexandra in the hallways, she looked right through him, as though he didn't exist at all. A few times he thought of saying something to her, but he didn't know what.

What should we make of this incident? Shouldn't Alexandra have notified the police? Well, she was born five or six years too early for that; in those not-so-long-ago days, everyone assumed that when a young lady entered a man's room she politely left her civil rights outside like a wet umbrella.

I guess it's to Farid's credit, sort of, that he felt guilty. Anyway, the Farid that Mara met the following year was a chastened, subdued shadow of his former self. I would not want to go too far; he was not a new man, not a born-again human being in any sense. His teeth still flashed with carnivorous arrogance, his voice still alternated between seductive murmurs and icy razor slashes, and girls still flushed when his speculative eye came to rest upon them, unsure whether to hate or to want him. But the critical weight of his personality had shifted just enough to allow him to fall in love. Maybe he wanted its redemption. Maybe the game just wasn't fun anymore. The woman he fell in love with was Mara.

Mara was new that year. They shared two classes, and while Mara appeared to notice Farid not at all, he found himself watching her during class, and searching for her on campus the rest of the time. Mara was pretty, in a solemn and intelligent sort of way, and like his previous victims she was self-possessed, quiet, and intense. He sat down next to her in the cafeteria, on his best behavior, carefully restraining flash, sarcasm, and innuendo. Mara was polite but unencouraging. He invited her to a movie. She declined, citing a heavy study schedule. He invited her to a Pakistani dinner, to be prepared by him. She laughed with genuine amusement.

"Thanks," she said, "but I've heard about your dinner invitations."

"Just dinner," he said. "Really, I swear. Please come."

To her surprise, Mara agreed. There is a strain in women, Mara likes to say, that drives them to struggle for the domestication of men. It's what keeps civilization going, she believes: women's irresistible impulse to be the first to place their foot on the virgin soil of a man's heart. It's the female equivalent, she says, of wanting to be the first to walk on the moon.

Farid hardly seemed, on that first evening, to be much of a challenge for a female pioneer in the wilderness of men's souls. He served a nice little dinner, insufficiently salted and with only a timid breath of foreign spices. They ate sedately; then Farid suggested a movie. After the movie, Farid took her home, delivering only the most chaste of kisses to her cheek. The second time she came to his apartment, Farid unbuttoned her blouse and pushed her toward the bed. Mara took her bag and left the apartment without a word. For two weeks she refused to take or return his calls, or respond to his notes; in class she avoided his eyes. Finally, Farid caught her alone and apologized. They went out again, and he asked her to marry him.

"There is a strain in the female personality," Mara says, "that thinks destiny wears a necktie."

Mara did not, at that point in time, know what to do with herself. Life loomed ahead, a vast expanse of American vanilla. Mara wanted to do good deeds, but social work seemed tacky, street workers were out of style, and anyway she felt intimidated by American slums. Pakistani slums seemed by comparison more glamorous. Mara agreed to marry Farid. They finished their degrees, then off they went to live in Pakistan.

"The same thing would have happened if we had stayed in America," Mara always insisted of their separation a year later. She had no horror stories to tell, as do some American wives. She was not locked up in a mud hovel and forced to make dung patties to fuel the clay stove; in fact, she was barely allowed to enter the kitchen. She was not abused by in-laws, forced into purdah and guarded by eunuchs, or dragged off to some remote village and compelled to bear ten children. What happened, then? "Nothing," Mara said, shrugging apologetically at her inability to explain it any better. "Really, nothing. The pieces just didn't fit."

Farid: in New York he was just a young man from far away, but in Pakistan he was at home, and easily reassumed the role of eldest son in his large and prosperous family. Immediately his voice seemed deeper, his statements bore more authority, his features took on dignity and importance. When he was annoyed, he had only to frown slightly, and his three younger sisters fluttered about in a panic of appeasement. If he got his own glass of water, if he set his own tea water to boil late in the evening, when the servants had been dismissed, then a sigh of awe went through the room and eight pairs of slightly envious, slightly reproachful eyes focused on Mara, ever so politely, at oblique angles. What a man! What a jewel! What a prize! Not that they were not nice to Mara; they were. Smiles, she never saw anything but smiles, until she positively longed for a glimpse of bad temper, an impulsive insult. "But I was a kind of prize, too, in my way," Mara reflected. "Like a tropical fish, halfway between an asset and a liability. Interesting, unusual, a conversation piece, but much too sensitive, too fussy, too much work." She was there because of Farid; everyone loved her for the sake of Farid. Farid, though, was becoming ever more remote.

"Haven't you got any interests?" he snapped impatiently when she complained of boredom. Despite the ethnological briefings he had delivered to his family on the subject of Western brides, he found himself lacking sympathy for this particular complaint. Boredom? That wasn't a grievance, that was a splendid luxury. 99 percent of the female population of Pakistan would give anything to experience an hour of what Mara called boredom. Still, fine, she was different. "So do something," he curtly advised.

Well, all right, then, she would. Mara took a job working with Afghan refugees. Farid forbade it: his party was opposed to the presence of the refugees, and her job would be a political embarrassment. Mara ignored his objections; what was political, she asked, about pregnant women with health problems? Every morning, a Jeep containing a Danish doctor, two American nurses, and a German volunteer picked Mara up from the house. Farid forbade it, saying that she embarrassed him by

45

driving in a car with laughing and joking foreign men, embarrassed him equally by wearing the silly fundamentalist scarf required of all refugee workers, embarrassed him by being employed by the American government, which sponsored the project, and by working for the refugees, who were just puppets of American foreign policy. He did not issue ultimatums, threaten, or become violent, but he sulked, argued, and stayed away from home. And once, as she was getting ready to leave in the morning, he tore off her scarf, a gesture full of such irony that both of them laughed, seconds later, and embraced with a brief return of their former camaraderie.

Farid's sisters begged Mara to stop making these problems; they all loved her so much, they said, so very much, and why didn't she have a baby, and take care of it, and stop worrying about those awful refugees.

Farid's sisters: they, especially, liked the fancy tropical fish their brother had brought home, and spent hours trailing behind Mara in pursuit of information unobtainable elsewhere: information about love, and sex, and birth control. "The Dr. Ruth Westheimer of the North-West Frontier Province," Mara titled herself; I'm sure she liked the role. In fact, the husbands for these sisters had long been selected; they could love them or not, as they chose. Farid was sympathetic to Mara's protests but refused to get involved. "What's their alternative?" he would say, and be right. Young people of good family did not meet casually, or go out on dates; the families arranged for sedately chaperoned trysts, and while you could turn down a candidate you hated, it was best not to hold out for one you loved. "And anyway, what's love?" Farid would say, neatly distracting Mara from the plight of his sisters by making her worry about herself.

46

Farid's sister Hamida had her wedding date set, and spent ten days crying in Mara's bedroom until Mara, unable to bear it any longer, told her to come and live with them; she could go to the university, she did not have to marry, Farid would support her decision against their father. Hamida looked up through tear-swollen eyes in utter amazement. Oh, but she wanted to get married, and her husband-to-be was very nice and handsome, it was natural for women to be worried and nervous beforehand, everybody was. Farid laughed when she told him, and said nastily, "Americans, the nation of meddlers," and then, realizing that he had been too harsh, or too honest, hugged her and said, "My little meddler."

But all Mara could remember was his voice asking "What's love?"

Few people among Mara's former friends and acquaintances in New York were aware that her marriage had, to all intents and purposes, failed. Had they known, most of them would not have been too surprised. Even if her husband and his relatives did not abuse her, how could she adapt? Though there is even some controversy about the notion of adapting. Once, at a party in Tokyo, I met a very bitter forty-five-year-old woman from Philadelphia who shared with me what she had learned from marrying into a traditional Japanese family. The key, she said, was not to adapt at all. The secret was to remain totally and completely unyielding and unadjusted; something she had learned, she said, at great personal cost, and too late. If you did not adjust, she explained, then they had to come to terms with you. And they wouldn't be able to judge your worth, either, because they would lack any unit of measurement. Whereas, as soon as you did things their way, you inevitably fell short. There was no such thing, she insisted, as meeting them halfway. If you tried to please them the littlest bit, they would demand total surrender. "Wear a white wedding dress!" she called after me in parting, intently. "If you get married in a kimono, all is lost!"

Mara, on the other hand, always insisted that being a "foreign wife" had nothing to do with the breakup of her marriage. There was only one really Pakistani reason for her departure, she said. Khadija.

"How could you not tell me?" Mara wailed, when she first learned about Khadija. And Farid would say, "I forgot. It's nothing. There's nothing to tell." Khadija was Farid's fiancée, engaged to him when they were both eleven. Mara didn't blame him for Khadija, but she did blame him for never mentioning her, for not wanting to hear about her even now. "Oh, for God's sake," he would say, knitting his brows in irritation. "What is there to say about it. I can't believe that you, of all people, would pay any attention to superstitious nonsense of this sort. It must be your scarf," he would add, nastily, for by that time Mara had begun her refugee work. "Ever since you wear that scarf, there's a shadow on your brain."

Ridiculous, superstitious nonsense; of course, in a sense that was perfectly true. How could he be expected to take seriously, let alone abide by, a silly piece of outdated nonsense contrived by his father when Farid himself was just a child? His father does not blame him for reneging; times have changed, he realizes that. In Islamic countries, good friends often find it fortuitous that one of them has a daughter, the other a son. Good friends often feel that it would be charming if the two children were one day to marry. Everybody has his own ideas about principles, and everybody has his own ideas about romance. "Homosexuality," Mara has been heard to comment, concerning such arrangements. "They really want to bugger each other, but they don't dare, so they put the poor kids in bed together instead." It is to Farid's credit that his face merely darkened another shade in anger when he heard his culture thus maligned. We can even sympathize with him, I think, when he found this view incompatible with Mara's insistence that he divorce her and marry Khadija. Really. Of all people, how could Mara take such a ludicrous arrangement seriously. "It was just the stupid idea of my father and his stupid old chum," Farid snaps. "It meant nothing. Why should I have told you about it? What would be different if I had told you? It was a silly, old-fashioned idea, and it means nothing."

"To you!" Mara would counter. "It means nothing to you."

Well, sure, it was sad for the girl, Farid knew that. An engaged and then rejected girl; what self-respecting Pathan man would have her? But was it his fault that he found himself the unwilling owner of a girl he did not want, had not seen since childhood, had never touched? The last time he had seen Khadija, she had been eleven years old, a pretty, spoiled little girl with hair down to the waist. And so she remained, in Farid's memory, accursedly conjured by Mara: a spoiled, bland, uninteresting child who had been gifted to him, a primitive little faceless Amish doll laid on his pillow.

"She's on our conscience," Mara would wail, absurdly. "I'll leave you and you can marry her," she would say, knowing all the while that this argument was not really about Khadija at all.

What was it about, then? From the whole long story of this failed intercultural marriage and the subsequent act of adultery that allowed Iqbal to put the American woman on the spot, Lilly understands what Mara means

49

her to understand: that her brief affair with this Malone person was the product of loneliness and confusion.

Meanwhile, things are happening on the home front. Before his departure, Malone had announced that his trip to Pakistan would take three days. "Three days tops," to quote him precisely. While agreeing indulgently that why of course, this will be such a brief business trip that Malone will hardly even notice that he has gone anywhere, his boss had mentally extended Malone's anticipated absence to five days. Pakistani partners are notoriously inefficient. The trip is long; jet lag and tummy problems can easily knock you out for a day or two. So George Hamish does not expect Micky back after three days. But two days later, and no phone call, he is starting to worry. George's secretary, Josie, tries Micky's home number at ever-shorter intervals, without success. On Day Six, she and a co-worker are dispatched to stop by his place; there is no sign of him and the neighbors haven't seen him. This is absolutely unlike Micky. Others may allow their business trip to extend itself fortuitously into a weekend in Manhattan and conceivably even, for a lark, to a foray to the thrilling Khyber Pass, but definitely not Micky. Even if you sent him to Miami, more likely than not he would return a day early, settling back into his swivel chair with a sigh of relief.

With George hovering over her in some anxiety, Josie calls the airline and learns that Malone was a no-show on the Islamabad–London–New York–D.C. route, reservation neither canceled nor changed to a later date.

It's time to take steps, but nobody is quite sure which ones. This has never happened before. What's going on? Why hasn't he called?

Assisted by Stefanie from the travel department, Josie calls the Inter-Continental Hotel but is unable to communicate her problem. They are just on the line to Inter-Cont. corporate headquarters to request intervention when the State Department desk officer calls on another line, asking for George Hamish.

In order to tell him that his employee has disappeared, that his blood and a message have been found in the hotel, that Pakistani police are investigating. And in order to query him about any information he may have concerning Malone, their foreign partners, or this particular transaction that could help explain what may have transpired.

West-Fab is in an uproar. Micky is low-key but popular. The news that he has gone missing, may have been kidnapped, could be dead, triggers stunned silence by the vending machine, compensated by a ground swell of E-mail messages zooming electronic dismay in all directions. In a kind of spontaneous totemistic act, the secretaries file by his workstation to garnish his Macintosh with their favorite stuffed animals. Soon his monitor is draped with bears, zebras, and undefinable cute fluffy things, some of them with improvised little yellow ribbons attached to their furry torsos with safety pins.

Co-workers bravely assure local television reporters that they are confident of their office mate's safe return, until Josie breaks down and sobs into the microphone that he didn't want to go on this trip in the first place, because probably he had a premonition.

J ulia is in Croatia while all of this is going on. She doesn't even know that her brother has gone on a business trip; as far as she is concerned, he is alive, well, and in Maryland.

She is researching a story on war crimes. Theoretically, she has a hotel room in Zagreb, and her office has the phone number. But when her frantic mother tries to reach her there, she isn't in the hotel—she is off with a delegation, touring mass graves. She is unreachable, and doesn't come back for a week. There are about 150 messages waiting for her at the desk when she finally returns from this grim field trip; none of them make any sense, but cumulatively they obviously add up to some kind of a disaster. With trepidation, she gets an outside line and calls her mother. It should be about 1:00 a.m. in the States, she figures, so if no one answers by the third ring, she plans to hang up and try again at a more civil hour. But the phone is answered immediately, by her mother, who instantly breaks out in sobs when she hears her daughter's voice and is unable to speak. This is followed by some clucking and exclaiming in the background, and finally Julia's aunt takes the receiver and tells her what has happened. It is a bad connection; there is a lot of static, and an echo that repeats the last words of every sentence back.

So the awful message comes across like a hysterical kind of telegram, repeated many times over. Micky. Had to go to Pakistan. Disappeared from his hotel. Blood found. Intense police search. Further bodies. Murderer on the loose. Micky dead, presumed dead.

Later, Julia can't remember anything about the flight back home. Customs, getting her luggage, getting a cab—it all goes by in a blur. The first thing she consciously registers is walking into her apartment. It is dark inside, except for two dim sources of light. The aquarium bubbles silently; Julia disconnects the automatic feeder and absentmindedly throws in a pinch of food, for no good reason. The answering machine blinks red five times; she pushes REPLAY without much interest.

The first call is from Jeff, her sort-of-serious current relationship. As she knows, he is on a business trip. "Things are getting complicated here," he tells her. "These people can never stick to a deal. Looks like things will be delayed by at least ten days, so you'll probably be home before me after all. So I'll get back to you then, babe."

Babe, uh-huh.

The second call is from her friend Beth. "I know you're not there," she says. "I'm just reminding you that my fabulous show, after which I will be incredibly famous and won't have much time for the likes of you media rabble anymore, opens on the seventeenth, and you'd better be there, girlfriend!"

The third call is from Micky. Julia is just lifting her suitcase when his voice comes on—she lowers it in slow motion, hypnotized by her brother's voice.

"Hey kid," he is saying, "you won't believe where I am. I'm in your neck of the woods. I'm here in Pakistan in a place called Peshawar." He pronounces the "a"s in "Pakistan" like the ones in "Pac-Man," instead of like that in "aah." For "Peshawar," he puts the emphasis on the first instead of the second syllable. Julia hates herself for being able to notice something like this, under the circumstances.

"Well," he is saying, "I need your advice here on something, so why don't you call me at the Inter-Continental Hotel. It's, well, it's kind of urgent," he says. Then he repeats that he is staying at the Inter-Continental, pronouncing it very slowly and reading out its phone number. That's it. She checks the date on her machine. Calculating quickly, Julia figures out that he must have called her the day before he disappeared. She would give anything, anything, to have been there to take that call. Even uselessly, in retrospect, she would give almost anything to know what he had wanted. How alone he must have felt, when he called and got an answering machine; when she failed to call him back. She would have called him immediately, had she gotten his message. If advice hadn't been enough, she would have flown there right away. He knew that, didn't he? Julia tries to comfort herself with the knowledge that he certainly must have known that.

She barely registers the fourth call, which is for Jeff anyway. And then, suddenly, the energetic voice of her Pakistani journalist friend Lilly comes booming out at her. "Maybe this has nothing to do with you after all," she has yelled into the receiver much too loudly. "But I've got this APA report in front of me about a Micky Malone from Bethesda. That isn't your brother, is it? Well, if it isn't, then I won't hold you up, but why don't you let me hear from you again sometime. Are you coming this way anytime soon? But if it is your brother, then listen, I'm on my way to Peshawar. I assigned myself to cover the murder. Oh shit, if it is your brother, I hope you knew about it already. I'm not telling you something new, am I, oh shit. Oh God, I'm such an idiot! Oh God, Julia! If there's anything I can do for you, just say the word."

This garbled message comes across to Julia like a precise call to action. Her direction suddenly seems as clear as day. She picks up the receiver and books herself onto the morning flight to Pakistan, 10:35, Dulles–Amsterdam–Karachi–Islamabad–Peshawar. Energized by this taking of action, she exchanges the contents of her suitcase for cleaner, cooler things, asks her aunt to continue taking care of her mother, putters around her apartment for a while doing this and that, and finally even feels ready for some sleep. Going to Pakistan feels right, feels like the right thing to do, and gives a measure of comfort. She doesn't have an agenda, anything concrete she hopes to accomplish. If you asked her to explain her purpose, she would probably say that she wants to be close to Micky one last time: to commune with the spirit of her brother; to stand on the ground that swallowed him up.

Motives are usually complicated, as I'm sure you know. A little bit of sibling guilt, a wish to get away from her mother's hysteria . . . but let's not overanalyze. In the end, she goes because her brother called her. Since she couldn't go to him in time, at least she will go now, too late.

3

Aunt Sonia is one of those gracious, well-groomed upper-class ladies that you find in all countries with imperial traditions, like England, India, Turkey, or Spain. As different as their nationalities may be, they resemble one another amazingly in their erect carriage, their poise, their quiet style of command. They even have the same hairdo—an immaculate, gently graying black knot. They have that special kind of serenity which comes from having been obeyed, respected, and waited on for the last nine or ten generations. Here's my theory about wealth: the first two generations, it makes you aggressive and arrogant. The third and fourth, it makes you lazy and stupid. Then, if you weather that, you start to turn mellow. Royal families are excepted from this rule; they rarely seem to get beyond step two.

At any rate, Gul dearly loves her Aunt Sonia. From the time she was five years old, she spent some of her best vacations here, being coddled, shopped for, chatted with, allowed to dream on the shady veranda while the elegantly dressed and sweetly scented lady friends of Sonia murmured to one another about the marriages, infertilities, infidelities, mergers, economic setbacks, and other large and small events of local high society. Now in her seventies, Aunt Sonia remains poised, perfumed, and quietly in command of a perfect household with soothing rhythms that unobtrusively punctuate the day. It surprises no one that a masseuse arrives every morning at six-thirty, to gently pummel Aunt Sonia into a state of waking. They have come to expect the delicious meals, served on very old, limp white linen by very old, absentminded servants. The polite visits by the neighbors' children, who stop by to decorously demonstrate their newly learned traditional dance movements and collect her pleased approval, are very charming. Only Sonia's new entertainment preference is initially startling to her city guests, though they really shouldn't be surprised—didn't she always have her manicured finger on the pulse of her times? "Oh," she says, as they sit in her living room after another perfect lunch, "it's time for the Maulana."

Tired smiles greet her announcement, changing to incredulous groans as she rises to put on the television. "Please," Lilly says, "you can't be serious." "I never miss the Maulana," Sonia replies. "He is an important part of your country and your times, my dear, whether you like it or not."

The preceding program is still on. As Sonia takes her seat again, the picture emerges, showing five women with tightly wrapped head scarves sitting on the floor in a circle while one of them reads gloomily from the Koran. This thrilling media event is evidently being filmed live in front of a studio audience; occasionally, the camera pans back to show ten deathly bored individuals sliding back and forth restlessly on their seats. A few commercials, and then the Maulana's smug countenance fills the screen. The topic on this day is one of his perennial favorites, soccer.

Soccer, the cherished colonial legacy of the Pakistanis: in the Maulana's eyes, the gateway to hell. When he describes the game as he sees it, it really does sound like some totally depraved undertaking. The naked legs of the players, thrusting toward the ball. Their bare thighs pumping as they race in its pursuit, their bodies to which sweat-drenched T-shirts cling. But worst of all is the way they slap their thighs when points are scored, a gesture that cannot fail to incite lustful and lewd thoughts in the viewers. This assault on the purity of the country has to be banned, the teams dispersed, this indecency forbidden! Soccer must go!

By the time he is finished, Lilly and Gul are in paroxysms of schoolgirl giggles. "Mmmmh, those naked thighs," Gul moans. "Ooooh, that sweat," Lilly pants. "You may be as foolish as you like, ladies," Sonia interposes, "but the fact of the matter is that he has a very considerable following, and has already succeeded in having two regular television programs canceled for good."

"*Wonder Woman.*" Lilly nods. "He went to the TV station with his little band of the faithful, and managed to get it thrown off the air because it was indecent to show a woman in a bathing suit, and fighting with men at that." "And winning," Iqbal adds, very solemnly. "That was the part that hurt. I'm not narrow-minded, I didn't object to the swimsuit at all."

Iqbal pursues his investigation, but to fill the hours,

he really has to stretch things. The fact is that he has very little to go on. There are no real witnesses. If Malone was in Peshawar to do anything other than sell prefab housing, there is no evidence of it. The clearest link between the two murders is the message. "YOU ARE THE DUST," Toufiq proclaims, at least a dozen times a day, as if the repetition of the incantation may, in time, reveal the spell. "You are the dust, you are dust . . ."

His theory, which Iqbal cannot refute, is that the writer of the message does not possess a very good command of the English language. " 'You are the dust,' it is meant to be an insult," Toufiq believes. "He doesn't mean dust, he wants to say scum, dirt, vermin. You are dirt," Toufiq spits out contemptuously, in illustration of the murderer's linguistic intention. If true, this is still not immensely helpful. How do you find a person, only moderately fluent in the English language, with a reason to hate both an American who has been in Peshawar for only a few days and a lawyer who has been on the scene for years? There has to be an answer, Iqbal believes this unshakably, but where is it to be found? In America? In Pakistan? In their personal affairs, or in their business lives? There is only one thing to do: accumulate as much information as you can about both of them, and hope for some kind of picture to emerge. What Iqbal really wants to do is to go back to Islamabad; his superiors won't let him. "There's nothing for me to do here," he huffs. "This investigation can be handled perfectly well by Toufiq, and I can keep an eye on it from Islamabad if they really insist. There is no need for me to sit here. I'm a human sacrifice for the Americans," he continues with deep pathos. " 'Don't worry, Mr. Ambassador, our top man is in Peshawar handling the investigation, results expected any moment now,' what a farce."

Meanwhile, to Iqbal's annoyance, his ladies have become devoted fans of the Maulana's television show. When Iqbal grumbles, Sonia tells him to be grateful— there's an evening show with the Maulana, too, but he will be spared that one, as it conflicts with her dinner hour. But they watch him unfailingly, every afternoon; the damned show is timed for the afternoon siesta, so Iqbal is almost always at home then, too, to enjoy the dubious pleasure of the Maulana's ramblings. There he sits, squat and smug in his oatmeal-colored robes, a latter-day Calvin, raging against the flesh. Each time, he chooses some harmless pleasure from the world around him and inflates and distorts it until it is the most vile, the most disgusting perversion imaginable. Female college students wearing slacks and lady television announcers are two favorite grievances, besides the thigh-slapping soccer players, of course. He has a large following, and can look back on many absurd victories. His goal is to remove women from television entirely; he has demanded a media ruling forbidding the display of the female face or form in print or on the screen.

"I'll bet you he's a really vile person, leading a really vile life," Lilly speculates. "Anyone with that graphic a sense of sin has got to be speaking from firsthand knowledge."

How astute of her. If she could peer into the recent past, she would find that her glib, irreverent theory is amazingly close to the truth.

4

The Maulana. As Lilly has sensed, he is a nasty little man, and he has a nasty little secret. He may rant on about soccer players and lady television announcers, but that's not really his thing; he prefers the young village girls brought to work in his household and duly terrified of their master, the Pillar of Islam. At first he ignores them, like the irrelevant nonentities that they are, perhaps issuing gruff instructions now and then but in general looking through them, past them, beyond them, entirely preoccupied with lofty thoughts of godliness and salvation. But sometimes they will find him watching them. He will begin to take an interest in them, to find fault with their clothes, to ask them about their families. He will ask probing questions about their behavior, their thoughts, their fantasies; this will not strike them as unseemly, since of course their souls are his provenance just as their work is his property. With stern, fatherly concern he will note that they lingered rather too long in the hallway yesterday, when the young man from the university students' league came to visit, trying to tempt his thoughts to their young bodies. Well, it comes as no surprise to him, nor can the young girl be blamed; the times are bad, corrupting, sinful. The girl, terrified and nearly dead with embarrassment, shrinks back, but the Maulana allows no escape. He must concern himself with this; her parents have entrusted her to him for moral and spiritual guidance, a responsibility he cannot, will not shirk. The girl is ordered into his study. Her father told him she is engaged and will be married in a year's time. No doubt she thinks about this often, and tries to imagine what her husband will be like. No doubt she thinks about him, at night in her bed. That is . . . he hopes she is a virgin, in spite of some of the improper behavior she has recently displayed? The girl, frozen with panic, rarely manages a coherent reply; certainly she manages no resistance when her inquisitor, nearly frantic by now in his misery over the disobedience, impiety, and shamelessness of his country's young womanhood, begins to slap and strike at her. When he yanks at her clothes, and at his own, and forces her down beneath him, the girl may not immediately realize what is happening to her, but may think it is still part of the chastisement she must somehow, in some way, have led him to believe she deserves. Afterward the Maulana will push the girl to the floor, throwing her clothes after her. Sometimes he is angry, and beats the girl some more for her lustfulness, which did not make a halt even before a man such as himself. More often he will look at her sadly, and quote for her the saying that when a man and a woman are alone together, the Devil is always the third one present. She has made him weak, she has driven him to this, but it is not really her fault; that is her nature, which is why, of course, she must be concealed from the eyes of men and strictly controlled. In particularly mellow moods, he may even clutch the girl to him and suppose that since Allah has made her a woman and made women the way they are, it may be that He will forgive her.

After several months of these ménages à trois, woman-Maulana-and-Devil, the girls begin to change. Some become disrespectful and lazy, indifferent to the moral authority of their master, and have to be beaten more and more often, and have a contemptuously knowing expression on their faces even then. Others become sallow and weepy, and slink along the edges of the walls; their skin becomes yellow and unattractive, and their look of resignation seems to mock his fervor, when they lie limp and miserable underneath him. Then it is time to marry them off, usually to some devotee of the Maulana who, after receiving a stern lecture on the weakness of women, which does not allow them to be held fully responsible for their deeds, and on the need to be firm and unyielding in one's supervision of them, is willing to accept a ruined woman—along with some appropriate story about a dead fiancé who just had time, before his demise, to impatiently claim a husband's prerogative—in exchange for the uplifting feeling that her body, her soul, her life even beyond the grave have been placed by no one less than the Maulana into his firm masculine hands.

Some months before Lilly has occasion to reflect upon the presumed moral qualities of the Maulana, he had received a new victim. Fatima, who has just turned sixteen, is taken to Peshawar by two of her brothers to work in the household of the long-widowed religious leader. Before her departure, lectures about the splendor, the fame, the sanctity, and the inestimable importance of the Maulana have been drummed into her ears, and during the trip the brothers repeat their injunctions to please, to obey, to serve, to display only the deepest humility, the most self-effacing servility, and of course the modesty and shame befitting a marriageable female of virtue and piety. Fatima is nearly catatonic with shyness and terror by the time she reaches Peshawar, and when they actually enter the Maulana's house and come into his august presence, her heart pounds, her hands tremble, and it is fortunate that speech is not required of her, since she would certainly not be capable of it.

Fatima, young, vulnerable, poor; the analogy of Cinderella comes to mind, also obliged to serve the Undeserving. It is easy to think of Fatima in slightly mythical terms. Lovely Fatima; it is easy to imagine a whole crowd of envious fairy godmothers showering poison kisses on her as she lay, raven-haired and bright and beautiful already, and helpless in her cradle. Fatima is beautiful; that can be a misfortune in itself. She has another: an imaginative mind that dreams, at times, of possibilities beyond the certainties life holds in store for her. She has a third: a strange older brother named Isa. When he was eight years old, he put himself into a school run by Irish missionaries, pleading a burning interest in Christianity to make up for the lack of tuition money or parental approval. Ultimately, this led to a scholarship to study in England, where he is right now; in the summers he usually comes home, to his village, though little connects him anymore to his family, his neighbors, his country. Except for Fatima.

During these visits he makes his favorite sister into his own personal home improvement project. The visits are not long, perhaps four months each time, but they are sufficient to baffle her with stories about the lives of girls in England, to confuse her with heretic interpretations of Islam, and to dismay her with conglomerations of Fabian, Marcusean, Leninist, Virginia Woolfish theories applied to the future of Pakistan, womanhood, and the world.

Fatima loves Isa, regarding his appearances like the flash of a meteor blazing across the eclipsed night of her sky. Fatima loves to listen to Isa, though he frightens her, though he is to her like a prophet, babbling on in a delirium of enlightenment incomprehensible to mortal humans. It does not occur to Fatima that there is even the most tenuous of connections between the words of Isa and her own life. Isa believes that men and women are equal. Isa believes that girls should go to bed with boys, for their own pleasure, whenever the mood strikes them. Isa does not believe in virginity, arranged marriages, or the chador. Isa believes in land reform, elections, the triumph of the Third World, socialism, and birth control. These beliefs, of course, are fairly recent. When he was seventeen and Fatima was eleven, he slapped her once for talking with Ali, the eleven-year-old son of their neighbor, and a few days later slapped her again, for going to the brook without the proper scarf on her head. He remembers these incidents with great shame and considers them in the nature of a debt he must repay by educating her and informing her of her status as a human being endowed with the United Nations' proclaimed human rights.

Fatima accepts the news of her emancipation as she accepted the slaps: all part of the behavior of men, who may do as they please and call it justice.

Fatima's three unfortunate traits will affect her life in the order listed; beauty, intelligence, and the love of her brother are waiting to do Fatima in.

It does not take the Maulana long to notice her beauty.

If you think that even the burqa, that unwieldy coarse full-body wrapping worn by traditional women in Pakistan, conceals the individual woman beneath, then you are not reckoning with the schooled eye of the connoisseur; and of course Fatima does not wear the burqa inside the house. Even in the first five minutes, confronting the terrified girl shrinking behind her brothers in his living room, the Maulana sees slim wrists and slender fingers, a straight body and a graceful neck. And in the first days and weeks of her employment, these impressions are expanded into a lavish extravaganza of erotic detail. A man of the Maulana's disposition is like a man on drugs: colors, odors, shapes stand out with unnatural clarity. To the Maulana, Fatima's hennaed hair—and henna, as those of you who have used it know, smells like boiled spinach—gives off a scent as aphrodisiacal as musk. To the Maulana, Fatima's every nervous motion and every timidly whispered reply is an incitement to immediate intercourse. To the obsessed eye of the Maulana, the world is one enormous Times Square, ablaze with licentious invitation. Fatima slapping dough into flat breads in the kitchen evokes the sound of copulating flesh slapping on flesh; Fatima unobtrusively crossing a room might as well be swinging her hips, dropping items of clothing as she goes, and gyrating before him at last dressed only in tassels. To persuade himself of the fatherliness of his intentions, the Maulana orders her to relax her attire; he pats her cheek benevolently when she serves him tea; he detects an imaginary limp in her walk and orders her to go back and forth across the room so he can check her posture, and Fatima cannot say why his scrutiny evokes in her such a paralysis of embarrassment that she really does limp, as well as stumble, catch her slipper on the carpet, and feel a suffocating weight settle around her throat. The real Fatima keeps her eyes downcast and her voice lowered. But in his dreams, the Maulana sees another Fatima. In his dreams, he finds her in his bed, smiling brazenly as she lets the sheet slip lower and lower down her unclothed body. In his dreams, the Maulana kneads her breasts, fills his mouth with her henna-red hair, and then pounds away at her inflamed body with a slap-slap-slap of dough being beaten into chapatis. In his dreams, a taunting, teasing Fatima enters his room and stands in the doorway, undoing her rope of hair, laughingly lifting up her shirt to expose pale circles of breasts; in his dreams, the Maulana slaps her deceitful, beguiling face with the sound of hands slapping dough into circles of bread, he beats her and beats her until their clothes loosen and fall away and she—

"Daughter," he says to her, coming abruptly out of his reverie, "you are a good child. Go and bring my tea." And Fatima cannot say why his voice, smooth and rich and benevolent, sends a shiver of revulsion down her spine. In Fatima's dreams, Isa comes to Peshawar to get her. He appears suddenly at the doorstep to take her with him, far away, to London, to keep house and cook for him and the strange, free foreign girls who flutter through his apartment and his life like exotic, chirping Western birds.

This does not happen.

Dreams, you may think, are free; a luxury that even the most miserable of God's creatures can indulge in. This, unfortunately, is sentimental nonsense. Dreams, like everything else in this world, belong to the powerful. The Maulana may dream, and see his dreams become reality. Fatima, on the other hand, will lose even the pleasure of her dreams. Inevitably, she meets the fate of her predecessors. It takes a certain innocence to dream. The Maulana has it; his is the innocence of total self-absorption. Fatima has lost it, burned away by self-contempt, humiliation, and hate. Fatima is dishonored; and Isa's theoretical attitudes, would they stand up to the test of Fatima's reality? She would rather not find out, not even in a dream.

The third murder victim is again not an American. This time it is a Pakistani banker of minimal distinction. Khan has employed him on occasion, but would not compose too enthusiastic a eulogy. He was useful but unpredictable, corrupt but unintelligent. He never really mastered the rules: that you can allow yourself to be bought, and can haggle for a better price, but that you must show some finesse, because otherwise you will find yourself without a protector. This, Khan comments to his lackeys, is what had happened to Nang, and if they are wise they will learn and profit from the lesson. You have to belong to somebody; otherwise you're fair game for anybody.

Too bad; if he had been less greedy, more adaptable, Nang could have done very well. Khan himself tried to be his mentor, to educate him in the ways of the world, but he was stubborn, stubborn and thickheaded. He had a nasty streak, too, without the power and importance that would have allowed him to get away with that. Actually, it was just a matter of time until somebody did him in.

This time, the message next to the body reads: BRING YOUR ENEMIES TO FALL! It is written on the torn-off corner of a greeting card. One side is metallic green with gaudy golden letters spelling out "Best Wishes for a

Happy Eid." On the other side, in smeared ink, is the murderer's message. Eid is the Islamic feast of sacrifice; perhaps the murderer has a sense of humor. The card, which at first seems unusual and a promising clue, turns out to be available in bulk in nearly any stationery store and bookshop in Peshawar, a special local import from Islamic Africa.

So let's see, what have we now? An American businessman, an Afghan lawyer, a Pakistani banker. An apparently straightforward importer-exporter of legal goods, a corrupt immigrant, and a minor relation of an established Peshawari banking clan.

Toufiq and Iqbal sit before their files, pondering the picture and finding no pattern. All three men retained valuable items of jewelry or money after they were killed, so none of the crimes include robbery. The notes are strange, but not really kinky enough to point to a madman.

Malone was abducted from the hotel, then probably killed somewhere else; there wasn't enough blood in the utility room to account for a quick death. The lawyer was killed in his rooms. The banker was killed in his office. That seems to indicate that the killer knew them, that they weren't just random victims picked out on the street.

The heat is off, a little, since the other victims are not Americans. The embassy has been told that Malone's death must have been an isolated, perhaps accidental, event; nothing points to terrorism against Americans. On the other hand, Islamabad is making no move to recall Iqbal. Clearly, he is expected to solve this case, and to stay in Peshawar until he does. His professional pride makes the same demand on him. There is a lot to do, but nonetheless Iqbal does not feel that he is making progress. Interviewing witnesses and informers, researching the murdered men, Iqbal does not feel that he is amassing facts; he feels that he is digging in a swamp, loosening up the quicksand that he himself, with every shovelful, sinks deeper into. There is a lot to be learned about Nang: witnesses he has bribed into perjuring themselves, victims he has blackmailed into silence, fights his bad temper has gotten him into. There are whispers about a kidnapping and a rape he may have engineered, though that particular trail runs up against the cement wall that Pathans erect in front of anything having to do with women and scandal. There are plenty of people who hated the Afghan lawyer, and there are people who hated the banker, but they are not the same people. And no one can be found who hated Malone.

But the most exasperating "clue," without a doubt, is the ubiquitous woman in a green chador. "Did you notice anything else, anything at all?" Toufiq or Iqbal invariably asks anyone who has been in the vicinity of the murder. The person then purses his lips, looks thoughtful, shakes his head, and says, "Well, there was a woman in a green chador . . ." It is tantalizing, it is frustrating. The probability that it means anything at all is so slight as to be almost nonexistent. A woman in a green chador—so what? That's like seeing a man in a business suit in Manhattan. Iqbal suspects there must be something a little bit different about the woman, a little bit off, otherwise the witnesses most probably would not have noticed her at all. There must be something about her that sets off subliminal bells, something too subtle for them to consciously register. So yes, she is definitely worth looking for. Except that there is no way, no way at all, that you can look for a woman based on your knowledge that she wears a green chador.

When Iqbal dwells on this annoying situation, Lilly just laughs.

"Oh dear," she says, "wearing a chador is certainly very inconvenient, isn't it? For *you*, I mean." And she laughs again, a nasty, bitter laugh. Causing Iqbal, never slow with his retorts, to remain silent.

I can understand Lilly's snippiness. The veil is an emotional topic for a politically engaged woman like her. In her hometown of Islamabad, the strongest compromise you will ever have to make will take the form of a gauzy shawl that you can drape loosely around your shoulders in a sort of insouciant compliance with the general idea of covering yourself up. In Islamabad, even the most traditional situation can be managed by pulling a tip of this gauzy shawl loosely over part of your hair. And the shawl matches your outfit, so you can pretend it is a voluntary accessory. But in Peshawar it is quite another story.

In Peshawar, two styles of chador are vying for dominance this season. There is the burqa, the traditional style of the area, and then there is the Afghan burqa, more properly called a chaddri, brought in by the refugee women and gaining fast in popularity. The Pakistani burqa is made of coarse cloth, the quality of a flour sack and the shape of a round tablecloth. It has a sort of embroidered lacy edge on the bottom, making the wearer look like a walking doily. It comes in white, blue, and black, and costs 100 rupees. The Afghan burqa is made out of finer fabric and comes in more attractive colors, which I suppose explains its popularity. It is made from thin and shiny stuff resembling parachute cloth and is pressed into very tight, permanent pleats. There are two sizes: short and tall. There are two qualities, costing 150 and 300 rupees respectively. It comes in olive green, grassy neon green, gold, navy blue—and those are just the standard marketplace colors. You may see them in purple, and pink, sky blue . . . nearly every imaginable shade. Both the burqa and the chaddri have a stiff, flat embroidered circle at the top, to center the thing on your head. And they both have a panel set in front, at eye level, a kind of visor, made out of tight, hard mesh, through which you can attempt to see.

I have always considered the burqa, and the chaddri even more, to be the most absurd garment ever devised for the confinement and humiliation of women—with the possible exception of the little leather miniskirt I used to wear in high school, and nobody ever said they would kill me if I didn't wear that.

In these outfits, your hands are not free; you are a moving blob. Behind the mesh, even your eyes are muzzled. Of the constant sounds in the cacophonous medley of noise that defines Peshawar, one element is the perpetual shrieking of brakes, as drivers skid around terrified women who are trying to make their half-blind way across the streets. The Iranian veil, more familiar to Americans thanks to our interlude with the Ayatollah, is actually quite a bit better. At least it leaves your face and your eyes free. It does tie up your hands, since you have to hold it shut in the front, but Iranian women solve that little problem by clenching the fabric in their teeth. That may look a bit strange, but it frees your hands. All those newscasts of the Iranian revolution plagued me with one persistent, obsessive thought: why didn't any of those grim, determined women sew buttons on their chadors? A button couldn't possibly be anti-Islamic, could it? Why did they run around with their clothes clenched between their teeth when a few little buttons and loops on the front of the chador would so easily solve their problem? You might find this question trivial, but I must tell you that for me it was very absorbing. Never mind the debate on women artists, women inventors, women composers. Faced with millions of women gripping their chador in their bare teeth, I feel the issue is more basic and the question is this: are women too stupid even to button their own clothes, if men don't show them how?

But Iqbal has more serious problems than the question of dress. The murder he was sent to solve is still a riddle, and two new murders have been committed on his watch; how embarrassing.

Dinner at Aunt Sonia's house is becoming a gloomy affair. The women exchange glances of motherly exasperation aimed at the shadowy figure of Iqbal, who sits sulking in the farthest corner of the living room. Gul's worried consolation and Lilly's businesslike annoyance eventually move him to his place at the table, but he is hardly an asset to the conversation anymore.

"When Muslim men want their 'mommies' to worry and fuss over them," Lilly comments with irritated impatience, "they lose their appetites. 'Oh, poor little Iqbal,' we are all supposed to exclaim. 'He won't eat!' "

Gul tries to be sympathetic. "What's wrong?" she asks her husband, studiously ignoring Lilly's look of disapproval.

"It's one thing to be a human sacrifice for the Americans," he grumbles, in reply. "I'd almost come to terms with that. But now they want me to be a fool as well."

Islamabad, it seems, has come up with an idea to counter the American reproaches. Far from the scene of the crime, and apparently without the slightest little bit of concrete evidence to support such an idea, it has decided that the killer is not a Pakistani at all but a Westerner.

Actually, Iqbal soon warms to this hypothesis. It is true, he agrees, that no motive has thus far presented itself, and no local group has claimed credit or demanded money; there is a case to be made for the idea that some disoriented foreigner is involved. And certainly there are enough of them in Peshawar. "I don't know," he says, "somehow my heart still isn't in it, and it just doesn't feel quite right, but on the other hand my intuitions haven't got me anywhere either yet, so I might as well explore this track."

Iqbal makes the rounds of committees, offices, clinics, and clubs. He drives back to Islamabad once to talk to Western embassy staff and to journalists. He collects files about suspicious, disoriented, and extremist Westerners in Peshawar.

In the evenings, in Sonia's garden, he entertains his audience with his red herrings of the day. "There's a fifteen-year-old carpenter's apprentice from Erlangen," he tells them, "which, as you may or may not know, is an industrial city in West Germany, who has been picked up three times on the Khyber Pass. He considers himself a subject of the Afghan king. In Germany he was institutionalized three times following unsuccessful suicide attempts; then he somehow made his way here. His plan is to kill himself in a suicide mission against the fundamentalists, and he can't understand why the royalists, instead of embracing him as a heroic brother, keep turning him in to the German consul. The German honorary consul, getting tired of this, has sworn to send him home in handcuffs if he is found near the border one more time. The French committee considers it entirely possible that the Austrian committee may harbor one or more 'Maoists or murderers,' I quote, and the Austrian committee believes the French committee to be composed of 'psychopaths and fascists.' " Iqbal sighs with mock distress. "Then I followed several promising leads on foreigners buying weapons and chadors in the bazaars. But every one of them turned out to be an innocent tourist purchasing souvenirs. You know, a few Afghan daggers to hang above the sofa, and chadors for God knows what." Iqbal shakes his head. Everybody's crazy. East, West, everybody's nuts, and that's the multicultural truth of it. And he's supposed to puzzle it out.

5

———————

J ulia, spurred by the posthumous message from her brother, flies to Islamabad. She changes planes and continues on to Peshawar. Well, I'm not sure you would classify the vehicles that fly the Islamabad–Peshawar stretch as actual airplanes. They are contraptions with wings, and sometimes, not always, they become airborne. Your fellow passengers could be goats and chickens; the cockpit is generally occupied by a crazed-looking individual in quasi-military dress with a suicidal look on his face. It is generally safer to take the overland route, which I have described to you already. Yes, even that is safer.

But on this trip, Julia isn't thinking about her safety. Her seat neighbors are an Omani and his falcon; the bird has trouble with the concept of flying; that is, he seems disturbed to be ascending into the air without any effort of his own, so upon takeoff he commences hysterically flapping his wings. His owner speaks to him soothingly while snapping at Julia that she must at all costs avoid looking into the bird's eyes. Usually she has something to say to people who snap at her, even and especially Omanis, but she's tired. She just nods.

The passengers arrive intact, some of them minus a few feathers.

Julia checks into Green's Hotel and makes some phone calls. She has a long conversation with Lilly, who brings her up to speed on the investigation, but Julia doesn't want to see her yet. Iqbal has gone to Islamabad for a day or two, which Lilly apologizes for profusely. But Julia doesn't really care. There is no urgency. It is already too late.

Julia unpacks her small suitcase. Then she goes looking for Micky. For his spirit, his aura.

First she goes to the Inter-Cont. She sits in the lobby. She remains there for an hour, watching people enter and depart. She tries to imagine Micky, in Pakistan, tries to imagine him here, right here; it is almost impossible. He didn't belong here. He shouldn't have come. This was just not his intended ecosystem.

Then she roams the hallways for a while. She walks up and down each floor, trying to sense which room he might have slept in. She rides the elevator. She walks down the stairwell. She finds a bench in the neglected, dusty garden and circles the pool, whose dingy water has obviously not attracted many swimmers lately. She isn't looking for anything in particular and she has no expectations, beyond wanting to be where her brother has been and to feel her grief. How alien this place must have seemed to him, how desolate. Even in the best of circumstances he would have felt very uncomfortable here, and Julia can only speculate on how desperate his circumstances in fact may have been. Did he know he was in danger? If he had been able to reach her, would it have made a difference? Might she have saved him?

This last thought is the most anguishing. Julia was close to her brother, yes, but here, in this drab hotel garden, it suddenly strikes her how one-sided the closeness was. It was never a two-way street, not really. They talked a lot, but rarely about him; he was always reticent about personal matters. He had girlfriends, but if Julia tried to engage him in a conversation about them he brushed them off as "nothing serious." He was always "fine." There was "nothing new" at work. Maybe no man is an island, but Micky was about as close as you can get. Why did he want it to be that way? What was he guarding? And: Why had she never seriously asked herself these questions before? Why had she so readily assumed that he was just an introverted sort of guy, content, unimaginative? And now he had called her, for the first time. She used to phone him if the paper in her fax machine got stuck, and he always had time and advice. He only phoned when it was a matter of life or death—and that one time, that one fateful time, she had missed his call.

The next day, Julia goes walking through the town. She puts on long, dark clothes and nobody bothers her. She walks through the bazaar, across a park, along the wide boulevards. She breathes the polluted air and lets the scooter taxis spit their black smoke on her. Dust and ashes cover her head and her clothes, penitence from head to toes, but her pain does not lessen. She wants her brother back. Also, she is getting restless. She had intended to just be here, but now she can feel her curiosity and impatience growing. What the hell happened to him, anyway, exactly? What the hell is the *story* here?

Micky and Julia weren't always close—and they never were what you might call compatible. As children they were just over a year apart, but they might as well have belonged to two different families. There was a brief period when both were pale blond and roughly the same height and liked to walk around together in the hopes that people would mistake them for twins, which sometimes actually happened. But mostly they just ignored each other. They didn't truly discover each other until they were all grown up. One could even put a date on it, if one cared to: it was the third of April 1987, and Julia was a mess. Her love life, her job, everything had more or less collapsed around her and she hadn't been prepared for it—well, I guess one never is. It was late at night; she sat there in the wreckage of life as she had known it and felt a totally uncharacteristic urge to cry on somebody's shoulder. So she reached for the phone, only to realize that no suitable candidate came to mind. It had to be somebody who was not involved in her crisis; somebody who wouldn't, on some mean-spirited level, draw satisfaction from her decline; it couldn't be somebody—such as her mother—who would get *too* upset, either; and it couldn't be somebody she needed to face again in the future with her image intact. That narrowed it down, as far as she could see, to exactly nobody.

She was shocked by that realization. It couldn't be true! There had to be somebody, somewhere on this planet, who would love her even in her present state of disarray. Who would not secretly laugh at her or condemn her. Who would just be nice. Whom she could call tonight, and they would still respect her in the morning.

By this time she had drunk quite a lot of wine, which

was also pretty much out of character, and in that condition she suddenly remembered Micky. A brother, by
God, she had a brother after all! I'm not sure what she
expected from that phone call, but whatever it was, the
results dramatically exceeded her expectations. Micky
was, purely and simply, great. First he let her talk for a
while, interjecting only the occasional therapeutically
correct noncommittal grunt. When he judged that she
wasn't going to throw herself off the balcony, he announced that he was coming over now and hung up
before she could demur. Making no further reference to
the crisis, and acting as if they had simply planned to
spend the weekend together, he collected her and an
overnight bag and installed her in his guest room. He
fed her tacos and ice-cream bars, things she hadn't eaten
for years but had loved as a child, and told her a lot of
pretty silly jokes; he let her rearrange all of his furniture;
and by Monday she was a new woman.

And the best part, as Julia found, was that she wasn't
embarrassed about her breakdown. First of all, he
treated the whole thing like a casual non-event, which
was very relaxing; second, this after all was somebody
she had seen in diapers. She had protected him that Hal-
loween when he thought Andrew from next door was
really a vampire who would suck his blood out. She had
heard him cry himself to sleep in hotel rooms because
his terrycloth kitten had been forgotten at home. There
really didn't seem to be any call to be embarrassed in
front of Micky.

Anyway, after this incident he became her all-purpose
best pal. He fixed her computer glitches and gave her
financial advice and vetted her boyfriends. His expertise
in real-life matters was quite astounding; she was constantly amazed by what he knew about spark plugs and

software and rebates. He had other virtues, too, as she discovered by and by: a dry sense of humor, an irreverent approach to politics, and the ability to enjoy youthful pleasures. His leisure activities often reminded her of that bumper sticker slogan that "it's never too late to have a happy childhood." To her surprise, she discovered that she enjoyed them, too—sometimes, as a respite. After the endlessly boring meals she was forced to share with tedious show-offs in trendy would-be trattorias, it was a relief to have brunch with Micky at the International House of Pancakes, to watch him soak his spongy meal with syrup and wash the whole thing down with iced tea. Meanwhile she would do imitations of her latest interview partners to make him laugh. On the occasional Friday, they would watch something like *Ace Ventura* on video and eat popcorn. Or they would play Myst. When they got stuck on the third island, Micky borrowed a cheat book from one of his friends and then, armed with all the secret levers and buttons, they triumphantly solved the puzzle.

Julia kept a case of root beer and several bags of greasy, salty, orange-colored foodstuffs in her kitchen cabinet just for him. He went with her to the sushi bar and perched uncomfortably on the barstool trying not to watch while chunks of raw fish were sliced into confections that his own sister was seriously planning to eat. They brought out the best in each other. Before you scoff, consider how many people you can say that about.

But now, in retrospect, it seems to Julia that this relationship was entirely one-sided, their intimacy a lie, their friendship lopsidedly and unfairly to her advantage. She called on him often, but when had she ever helped him? And now he is dead, and it is too late, too late.

6

———

The Maulana loves Fatima. He did not love the others, but this girl, with the soft rope of hair and the tragic eyes of a gazelle about to be pierced by the hunter's arrow—and I beg your pardon for the phallic imagery, but I am merely the narrator here—this girl is different. Even to the Maulana's sludge-clouded eyes, even afterward, when he has once again freed himself of his feverish heat and has once more cursed the demon who possesses him, Fatima appears clean like an opal, pure like her namesake, the blessed daughter of the Prophet himself, may-peace-be-upon-him. Can the Maulana be feeling guilt, self-doubt, remorse? But no. He does love Fatima, though, so he blames the Devil, who is the third member of their party, more than he blames her evil and seductive womanness.

It has even occurred to the Maulana, in the moments of utter calm after the assaults and after the demon expulsions, that he might marry this girl. He pictures those eyes, liquid with gratitude, the speechless worship she would feel, were this incredible event to take place and redeem her. He pictures the meek obedience, perhaps even the girlish, timid delight, with which she would then welcome his caresses, once the two of them were blessed by Allah instead of cursed by the Devil. He pictures the wedding, the hysterical servility of her relatives, the adulation and cringing with which her parents would give homage to this illustrious son-in-law. He pictures his wedding night, the shy eagerness with which Fatima could finally permit herself to welcome him, in place of the desperate struggles with which she now attempts, so fruitlessly, to camouflage her own wanton desires.

Shall he do this? The Maulana cannot decide. Marry a woman who has writhed beneath him, witness to and undoubtedly, in spite of her show of distress, active seductress of his lust? The Maulana cannot decide. In the meantime, nearly daily resolutions of abstention are broken as soon as they are made, somewhat dimming any urgency of reaching a decision. The Devil, after all, has his merits, too.

Women's tragedies tend to be so trite, don't you agree? Sexual molestations, unwanted pregnancies, abandonments by lovers and husbands . . . Fatima, I am sorry to say, cannot add anything to our repertoire: she is merely pregnant, one more pregnant girl in the monotonously banal history of women. No wonder there aren't more departments of women's studies; what is there to study, after all? You'd have to link them to the medical school and staff them with gynecologists.

Fatima, as I have said, is pregnant. She does not have a glow. She is not passively resigned to her fate. Her months of fatalistic despair are at an end. Fatima is a woman at war, but she cannot locate the enemy. She does not feel as if she is carrying a baby; she feels as though the Maulana, like a disgusting kind of tapeworm, has broken off a piece of himself inside of her. Fatima feels that some horrible thing is inside of her, where she cannot get at it to scrub it out or expel it. Fatima is not sick in the mornings; she is sick all day, she is sick all night. The baby is much too small to merit such vehemence, being at the moment barely larger than a thought, but Fatima imagines that she can feel it, gloating and fat inside of her like an adder, like a slug, like one of the repelling slithering creatures forbidden to Muslims by the Holy Koran.

The Maulana does not know of Fatima's condition, of course. What would he do if he knew? It is hard to say. This, a pregnant unmarried girl, is not infrequently the topic of his sermons; in his sermons, the Maulana knows no mercy for such creatures of godless sin. A newborn infant abandoned in front of a mosque was once stoned to death by a group of the faithful, and some newspapers blamed the Maulana's uncompromisingly fiery sermons for sowing such intolerance among the Muslims of Pakistan. But while in his sermons the male involved in impregnating the hypothetical unwed pregnant sinner is generally absent, in this particular case that male is only too well known to the Maulana. So far, he has inflicted on his followers a number of wives with the blemish of non-virginity; could he, in a special effort of oratory, persuade one to take a wife already pregnant by an unspecified other? Well, who knows? Mullahs can get their followers to blow up airplanes and embassies. They can talk their followers into standing on street corners, waiting for a crowd to assemble, taking note of the schoolchildren among them, and then detonating themselves in a shower of blood and bone. Compared to that, persuading somebody to marry Fatima is hardly a challenge.

On the other hand, the Maulana is a widower, whose wife during fifteen years of marriage remained barren. After all, the Maulana has already thought of marrying Fatima. It is not impossible that he might increase her humble, inarticulate delight at becoming his wife even more by adding to it the inconceivable kindness of snatching her from the very edge of despair. It is her only chance; she had better throw herself on his mercy quickly, while the pregnancy can still be passed off as a sanctioned marital one. It would surprise the Maulana no end to catch even the tiniest glimpse of Fatima's feelings for him. He disgusts her. Not even in her present despair does a lifetime at his side appear to be a desirable alternative.

Time is passing, meanwhile, and Fatima cannot think what to do. She is pale, she is listless. An inner rage, having no other outlet, contents itself with placing volcanic red spots of anger on Fatima's cheeks, spoiling the previous pallor of her complexion. Tears and hormones redden her eyes and swell her wrists and ankles. The Maulana forgets why she seemed so different; every day she appears more and more like all the other girls he has had. Marry her? Well, that is something that will have to be very carefully considered. As he studies Fatima, whose face is puffy and whose hair hangs limp, it occurs to the Maulana that the idea of marrying her may well have been whispered into his ear by the deceitful demon who shares their illicit bed.

There is someone else, besides the Maulana and the demon, who lives in this household, and that person registers the changes in Fatima with an interested and

knowledgeable eye. Jamila has been with the Maulana
for twenty-two years, ever since she herself was sixteen
years old. Jamila has a crippled hand from polio, but
this did not stop the Maulana, when she was a timid
and fearful, unmarriageable sixteen-year-old, thrown
into the charitable embrace of the saintly Maulana, from
giving that embrace its very literal intent. Today, Jamila
is no longer timid, no longer fearful. It has been many
years since the Maulana last touched her, but she is in-
dispensable to him anyway, not least because her discretion is as great as her domestic efficiency. Jamila has
seen many girls pass through the Maulana's house,
his kitchen, and his hands, and Fatima is not the first
to experience unfortunate consequences. The Maulana
never knows and does not make it his concern to know;
Jamila attends to this as she attends to the other inevitable household items requiring disposal, such as
chicken necks and mildewed food. Jamila helps the desperate young girls who have something of the Maulana's to dispose of.

Not out of pity; Jamila does not know what pity is, or
compassion, never having encountered either of them
herself. And today Jamila neither wants nor requires
pity and compassion. She is highly satisfied with her
life, which brings her stature in the community as the
housekeeper of this prominent man, security, since her
discretion makes her irreplaceable, and opportunities,
many opportunities for advancement. Jamila is something of an entrepreneur; she deals in those commodities
a traditionally male society assigns to the economy of
women: lust, hypocrisy, and fear. Jamila enters the bathroom when she knows Fatima to be bathing. Jamila has
authority and does not shrink from its exercise; she
thrusts the young woman energetically from her, holds

her at arm's length, and studies her waist and belly while Fatima blushes and tries to pull away.

"I thought as much," Jamila says then, accusingly, though there is nothing for her to think here, since only Fatima herself could possibly register the minute widening of the waist that a fifth week of pregnancy can bring. But Fatima, neither composed nor biologically informed enough to call any bluffs, begins to weep, and to reach feebly for her clothes. Jamila, a self-made woman in the art of psychology, pushes them beyond Fatima's grasp and allows the girl, naked in every sense and miserable, to cry for just the right amount of time. "I know someone who can take care of these things," she says then. The sisterly note in her voice encourages Fatima to stop sobbing just as Jamila's next sentence, coldly pronounced, makes the tears flow once again: "You must pay her five thousand rupees."

Under the guise of midwifery, Jamila delivers astutely prodding injuries to Fatima's exposed breasts and belly before, on the pretext of calming her, placing a few resounding slaps against her cheeks. "All of this crying won't help anything, girl, it's too late for that," she says, comradely once again. "It is possible for you to get this money, and enough to get away from here besides." Fatima makes another halfhearted attempt at her clothes, but Jamila stands in firm control of them. "These are not clean, girl," she says, pretending to examine Fatima's scrupulously washed garments. "I will myself bring you new ones," she says, and leaves Fatima alone for half an hour in the tiled bath with a body that seems to swell, and a heart that seems to shrink, by the minute. When she returns, she judges Fatima ready to absorb the pivotal bit of information.

"You can have a lot of money, girl. Enough to take

care of this little problem, and to get your freedom besides. A little shop somewhere, you will say you are a
widow, soon your neighbors will find a nice man for
you." Fatima only shakes her head, which feels so full
and so crowded that it almost seems the Maulana's off-
spring has made her brain instead of her uterus its
home.

"A woman can see that you are pregnant, but a man
cannot," Jamila says, judging that the moment for blunt-
ness has come. "There are men who will pay for you.
You need do nothing, I will arrange this, to help you.
What have you to lose? In three or four weeks you can
have enough money to be rid of this problem," she says,
prodding Fatima's belly roughly one more time. "A bit
longer, and you will be a wealthy lady, rich enough to
get away from here forever."

Never does Fatima actually agree to this course; both
women take the acceptance of her clothes from the
greedy hands of Jamila to equal the shaking of hands,
the signing of a business deal.

Jamila, businesswoman in the shadow economy of the
patriarchal bazaar, likes to make herself useful to important men. One such man is Walid Khan.

Starting from a respectable but not overwhelming position on the lower margins of the upper class, Walid
Khan has clawed, bartered, maneuvered, and dealt his
way to the very top of the Peshawar power pyramid.
Looking at him, you would never suspect that; from his
urbane demeanor, the confident smile on the handsome,
fifty-two-year-old face, and the ease with which he deals
with the other Mighty and Powerful, you would think
he had been born right where he is, right at the very
top. Jamila cultivates him. He is never stingy, and it's
important to have a friend like that, just in case. And

Walid Khan is a good customer. Getting his girls from the Maulana's household amuses him; it's a great joke. If he knew that he is quite literally sharing the Maulana's girls with his enemy, that pompous and self-righteous religious opponent, his pleasure would be increased even more, but of course he doesn't know that, though he ought to be able to figure it out. Why else, after all, would the Maulana's household—of all places—provide such an unending stream of fallen women?

But Walid Khan does not think about it. His pleasure in paradox is great enough—the Maulana's maidservants, wonderful! Jamila makes a great to-do about taking any money from him, part of the ritual of feudal obeisance. Never mind; he pays, and pays very well, and she pockets it after her elaborate display of subservience and reluctance. Walid Khan likes to receive the visits from Jamila's girls in his office. He finds it enormously entertaining to see them waiting, huddled in their burqas, in the midst of the crowd of petitioners and other hopefuls. It amuses him to disport himself with some little grubby, illiterate village girl in his office, while at home his educated, politically chosen wife peruses Western magazines and wonders why her husband never sleeps with her anymore. It amuses him to have these girls on his sofa, while outside the door, only inches away, his advisers and secretaries wait, unknowingly timing his rendezvous into a perfect schedule. It amuses him to appear, unruffled and serene, in the doorway of his office, afterward, and instruct his assistant to give this woman so-and-so-many rupees, as though it were some charitable donation he were making to the poor destitute widow who has just wrung her veiled hands at him in his office.

And he likes to think of the girls, who have just

obliged him, carrying these memories of themselves home under their burqas to whatever little mud hole they share with their peasant husbands—or home to the house of the Maulana. Fatima, the first time she leaves the office of Walid Khan with her little envelope of rupees, feels almost nostalgic for the Maulana. Khan seems even more alien and intimidating, and he laughs a lot and you don't know why. At least with the Maulana she has the dignity of resistance, while now the trace of a forced smile on her mouth feels as sticky and is more lingering than the more tangible trace of Walid Khan's pleasure elsewhere on her body.

Walid Khan, the first time Fatima leaves his office, is well pleased with this new girl. Once again installed behind his desk, he glances for a satisfied moment at his couch. Often, when a delegation of particularly unpleasant tribal leaders, a group of particularly obsequious and undeserving constituents, a host of especially self-righteous and tedious religious functionaries is lodged on his sofa, it pleases him to superimpose the image of himself energetically copulating on the very spot now occupied by the stuttering owner of a cement factory, the dean of the agricultural department of the university, the sonorously lecturing, semiliterate mullah, and he can already anticipate that willowy Fatima will be the pornographic phantom most favored in that place.

Fatima, our little Fatima, has embarked on a promising career. It only took a week to earn enough money for cutting short the Maulana's chance of progeny, and Jamila has provided her new protégée with the wherewithal to prevent such mishaps in the future. Fatima, her mind muddled and her body still bleeding, lies on her mattress and tries to think. What happens now? Stay here, serve in the Maulana's private sexual melodrama until he tires of her, and then return to her village to marry the unknown fiancé, who may or may not be merciful enough to spare a woman found to have been delivered in spoiled condition? Jamila never assumes that Fatima might even entertain such a notion; nor does she suppose that this girl will go meekly into the bed of one of the Maulana's lackeys. There is a streak of rebellion in Fatima, and Jamila has not taken long to note it. Some savings, and then she can go away, far from the Maulana, far from her village bridegroom, too. A little shop, and her freedom. And after all, what is there to lose now that has not been lost already; might as well turn the situation to her advantage. In Fatima's muddled brain these intrusive ideas, for lack of any others, make their home, settle in, become almost familiar. The politician is a powerful man, with rich and powerful friends. Oblige them for a little while, and she can have her freedom. It may not be nice, it may not be enjoyable, but after all, does Fatima suppose it will be any nicer, any more pleasurable, with the self-righteous lout of a village boy her parents have lined up for her? Will she not have to do the same thing for him, and without getting paid for it? Khan and his friends, Jamila warns, are exquisite gentlemen in comparison to what awaits her in her husband's bed; cultured, well traveled, elegant, and polite. Her husband, on the other hand, likely as not will be a younger version of the Maulana, all bent and twisted with his own confusing thoughts about sex, women, and virginity, and ready to take it all out on his personal victim.

The Maulana, the politician, virginity: Fatima cannot think straight at all; the still-painful throbbing in her inexpertly plundered uterus makes her feel that she has lost her brain altogether, and that the center of herself has slipped right down into her belly and, from there, been bloodily scraped away. Jamila at least still seems to have a mind, and to see things clearly with it; Fatima, for lack of a better alternative, accepts Jamila as her brain. Jamila, efficient and almost motherly, takes charge of Fatima and her body. Poultices and potions heal her wound, and soon Jamila judges her fit for work. Her career is managed with the proficiency of an expert agent. In the mornings, Fatima serves the Maulana's breakfast and bustles about for a while performing symbolic household tasks, so that he thinks things are normal. After he has left the house, Fatima is free for business. The politician has a firm booking for two days every week, and almost every day has at least one friend, partner, or incipient partner with whom he wishes to share Fatima's services. Jamila has her own list of clients, built up over the years, whom Fatima goes to visit the rest of the time. She is relieved of domestic tasks, which are performed now by a young girl Jamila has recruited in the neighborhood.

Fortunately for Jamila, the Maulana is not a spontaneous kind of guy. His days run like clockwork, according to a precise schedule. When he is home, Fatima is instructed by Jamila to don her simple drudge's clothing and be seen emerging from the kitchen on some trivial errand. Even her extended household duties have been greatly reduced; the Maulana attends to her much more rarely, having lost most of his desire for her during the time when she was so unattractively miserable and unwell. The same cannot be said of the others. On the contrary, Fatima is acquiring some renown in certain circles of Peshawar male society, and to have her arrive at your door, in the chauffeured car of Khan, is an honor and a distinction. Yes, over the past few weeks our little Fatima has made quite a splash. She is an income-generating project all on her own.

The moment she hears Iqbal pull into the driveway, Lilly is on the phone to Julia, assuring her that Iqbal will meet her right now and give her any and all the information he has, if he knows what's good for him. Soon they are ensconced in the living room. Julia finds Iqbal nice enough, and earnest, competent, too, she supposes. He reviews all the facts and offers to take her to the station for a still more extensive briefing. He says that her brother, in his view, was a random victim, perhaps of some kind of a misunderstanding.

Then he makes some phone calls, and drives Julia to his office. His colleague, a short efficient little guy named Toufiq, is already waiting, along with several other investigators. They are not going to alienate this American relative. They are going to show her that they are taking her brother's case very seriously, very seriously indeed.

Things are a little stiff at first, but Julia isn't a journalist for nothing. Her first goal is a paradigm change, so to say. She wants their cooperation, which as all journalists know is something you can achieve either by intimidating somebody or by becoming their temporary best friend. And since she follows the Barbara Walters, not the Oriana Fallaci, school of journalism, she employs the second method. They chat for a while about crime in general, and about the unfair treatment of the police in the media, and pretty soon things are getting cozy. They tell Julia their theories, and why they have had to abandon most of them; bathed in her professional empathy, they admit that they are basically stumped. They bring out the dossiers and describe the other victims. In the end they even show her the morgue reports, complete with photographs of the bodies. I suppose they think this is okay—if they are thinking about it at all— since she is such a level-headed professional, not the hysterical relative of a victim at all, and since her brother's picture is not among them. But it doesn't take much imagination to add Micky in. Has he, too, had his throat slit? Is he lying somewhere, undiscovered, his meticulously wrinkle-free shirt soaked in blood?

It takes all of Julia's strength to get through the end of that meeting and back to her hotel. Her plan is to shut the door and have a proper breakdown, but when she is finally alone, the tears refuse to come. In fact, Julia can barely even breathe. She feels as if she is in the grip of some unspeakable nightmare. She can't sit still, but she can't get her heavy limbs to move around, either. She doubts that she will ever experience a good night's sleep again.

Soon, she finds herself thinking about Mara. Lilly had told her about Mara right away, and now Iqbal has confirmed her presence in Micky's life. Julia can't quite believe that her brother, of all people, found himself a girlfriend so quickly, here in Peshawar, of all places. What kind of a woman could that have been? Julia is curious, especially since Lilly and Iqbal both seemed uncertain about the nature and depth of their relationship. Lilly was enthusiastic about Mara, though. A wonderful woman, she assured her friend, strong, determined, engaged in good works for refugees. This doesn't sound like Micky's usual type of consort, somehow. Or maybe it's just further proof of how little she knew him. Mara knew that Julia was here, Lilly had said. She was ready to see her at any time. She had specifically asked Lilly to tell her that, and to tell her also that she would understand perfectly if she preferred not to see her at all. A strange message. Why should she not want to see her?

If she hasn't seen her yet, it's not for lack of trying. Mara never seems to be in her office, and the first two private numbers Julia was given were wrong. Now, though, she returns to this project with new persistence. Iqbal gets Mara's correct home number for Julia without difficulty, and she calls her up. She does so in the firm expectation that she will be asked to come over right away. But such is not the case. This Mara woman is friendly, but she claims to be leaving town right this instant, to have been "halfway out the door when the phone rang." An appointment she just can't cancel, she explains, and it will probably be very, very late by the time she returns. Then tomorrow morning she has to leave at the crack of dawn, some sort of crisis in one of her camps, but the day after that! Why don't they plan to get together sometime then! The more reluctant she sounds, the more determined Julia is to see her. She pins her down for 3 p.m., the day after tomorrow. And then she takes some pills, something she really never does. She always carries a bottle of Xanax in her bag, though. It's more of an amulet than anything else, just in case she should find herself overwhelmed. So far she has always managed not to get overwhelmed, so the bottle is still full and probably expired, but she takes two tablets and then, expecting only to become a little more anesthetized, she falls asleep.

7

A new development in the life of Fatima. She has lots of men, that's nothing new, but now she has more than that, she has a lover. His name is Mushahed, and anybody could readily understand his appeal. He is young, as full of feeling as a cloud is full of rain or a young tree full of sap. On top of that, he looks like Isa. He talks like Isa, he is a student like Isa, and if this helped Fatima fall in love with him, then there is nothing particularly perverse about that, all things considered. Not that many men have been nice to Fatima; she doesn't have that many mental associations to fall back upon. Mushahed is a student of economics, and to earn some money, he works part-time for his uncle, as a kind of all-around assistant, secretary, and chauffeur. Mushahed's uncle is someone you have met; his uncle, in fact, is the person Malone knows as "Mr. Khan." Mushahed and Fatima meet when Mushahed is dispatched to collect her from the rendezvous spot behind the market and bring her to his uncle's house for a weekend party; the Maulana is away for a few days, and Jamila feels the money offered justifies the small risk.

Fatima has been told not to wear the burqa; she is in her shalwar kamees instead. This means that Mushahed, on that first encounter, can see her face. Mushahed is curious about this girl; for social and political reasons alone, as he believes, but we may surmise that her face has something to do with it as well. He is driving her to a weekend house in the direction of Quetta, a drive of one and a half hours, and begins to talk with her. Fatima, from the backseat, answers timidly. Mushahed knows she is a prostitute; he doesn't mind that, being prepared to find a prostitute a very romantic figure, in his Third World leftist student sort of way. Mushahed sees his uncle as a feudal lackey sort of figure, and thus is perfectly ready to embrace Fatima as his victim and as one of the Wretched of the Earth. Two days later, when he picks her up for the return drive, her appearance will do much to heighten this impression. She looks pale, ill, and exhausted, and isn't that a bruise on her cheek? Fatima cannot be mistaken for anything but a victim. Inwardly, Mushahed's feelings are stumbling over one another in their haste to escape the distaste they fear may be racing up to block their way. Pity, sympathy, political theory, and, who knows, perhaps the response of a sheltered young man to a lovely female face, they are all tripping over one another's feet, and out of the dizziness that results from this race against contempt and distaste, love is born. Mushahed is quite, quite certain, when that weekend repeats itself two weeks later and he is again assigned the task of delivering Fatima into the hands of her abusers, that he loves her.

And Fatima loves Mushahed. He is even better than her brother, in the sense that he knows everything about her and grants absolution; grants distinction, even, purifies and elevates her in his thoughts. Fatima is not some dirty bargain of a village girl being passed from hand to hand, she is the Third World, exploited by the Villainous and the Greedy. Fatima can hold her head up; it is the others who ought to feel shame. As he explains all of this to her, Mushahed's throat constricts sometimes, and it would be hard to tell what moves him more—her plight, or his own moral heroism in recognizing it. It doesn't matter, and what he says does not matter. It makes no more sense to Fatima, coming out as it does all garbled up with the history of industrialization in Poland, mill girls in Lancaster, and the necessity of arming the peasantry, than her brother's lectures used to. The gist of it, as far as she is concerned, is what she has already concluded all by herself: that what is happening to her is happening to a girl who was helpless, and therefore blameless; who did what she had to, who wants to survive.

Mushahed is fiery, more fiery even than Isa; he is very handsome, too. When I say he is her lover, I mean it in the Victorian sense; it has not occurred to him, not even for a moment, to make any claim on the much-claimed body of Fatima. Instead, he meets Fatima in out-of-the-way spots, where they listen to music on the tape deck of his uncle's car while Mushahed talks.

These chaste trysts do not seem strange to him; after all, in his frame of reference it is bold beyond belief for him even to be sitting alone in a car with the girl he loves. And, in fact, these episodes represent the pinnacle of Mushahed's erotic experience to date. It would surprise him enormously to know that one person, at least, thinks otherwise; thinks him a debauchee, a sophisticate, the true nephew of his uncle. I refer, of course, to Jamila. In order to be allowed to meet Mushahed, Fatima must tell Jamila that he is a paying client. Fatima has told Jamila the truth, more or less, out of necessity. She has told Jamila that Mushahed is a student, and the nephew of Khan; if he were not a student, Jamila would expect him to pay a lot more for each rendezvous, and if he were not the nephew of Khan, she would not agree to such an impoverished customer. Nor does she like it that Fatima is arranging for her own clientele, now; still, family counts for something, and Khan's nephew must be obliged.

After each meeting, Fatima has to hand over to Jamila her "earnings," although of course on such occasions there are no earnings, since Fatima would never take money from Mushahed and he is blissfully unaware of the arrangement. Fatima is paying Jamila out of her own slowly accruing savings for the pleasure of sitting in Mushahed's uncle's car listening to cassette tapes of poor quality and hearing impassioned summaries of the economics books Mushahed has recently read. But then, compared to some of the pleasures Fatima's customers pay their money for, who is to say that her own vice is any more peculiar?

Fatima's mind, as I have told you, is still quite cloudy. If it were not, she would not have told Jamila a story so close to the truth. Jamila must naturally assume that Khan is a benevolent party to his nephew's sexual introduction, and Jamila is not the sort of person to allow any opportunity to ingratiate herself go by. The next time she has dealings with Khan, she cannot fail to mention her usefulness in providing experience for his nephew, smiling conspiratorially all the while. Khan, adept at concealing his thoughts, does not show Jamila his surprise, but smiles benignly and pretends to know all about it. Afterward, he sorts his thoughts. After all, it is not a very important matter, and he himself has passed Fatima along to innumerable other men, but still, it is annoying to share a woman with this little boy, and still more annoying to have them meeting behind his back, without his knowledge, perhaps talking about him . . . but no, Walid Khan is not insecure enough for such a thought to plague him. Besides, any nephew of his will have better things to do with a pretty and cooperative young girl than gossip about his old uncle. The longer he thinks about it, the more harmless the whole matter appears. Mushahed is a healthy young man living in a sexually stifling environment. An opportunity arose, and he seized it; an admirable and perfectly normal response. Khan chuckles to himself as he imagines the meetings between Fatima and Mushahed, and nods jovially. Poor girl, after all, always thrown together with the flabby elderly men who can afford her. He is the last one to begrudge her a little sport with a handsome young man, for a change.

It is, therefore, with the utmost benevolence that he regards his nephew, the next time he lays eyes upon him. Mushahed, who has been sent for to drive his uncle and some associates to a meeting, wonders at the hearty clap on the shoulder, the wink, the jovial remarks he can't quite make sense of. It takes Mushahed quite a while to figure out what his uncle means; when he finally understands, he is overcome with embarrassment that his love for Fatima is known to his uncle, and cast in such a sordid light. When he comprehends that his uncle considers him just another customer of Fatima, he is first angered and then, when his uncle makes a joke about the "discount" Jamila has supposedly granted him, increasingly confused. Understanding dawns horribly: Fatima, then, has been paying for those innocent trysts, with money so painfully earned. Well, of course, he despises himself for his stupidity. Obviously, she could not just run off as she pleased; she is not free; how could he have failed to consider that?

Mushahed wants to slap the mouth of his uncle, who is at present speculating companionably about Fatima's various attractions. He wants to beat himself for his stupidity, and for increasing Fatima's troubles. He wants to put an end to the disgusting stream of his uncle's man-to-man chatter. He wants to see Fatima, to hold her, to comfort her, to apologize. Mushahed sees, as his uncle talks on and on, that he has been like him. He has used Fatima for his own games, he has talked and talked, he has pleased himself without thinking of her, he has not helped her. He has harmed her. He has moved her further from her freedom, instead of bringing her closer to it. Mushahed resolves solemnly that he will make it up to her.

One day, Mushahed has an idea. He will take Fatima out! He will take her visiting. Why is he hiding her? Isn't that hypocritical? He will take her out, to meet his friends.

Let me say that of all the ordeals inflicted on her by men who have bought her, this one strikes Fatima as one of the worst. The thought of being introduced to Mushahed's friends is bad enough, but she has been unambiguously commanded to do far more than this. She is to feel free and equal with them, he says; she is to state her views, unashamedly explain her situation, and otherwise discourse with these persons, a prospect which induces in Fatima the kind of nausea she has not felt since the terrible first days of the Maulana's attentions.

On the way to the house of Mushahed's college friends, that first time, Fatima longs for the wonderfully comforting and anonymous folds of her burqa. Fervently she begs to be allowed at least the surrogate comfort of a shawl, but Mushahed is relentless. No, Fatima must meet his friends with her head bare and her spirit uplifted, she is to look them straight in the eye and speak her views—oh, poor Fatima: what views?—forthrightly and loudly. Stealthily she pulls a ribbon of narrow scarf over her head, but Mushahed removes it adamantly. We might say that he is, in this at least, just one more in the long line of men who want to undress Fatima, but he would be horrified at this analogy, and perhaps it is unfair. Perhaps, though you might not think so if you could see the trembling misery in Fatima's heart as the car speeds her along to the house of his friends. But she does as she is told, of course; she does what the other men say because she has to, and she does what Mushahed says because she loves him.

Her devotion is rewarded by the intervention of kindly fate. Mushahed's friends, four college boys from his economics class, are not at home. Only Shabnam, the older sister of one of them, happens to be there, waiting for her brother. Shabnam takes one look at Fatima and understands all. She understands that Mushahed, this little boy, is playing with dolls, has found himself this little doll or, rather, a living little kitten that he carries around by the scruff of the neck, and loves, and pets, and squeezes, and feeds with cream whenever he remembers, and may inadvertently squeeze the life right out of. To her immense relief, Shabnam lets Fatima sit, in a little burqa woven out of silence, while she chats with Mushahed and gives the girl a chance to get her bearings. Then, before the four men can arrive, she whisks her two visitors away for a drive, sitting with Fatima in the backseat and talking in a steady stream that somehow manages to include Fatima without expecting anything of her. "Kind" is not the first word that would occur to Shabnam's friends when describing her, but on that day she is exquisite in her kindness. After dropping a profoundly relieved Fatima near her house, Shabnam moves to the front seat beside Mushahed and extracts the whole story from him, bit by bit.

Mushahed is meek with Shabnam, meek and deferential. Shabnam is exactly the sort of woman he populates Pakistan's utopian future with, in his dreams; face-to-face with the first prototype, he is stunned into near speechlessness. Poor Mushahed; what would he do if the world he fantasizes were really to come to pass, if women were free and held their heads up and spoke out clearly, as he has instructed the terrified Fatima to do? Poor Mushahed, face-to-face with even one such woman, he is at a total loss. Meekly he answers her questions, mumbles his story, slightly resentful over the dawning suspicion that he has done something very wrong, very stupid, when at the same time he knows that he has only done what was fair, and right. Shabnam, sensitive to the condition of her subject, is careful to express no judgments beyond an occasional sigh. The story of the audience between Mushahed and his uncle elicits a sigh.

Resolving to keep an eye on his little doll, on his scruffy little kitten, Shabnam commands Mushahed to visit her at her house very soon, and to bring his girlfriend with him.

As it turns out, these visits will become fairly frequent. Fatima, in particular, will often plead to be taken to visit Shabnam. She likes to be in the beautiful house. She likes to look at the pictures in Shabnam's bright, foreign magazines. Mostly, she likes to watch Shabnam. Fatima usually offers to meet Mushahed at Shabnam's house, and then she tries to get there early. That gives her time to be with Shabnam.

"Don't let me bother you," Fatima pleads eagerly, on those occasions. "I'll just wait." Because that's really all she wants: just to be there, near her idol.

You or I might feel funny in a situation like that, but Shabnam doesn't. In Pakistan, life for the wealthy is a little bit like life at court in Versailles. There is no real notion of privacy, because you have so many servants. You dress, you undress, you sleep, you eat in the presence of your minions, who are constantly there to massage you, bring things, iron things, button your buttons, run your bath. If you grow up that way, they don't bother you; it's just like being alone. You don't really have to worry about keeping secrets; these people are far too dependent on you, far too frightened of you, to do you harm. If Fatima comes early enough, she can sit in a corner, like furniture, and watch Shabnam check her makeup in the hall mirror; watch her drape her shawl elegantly over her dress; listen to her hum and sing and issue orders self-confidently by phone; and bask in her distracted, benevolent smile.

Where there's life, there's hope, the saying goes. It's true of Fatima, at any rate. She has hopes, tenuous, vaporous ones. They aren't much use. They hover about her like clouds, too intangible to touch, too insubstantial to support her, she can't stand on them, she can't cling to them, she can't hold them tight during the dark hours of the night. But they do exist, cloudy vaporous ghost-like formations, and if she were to think about them, she could visualize them as a kind of nebulous triangle. There is Mushahed, there is Isa, and there is Shabnam, three unlikely deities holding up Fatima's sad cosmos. She does not expect, she does not hope for, she dare not pray for, but she dreams of love and salvation, and when she does, she imagines it coming perhaps from one of these three.

From Shabnam, who barely registers her presence and forgets about her the instant she leaves. From Mushahed, to whom Fatima is also something in the nature of a cloud, a theory, a hormonal impulse transmogrified into a lofty political dream. And from Isa. Her brother Isa seems to her the most distant one, but actually, that is not so. Isa, as a matter of fact, is a lot closer than anyone thinks.

Isa. Although he is named after Jesus, whom Islam claims as one of its prophets, and although he was raised by staunchly pious parents, Isa claims to be an agnostic. Well, not in London; in London he generally finds it more stylish to be a Muslim, these days, and a self-righteous and unyielding one at that. It helps with the girls, he has found; it makes their eyes brighten, it makes them giggle with delighted apprehension. But at home, to the fury of his father, he proclaims his agnosticism. It's hard to know what to make of that. It's easy, I find, to develop your own view of God, or even to not believe in Him at all anymore. It's all the stuff that used to go along with Him that's so hard to abandon. Things like sin, guilt, and fear remain embedded in your cells long after God has left your heart.

It's August. The term has finished. Isa has been invited to spend the holidays in Ireland with a classmate. He has nearly made up his mind to do it when some impulse inspires him, instead, to go home to Pakistan.

Is Isa good at packing? He left God behind, he thinks. But has he freed himself of his feelings about the virtue of sisters?

Isa lands in Karachi. He changes planes and lands again in Islamabad. A succession of buses take him to his village. His parents are waiting to greet him. His brothers have stayed home to receive him. Isa drinks tea, distributes the gifts he has brought, and is puzzled by the absence of Fatima. Didn't she know he was arriving? Where is that girl? Isa is infuriated to learn that his sister has been rented out to the Maulana, of all people, that vicious backward idiot who will exploit her and fill her impressionable mind with nothing but nonsense. Get a dowry? Marry that dolt Mirza? Never! How could they even think of it! His mother weeps. His father shouts, blusters, and curses. Isa shouts, blusters, and curses back, then stomps off to visit like-minded friends. The next day he will set out for Peshawar to see about his sister; if she is unhappy he will bring her back, never mind the consequences.

"Don't ever come here to the house again" are the words with which Jamila greets Isa when he appears at the door the next day. They are his first indication that all is not well. "I will send her to you. How can you just come here like this! Don't you know how dangerous it is?" she scolds him, not too angrily, for after all he is— or so she assumes, faced with a young man who comes to the house asking familiarly for Fatima—a paying client. Isa makes a sarcastic remark about being unworthy to enter the house of his saintly uncle, about not knowing where the servants' entrance is, remarks that are not immediately comprehensible to Jamila but from which she does eventually glean the fact that Isa is a relative and not a customer. Her signs of confusion and distress further puzzle Isa.

Flustered, Jamila struggles to smooth things over. She informs Isa that his sister is not here right now. No telling when she will be back, with so many errands! And the Maulana is away, too; otherwise, of course, he would insist on welcoming his dear guest; unfortunately she, a woman at home alone, cannot ask him in. Perhaps it will be best if he returns in a few days? Isa departs without further comment, because he wants time to think this through. Something is definitely not all right here. A young girl does not leave the house in which she is employed, for an unspecified amount of time, alone. And because the young woman in question is his sister, his thoughts turn immediately—and correctly, let it be said—to illicit sex.

What is stronger in Isa, the old or the new? Will he loiter about in the streets, as a young man of the old order certainly would do, to spy on his sister? Or will he simply return the next day, as a young man of the new order might, and ask her straightforwardly what the matter is? When he finds out, will he stand by her? Will he help her? Has he really and truly gotten them out of his system, those compelling thoughts about honor and the virginity of sisters?

Isa takes a room in a cheap hotel. The room is small and dingy; the walls are stained and smell of mold. The mattress is a thin piece of foam, and the bed gives way when you sit on it, like a sponge. Isa is not used to this anymore; Isa is used to London now, to his pleasant little flat and his water bed. The light bulb flickers and has at most twenty-five watts; the room is steamy; the pillow is covered with stains that look like blood and nicotine. Isa is trying to think, but who can think under these circumstances? He leaves the hotel and walks the streets, his mind in confusion. It seems obvious he should wait until his sister reappears, go to see her, and simply ask her how she is; why, then, does the thought of observing her secretly intrude itself upon his mind so obsessively?

Well now, Isa isn't so bad at packing, after all. Wisely, he has left his British wardrobe behind. In a drab blue shalwar kamees, Isa takes up his post near the house of the Maulana. He buys a pan leaf from a shop across the street and leans against a wall, chewing and spitting. He waits in vain. Fatima uses the side entrance, and he never sees her at all.

The next afternoon he does better. He finds a better vantage point, from which he can survey nearly the entire house. At about ten o'clock, something green peers out the door, and then a green-wrapped person leaves the house, stealthily, creeping along an alley. She steps over mounds of orange peel and fish heads and moves past a group of boys trying to construct a kite. She walks quickly, followed at a considerable distance by a man in a drab blue shalwar kamees. She turns several corners, until she reaches a wider street, jammed with people, scooter cabs, and vendors of all sorts. There she hastens toward a preappointed corner, where a car is parked, motor running. She gets into the backseat of the car. The car drives off, leaving her fraternal pursuer perplexed and thoughtful on the street's edge. Was that even Fatima? Why would she be getting into a private car? Where could she be going? What the hell is going on?

8

Walid Khan is a worldly man, and likes to think of himself as having an excellent sense of humor. He is a solemn, even a frightening man, wielding much power, but he likes to think there is another, more whimsical side to his personality. The Americans, who cultivate this trait almost to excess, have a talent for bringing it out in him. He remembers a very amusing evening with Micky Malone's boss in Washington, D.C. So it is only natural that now, while he lets Micky stew in his hotel room for a while to loosen him up, this evening once again comes to mind. Washington, D.C. Khan had mentioned, quite offhand, that it was his birthday, and that night, his business friends had sent a "Belly-Gram" up to his suite. "Belly-Gram"—wonderful, these Americans! That funny American girl came into the room in her so-called Arabian costume, shaking herself ineptly but with spirit and singing "Happy Birthday," and they were well into their third bottle of scotch and everybody laughed and clapped and slapped Walid Khan on the back. And then they tried to give the girl some money to stay on, to go to the suite next door and show Khan "a really nice American birthday," but she got huffy and said she was a "dancer," and left. A dancer! Just imagine! These Americans—wonderful!

So he really should give this Malone the benefit of the doubt. Besides, Khan is a man of action. He had planned to just let Micky stew in his hotel room, until compliance came about through a sort of internal process of fear, doubt, boredom, and greed. But maybe it's better to take a more proactive role in the proceedings. Khan nods thoughtfully as he ponders the matter of Malone. Yes. He shouldn't immediately think the worst of this American. Probably Micky is just stubborn and provincial, not sneaky or dangerous at all. Probably he just needs to be nudged into the real world of real international business. Well, he will send him a Belly-Gram, a real one. One he won't quickly forget.

When Fatima comes to his office, he sits her down in a chair beside his desk, pats her hand benignly, and explains carefully her role in this wonderful joke. Feeling expansive, he even explains the parallel to the Washington Belly-Gram, a story that dins on Fatima's ears like a baffling, incomprehensible riddle. Dancing girls, Arabian costumes, girls who strip before strange men in hotel rooms but are offended when taken for a whore, Fatima cannot follow him at all. Never mind, her instructions are quite simple. She will go to the hotel room of this American to whom Khan wishes to give a present. She will enter the room in her chaddri, she will say, "I am a Belly-Gram" (the only really hard part). She will suddenly pull off the chaddri and be wearing nothing beneath it. Then she will go to bed with the undoubtedly speechless Malone, if he can manage that in his condition of utter shock (Khan laughs heartily, imagining it, and wishes he could be there). And for this, she will be paid twice the usual amount, because she is such a good, such a nice, such an intelligent girl.

And because the idea is so amusing, and because he cannot be there to see Malone's face, he has Fatima go into the little bathroom connected to his office, and come back wearing nothing beneath her chaddri, and practice her performance a few times for him. He laughs uproariously and adds a few refinements—a bit of a dance step when she gets out of the chaddri, a wiggle when she says, "Belly-Gram"—and laughs and laughs with delight and says she could make a killing in Washington, and that one day he may take her there.

Fatima has always felt slightly off balance with Walid Khan. He is so powerful, and everyone is so afraid of him, that her main emotion is probably awe. On the other hand, he is very generous to her, often pressing extra money into her hands. He is relaxed and jovial with her, telling little stories and jokes and tweaking her cheeks fondly like an uncle. Unlike most of the other men, he has simple tastes and seems to think nothing of them, acting neither furtive, nor angry, nor guilty about what he does with her. Today, though, Fatima feels as though the ground has shifted under her feet, leaving her afloat in deep space without air, without light, without a spark of warmth.

Made to strip and dance, Fatima feels a sick and horrible emptiness that seems to stretch from her throat down to her knees. She can identify some of what she is feeling, but she is at a loss as to the rest. She knows she feels humiliation, and shame. She knows that she would like to die, right here and now. She knows that however jovially Khan may laugh, inviting her to laugh with him, this joke—whatever it may be—is really on her. But the feeling that is strongest of all eludes her. She searches around for it, the way one struggles to name the one elusive spice in a new food one has tasted. You know what it is, you just *know*, but you can't pinpoint it; what an exasperating feeling. Likewise, Fatima just cannot seem to put her finger on the stirring in her heart.

I don't know why Fatima is having so much trouble identifying it. It's a perfectly simple, straightforward feeling.

Hate.

The Belly-Gram assignment is doomed from the start. Mushahed is supposed to drive her to the Inter-Cont., but when she looks out the window, she discovers that he is going the wrong way. "Mushahed?" she says, timidly. "That's wrong. I have to go to the Inter-Cont." Mushahed doesn't answer. He just keeps driving. "Mushahed?" Fatima repeats, a little bit louder. "Remember, I have to go to the Inter-Cont.? And later to the weekend house?" He keeps driving. Fatima starts to cry. "What are you doing, Mushahed? Where are you taking me? Why don't you answer me?"

"I'm not taking you to any more men," he announces, finally. "But, Mushahed," Fatima says, sobbing. "What will we do? How will we manage?" "We'll find a way," he snaps. "But, Mushahed," Fatima protests. "Jamila will throw me out. And Khan will be very, very angry. And I only need a little more money. Just a while longer—"

"Money!" Mushahed screams. "Money! Money! What about your pride! What about your honor! I can't believe this. I can't believe that you are pleading to be allowed to remain a whore! I'm trying to help you, and you, you want to be a whore!"

"Help me?" Fatima yells back. "How are you going to help me?" Mushahed has no answer for that. All he knows is that he cannot, will not drive her to any more of her assignations. He won't be her pimp.

"I forbid you to go to any other men," he pompously announces. Fatima collapses into the seat. She feels terrible. Do this, do that. Take your clothes off, put them on. Sleep with this man, sleep with that one, don't sleep with any of them. I love you, I love you, I love you.

Mushahed takes her home. Moments later, she leaves by the side entrance, looking about carefully in case he is still lurking outside. She runs down the alley and takes a rickshaw cab to Khan's office. She tells his assistant that Mushahed has suddenly been taken ill and cannot drive her. He sends arrogant, bossy Ahmed to drive her to the hotel instead.

There is a knock on the door. Though paranoid, Micky thinks nothing of it; even he can think of any number of harmless interpretations. Someone with towels. Someone to pick up the laundry order. Malone fears the telephone, which could be Khan demanding a decision, far more than he fears the knock on the door. Malone opens the door and finds himself facing a green apparition. The apparition steps into the room. Malone assumes the apparition to be part of the lunar hotel staff and allows it in with a shrug. The apparition removes its green outer casing. It emerges as distinctly female, with unfamiliar but scanty undergarments that make this attribution easy. The apparition begins moving around his room in what appears to be a dance, and begins removing aforesaid scanty undergarments with hands that glitter at wrist level and emit a harsh, faintly melodic sound.

Malone yells out a spontaneous "No!" and scampers across the room to retrieve the large green thing. He says, "Excuse me, miss, I think you have the wrong room," and holds the green thing up like a curtain between himself and the alarming spectacle. He advances very slowly, holding the large green thing insistently toward the apparition, which stops moving and accepts the slippery green fabric. "That's right," says Malone, retreating again, "that's good, thank you, excuse me, just the wrong room, that's all!"

Malone speaks softly, soothingly, but his body language has something different to say. As he speaks so softly, soothingly, his large body is flattened against the wall in a state of high alarm. The apparition regards him for a moment and the expression on its face, were he calm enough to attend to such details, might reassure him; it is benign, even tender. And then, swish swish, cloth swirls, the apparition disappears completely under a swish of green, and as Malone helpfully stammers out a "The front desk! Ask at the front desk! They'll give you the right room number at the front desk!" the door closes softly, and his guest has gone.

Malone breathes slowly in, slowly out. That's right, don't hyperventilate! He sits down on the bed and buries his face in his hands. He remains in that position for quite a while. There is some kind of a commotion in the hallway, but Malone does not attend to it, and it quickly subsides. A drink. Something cold to drink. Ice.

Malone heads to the hallway, he will get a bucket of

ice, he will have a Coke, a cold Coke. He opens the door with caution, a crack, another inch, enough to peer through. There is no one in the hallway. Holding the brown plastic ice pail, Malone moves quietly down the hall. He reaches the door to the room with the ice dispenser, he opens it, he enters. He sees the ice machine against the wall, he approaches it with his ice bucket, he recoils. There is a red smear of something covering the front of the machine, it looks like graffiti on the New York subway, but it is smeary, wet, and red; it looks like blood.

It says something: it says two words: YOU ARE. Malone hardly reacts at all, he is too stunned. He stands there, frozen in contemplation of this message, without the slightest doubt that this is blood, that he is the YOU, that this message is for him. He stands there, I don't know how long, maybe for a minute, maybe more, and then he begins to move mechanically backwards, as if someone had put him in reverse gear.

Malone backs right out of the cubicle, right down the hallway, right into his room. He reaches directly for the telephone. His first words are such a terrified squawk that Mara cannot understand him, squawk, squawk, squawk, until finally he squeezes out a "Get me! Help! Get me!" Then the receiver drops out of his hands and Malone, suddenly free again of his paralysis, grabs whatever of his possessions he can and stuffs them into the nearest bag, which happens to be a large plastic laundry bag. And then he waits for Mara, who, suspecting a coronary, is already on her way, mentally reviewing her CPR procedures.

Mara and Malone drive through the night. She is angry, he is frightened, there is little conversation. First they are on a road, then Mara veers off abruptly to the left and they appear to be jolting through open landscape. It is very dark. Once in a while Mara mutters a curse. Suddenly she kills the headlights. They continue in total darkness until Mara pulls up in front of a small building. Mara doesn't get out. She prefers to give him his survival briefing right here, in the dark car. Okay, she says. He thinks someone is after him, okay. It's not likely but it's possible, entirely possible. He needs help from the consulate, and the consul is not here, fine. He needs Mara to hide him for a week or so, very well. Here's the story. They are on the outskirts of one of the many, far-flung refugee camps. This is a storage shed, outfitted simply to accommodate one to two persons. He will find a bed, a burner, blankets, bottled water, and some food. She will come by in a few days and bring more provisions. He will be fine here, just fine. Most likely he won't see anyone, and no one will see him, but if he is seen, that is fine, too. The refugees will assume he has something to do with the committee. They will ignore him. She has turned out the headlights only because she doesn't want anyone snooping by right now and finding them together, a man and a woman, at night. Afternoons look like legitimate work, but night, there's no way to explain their being alone here together at night.

So okay, she urges impatiently. Malone can go now. What is he waiting for? The door isn't locked; he can go right on in, then bolt it from the inside. Go right on in? Go inside? Alone? Malone fears Mara's contempt, but there are plenty of things he fears even more. Snakes. Bandits. The dark. Mumbling further curses, Mara precedes him into the shack. The moonlight illuminates the room quite well, but with a contemptuous sigh, she lets her flashlight roam exaggeratedly into each corner. The irony is lost on Malone. He is still regarding his new domicile with stunned disbelief as Mara leaves, the car motor starts, its noise recedes, and there is silence. Malone makes his way to the cot. He pulls the malodorous blanket over himself. He thinks that he will never sleep, but, almost instantly, he does.

And what about his earlier visitor, you ask. What about the thrilling, terrifying guest whose visit set all of this in motion, sending Micky into flight, into the desert? What happens to his surprising green visitor? Well, after he ushers her nervously out, Fatima, clutching her chaddri around her, emerges from Malone's hotel room. As in all hotels, there is a staircase; as in all hotels, it is seldom used, because everyone prefers the elevator. Fatima approaches the staircase and finds the driver, who is sitting on one of the steps, smoking a cigarette. He has barely sat down, has only just lit the cigarette. So he is surprised to see Fatima; she cannot possibly have completed her assignment. Another driver might not care, but this one has a mean streak, and besides he likes to play the boss, so he challenges the young woman. Fatima stammers out her explanation; she tried to follow her orders, but the American sent her away. The driver becomes enraged. He curses her, saying that he will be blamed for her failure, which is untrue. He shoves her about roughly and orders her to go back. Fatima refuses. Very meekly, it's true, in an apologetic little whisper, but it's a refusal nonetheless, and the man is furious. He delivers a few blows in the vicinity of where he estimates her face to be, under the green cloth, and when she lifts her arms up to shield herself he punches her once or twice more. Then he shoves Fatima toward the door and orders her to go back and try again.

Fatima stumbles into the hallway and leans briefly against the wall. She doesn't know what to do. She won't go back to the room of the American, she can't. She is afraid to stay in the hallway, lest the driver come out and find her there. She spies a door that is ajar and, nudging it, discovers a sort of storage room housing a large white machine. Fatima ducks inside to take stock and shelter. In the quiet room, the misery of her situation washes over her. What just happened was so humiliating, and the American man felt it, too, and sent her away. Her head hurts a little where the driver hit her, and her arm hurts even more and feels sticky. Lifting her green garment over herself like a tent, Fatima ducks underneath to examine her arms. Most of her glass bracelets have broken under the impact of the blows. Several of them, in breaking, have dragged their jagged edges down her arm, which is streaked with blood; one shard has lodged under her skin, and when she pulls it out, more blood follows. Fatima touches the blood with her fingers, tracing this cut. It isn't deep, but it has torn her skin unevenly, and it hurts. Fatima sobs quietly, but really she would like to scream. How many ordeals can a quiet person quietly submit to? Feeling very sorry for herself and very abused, Fatima strokes her bloody arm and contemplates her miserable condition. She doesn't scream, but she takes her bloody fingers and starts to leave a message about herself on the gleaming white surface of the big machine that owns this little room. But then the sound of footsteps startles her and, in a final act of defiance against the loathsome driver, she flees down the narrow utility staircase and exits the hotel in a blur of anonymous green.

9

Mushahed decides to marry Fatima. Marry Fatima? A woman who has been with so many men, who has been bought and sold and borrowed and bartered? Never mind; Fatima was not a free agent in any of this, she is innocent. Mushahed knows that this will be a real test for him, a test to show whether he is just a talker, like the others, or someone who really lives his life according to his convictions. According to his beliefs, Mushahed knows, Fatima is pure, untouched. She has been plundered, like the Third World; in her, as in the Third World, there is a strength and purity that has been honed, not defiled, by her degradation. Mushahed's throat tightens with emotion to think himself capable of such lyrical thoughts; how many of his fellows, he asks himself, could display such intellectual nobility? He will marry Fatima, and together they will dedicate themselves to a life of struggle and resistance. After all, for such a purpose, for such a life, what other girl would do? Not the fluffed-up little bits of glamour, the spoiled daughters of good families, that his parents want for him.

As he reflects upon all of this, his plan does not seem impossible. Fatima, after all, comes from a respectable clan, though from its poorest and lowliest branch. Her family relationship to the Maulana will help his case with his parents. With increasing excitement, Mushahed begins to think that he just may be able to pull this off. His parents may like the idea of his marrying a village girl from the ultraconservative backwater of Pakistan. They may think that such a girl will calm and tone down their left-wing black sheep. What a marvelous, schizophrenic coup that would be! To impress his comrades by marrying a whore, while pleasing his parents by marrying an illiterate village girl!

But then, with a start, he remembers the flaw in this logic. His uncle. His uncle knows all about Fatima. Well then . . . he will just have to be silenced. Maybe he can blackmail him? Mushahed mulls this idea over for some time, but the truth is that he has absolutely no idea of how to go about blackmailing someone. No, he will just have to hope that his busy, important uncle will consider the matter beneath his notice. He will have a heart-to-heart chat with his uncle and ask for his discretion.

Mushahed makes an appointment to see his uncle. He wants to do this properly, formally even; this is not a matter to be haphazardly discussed over his shoulder as he drives. It needs to be presented carefully. His uncle receives him in his office, with perhaps slightly exaggerated solemnity. He likes this nephew, and if the boy is politically naïve and extreme in his idealism, well, that is part of youth. So he will treat him like a man, and receive him very solemnly in his office, and if he smiles just slightly, then there is more affection and indulgence in that smile than contempt. Affection and indulgence maintain the upper hand even when he has heard the ludicrous proposal Mushahed is forwarding, but it's a struggle. Anger and disgust well up briefly, but Walid Khan suppresses them. A child, he reminds himself, a child stands before him, though in the tall athletic body of a man and with the intelligent fiery eyes of late adolescence. And it's his first girl, of course, so he finds her romantic and sad. The uncle sighs and resolves to put a kindly interpretation on the whole affair instead of blasting Mushahed contemptuously for this utterly stupid and preposterous notion. Marry Fatima, indeed. A girl whom Mushahed himself has driven to the countryside to entertain his uncle's friends, well, it is just too absurd.

Kind, but blunt; Khan determines to be kind, but blunt. "Look," he says, "that girl is a peasant, a whore. It's sad, I agree. You're right to want to help her, I've been helping her myself, after all, helping her to earn the money she needs to get out of this and make a decent life for herself. She needs a man who knows nothing about her past, someone of her own class. I'll fix it up for her. We'll get a note from a doctor saying she's been ill, saying she's had some sort of a woman's operation that made her not be a virgin anymore." Walid Khan waves his hands vaguely. "We'll get her a nice letter with a lot of stamps and seals on it, and with that she'll get some nice fellow to marry her. We'll take care of that little girl for you, don't worry, and let me say I respect you for your kindness of heart, we must look after those who depend on us, that is the true responsibility of leadership."

"I'm going to marry her," says Mushahed. His uncle,

drawn so abruptly out of the beginnings of an eloquent speech on the responsibilities of leadership, feels his patience snap. Quite graphically, and with some coarse vocabulary unbefitting an orator and a statesman, he reminds his nephew of the precise nature of the activities of his intended bride; activities which, if Mushahed persists in his grotesque plan, he himself will make sure to describe to his parents in all exact detail, and to anyone else who wants to hear it, too. "I am going to forget this entire conversation," he winds up, finally, exhausted himself by the verbal orgy he has just perpetrated upon Fatima. "I am going to forget that you came to my office today. I will not remember it at all, not any of it. And one day, when we are working together as friends, you will say no more than 'Thank you, Uncle,' and we will both know that you are thanking me for not letting you make a total ass of yourself today."

Mushahed does not sleep that night. All night, he drives in his uncle's car. Images put in his mind by his uncle circle round and round in his brain as he circles round and round the deserted streets of Peshawar. It's true; he himself has delivered Fatima into the hands of all those fat and ugly men, he himself has chauffeured her off to be used by all of them. He scarcely allows himself to admit it, but it's true. Peshawar is a small place, a very small place, and if he ever does live a normal life, he will be constantly dealing with the men who have . . . And he, will he be able to look at Fatima without seeing in his mind the pictures of her that his uncle has so precisely drawn . . . pictures that—to be honest—were there even before? Perhaps it is better for Fatima to be with some simple man, who knows nothing about her, part of a community where her life will be completely new? And is it fair of him to plunge Fatima, who to be honest seems a bit, well, lukewarm on the matter of class war, into a life of political struggle? But on the other hand, how can he condemn her to the life of a peasant woman, slave of a slave? And besides, he loves her . . . doesn't he? So how can he send her away? After all, it isn't Fatima who should be ashamed, who must be banished. The men are the ones who have accumulated shame, who should hide themselves, not Fatima, who had no choice in the matter. The men are the ones who deserve punishment, including and especially his uncle, his cynical and corrupt uncle who has used Fatima like that, as a bone to be thrown to his equally corrupt cohorts, his uncle who has even managed for a moment to distort Mushahed's own thinking and confuse him. They are the past, his uncle and those other men; why concern yourself with the past when you have the future? And Fatima, Fatima is the future, too, the redeemed and beautiful future of the Third World when it rises clean and new from the avaricious, dirty grasp of its feudal past. Exhausted and at peace, Mushahed finally returns home near dawn to fall into a deep and sated sleep. From the ecstatic climax of his political insights, Mushahed sleeps as deeply and contentedly as another, less lofty man might from the profane consummations of sex.

Walid Khan, seeking to iron away the tensions between himself and Mushahed, casts about for ways to please the young man. One way is sure to please, there is one currency that pays for anything, as Khan knows. Besides, what the boy needs is to get the girl out of his system totally, so he will stop mooning over her and romanticizing her. Walid laughs contentedly to himself;

why bother with sports or cold showers when you can have the real thing? He will drown his impetuous nephew in a surfeit of Fatima. With a beaming and blinking Jamila, he arranges to book the girl for his nephew every day. Let him have her until he's sick of her, until he realizes what other men learn more slowly, that sex is pleasant enough but has no more magic than a pan leaf, which is pleasant enough, too, and offered up in the bazaar in just as many varieties. Then, after a little while, when the boy has had time to get bored with his daily diet of Fatima, Walid will send a different girl instead—someone with a bit more experience, perhaps that Lebanese dancer Zeyna—and Mushahed will see how foolish he has been.

The arrangement has its merits, as far as Fatima is concerned. She can see Mushahed regularly now, without worrying about Jamila. And it saves her money, too, since the uncle is now officially picking up the tab. But Mushahed cannot view matters in this light. Mushahed is disgusted and humiliated to have Fatima bought for him by his uncle. When he drives her to her morning assignations, now, he imagines the men to be sneering at him, and it is all he can do not to leap out and murder them, right there, with his bare hands. He could ask his uncle to get another driver, of course, but perversely he refrains. In agonies of rage and shame, he continues to deposit Fatima at the designated spots, knowing where she is going, knowing what she will do, and considering her more firmly than ever his bride. And Fatima, feeling his tension, is very much afraid.

And the rest of the time? What does Mushahed do with the gift of Fatima, so generously bestowed upon him daily by his uncle? He has the girl, he has the car, he has permission. What does he do? I can tell you what he does not do; he does not take Fatima to bed. She has been bought for him, very well, but he will not be like the others. As before, they just sit beside each other, listening to music and talking, or dropping by for a visit at the house of Shabnam.

Six a.m. in the Pakistani desert. Malone has awoken. He opens his eyes reluctantly, runs his fingers through his hair, and gets up to examine his new home. His inventory begins, despairingly, disbelievingly, with what there is not. There is not a sink, or any visible source of water. There is not a kitchen. There is not a bathroom, or any related facility. Nor is there a door that might lead to any such wonderful thing.

Thinking of prison cells, Malone searches for a bucket that might serve until he figures out what people around here do for a bathroom, but there is no bucket. There is an empty plastic Vichy bottle, a last resort. Malone does what he has to, then screws the cap back on fastidiously and stashes the evidence in a corner to dispose of later. After a brief mental pause while the details of his situation sink in, Malone moves on to what there is. There is a bed. There is a small, wobbly table, but no chair. There are some tins containing tea leaves, green ones in one box, black ones in another. There is a tin of sugar. There is some sort of contraption that can be lit, presumably for cooking. Behind a curtain there are shelves, storage shelves containing a large quantity of gauze and bandage strips, tubes of ointment, syringes of some sort. There is bottled water. There is a case of something called Australian protein biscuits thoroughly labeled and explained in English. There are some tins of beans, sardines, and sausages. Gingerly, Malone unwraps a packet of the biscuits for his breakfast, grimacing at the first one but then changing his mind; the tastelessness and the density make you chew, and chewing makes time pass.

Housework passes time, too. Malone straightens his blankets, wincing at the musty smell. He paces to the small window, looks out, paces away, paces back. He checks his watch, discovering that five minutes have passed. He examines the tea tins yet again. One of them is decorated with a picture of a mountain; the other one, with a rose. Malone stacks them one on top of the other, placing the round sugar jar to their left. He hopefully monitors his interior to see if he is tired; he is not. Boredom, like a steady droning hum, resonates in his head and makes his skin feel tickly. There is no way, no way at all, that he can survive days of this. He will go, is already going, crazy.

Mushahed no longer thinks about the future in purely global terms. On the afternoons spent in his uncle's empty apartment, he talks about his own and Fatima's future, too. They will be married. Boldly they will face down the disapproval of the hypocrites, the small-minded. His uncle will not really dare talk about her to his parents, for that would throw too much of a bad light on him, too; they will think of her as a peasant girl, but in time they will accept her.

Fatima preferred his earlier talks, about neocolonialism and industrialization. She can't say why, but his talk of their future makes her feel like crying.

Now, why would that be? Well, let's see. Mushahed has no money. His family has, but he himself is a penniless student living on an allowance; even Fatima has more ready cash than he does, with her slowly accruing stash of rupees. Mushahed has not completed his education, and even if he had, who would hire him, except, in the time-honored manner of Pakistan, the friends and associates of his family? A career in politics? His uncle would be only too delighted, but, of course, minus Fatima. If he works hard at his studies, then perhaps in a few years he can find employment in Saudi Arabia, and after a few more years, perhaps he will have saved enough to live a modest life in Pakistan, with Fatima. Lead the life of a rebel, committed to leftist ideology? That costs money, in Pakistan; only a son of the upper classes can afford it, funded by an indulgent father or funding himself with the income from inherited landholdings. Yes, leftism is the privilege of the feudal classes, in Pakistan. A rebel from his own class, though, must of necessity lead a very bourgeois life; he won't have the money for anything else. Will Mushahed marry Fatima? What do you think?

Despite these worries, Fatima is looking well these days. Love has given her back her sparkle, the sparkle she had thought was lost forever. To the tragic appeal of her face her former spark of joy returns, an enchanting combination. One day the Maulana's eye happens by chance to rest upon her and he is startled. The drab misery is gone; Fatima is back again, in living, breathing color. How could he have thought this girl was just like all the others? There is something special here, after all. Catching her one afternoon with a wistful, dreamy look on her face, he feels all his former lust surging back, and he moves to pull at the cord of her trousers with a confidently possessive hand. But what is this? Shouting a forceful no and snatching back her waist cord, Fatima runs from the room and takes refuge in the kitchen, where she wrests a mortar from the startled Jamila and begins pounding spices. Jamila, as we know, is unfortunately unsuited to the role of chaperone; nor does a little resistance discourage the Maulana. He calls Fatima back with a firmly shouted command; she stays where she is. "Go," Jamila barks, and pushes roughly at the girl's shoulders. Has Fatima gone mad? Fatima stays where she is. The Maulana appears in the doorway of his kitchen and sways there momentarily, repelled by the unfamiliarity of this female domain. "Come instantly into the living room," he orders, but Fatima, blindly pounding at the spices, ignores him. "Have you gone mad, girl?" asks Jamila, who in a panic already envisions her lucrative source of income sent away and herself blamed for the girl's unaccountable behavior. "You tell that filthy lecher to leave me alone," Fatima sobs, defiantly stomping tears into the garam masala. Speechless with shock, Jamila slaps her hard. The Maulana hovers indecisively on the threshold of the kitchen, and for a moment it seems possible that he might retreat, but then the sight of Fatima's passionately distraught face, lips reddened from being so violently compressed, cheeks swollen from the slaps, and eyes blurry from crying, fires him up again. "Jamila," he says, "go to your sister's house. Return tomorrow." Jamila withdraws in haste, still hissing curses and admonitions at the insane, the wretched girl.

Now the Maulana advances. The first thing is to get the girl out of the kitchen and into more familiar surroundings. Fatima has abandoned her spices and is backed against the wall. The Maulana grabs her arm to drag her into the living room. Reaching out for the table in search of support, Fatima's hand encounters the handle of the meat cleaver. The Maulana holds Fatima's arm; Fatima's hand holds the meat cleaver. With a cry of alarm, she pushes it from her, letting it clatter to the floor, and throws herself unarmed against the Maulana, scratching and struggling. Fatima's wrists flash with the reflected glow of thirty green glass bangles. The Maulana, increasingly furious and increasingly aroused, smashes Fatima back against the wall, her arm pinned between them. Six glass bangles shatter, tinkling gracefully as they hit the ground; six glass bangles cut Fatima's breasts and draw tiny drops of blood from the Maulana's arm as he slams the infuriating girl once, twice, three times against the wall. The next pushes propel her toward the living room, where she is hurled, finally, onto the foam cushions lining one wall. And in the brief frozen moment of silence that ensues as Fatima collapses dispiritedly onto the cushions and the Maulana gasps for air and contemplates his victim, it may well be that the Devil really is present.

Afterward, disheveled and breathless, the Maulana regards the huddled form of this girl and tries to order his thoughts. What is happening? Is he possessed by a demon? Is the girl, perhaps, a demon, a demon in female form? He regards her doubtfully as she lies limply before him, and is suddenly overcome by a feeling of fondness and calm. No, there are no demons here. It's just that he is a very passionate man, and this girl is his perfect partner. None of the others ever inspired in him such delirious extremes. Of course, things cannot go on like this. This is chaos, this is savagery. First she arouses him, because she, too, is filled with passion, then she resists him, because she is at heart a good and modest girl. He will snatch these pleasures from the Devil, and he will snatch the exquisite, the vortex-inducing Fatima from the dung-covered hands of whatever goatherd her parents have promised her to. In his pleasant condition of triumph and satiety, he is even inclined to view the girl's incredible behavior in a benign light. After all, he had ignored her for some time, giving her a chance to reflect on her failings; remorse and the desire to avoid further wrongdoing, not disobedience and revulsion, were undoubtedly what inspired her rebellion. She is a good girl, at heart. A girl to marry.

Fatima, exhausted and unhappy, has fallen asleep. Unfortunately, she dreams. She dreams about a hideous toad. The toad is huge and makes disgusting noises; with each noise, it spits out poison, and it is growing, growing, until it is larger than Fatima. Then it begins to sing, an ugly, toady, dissonant song, and every time it opens its mouth, bits of poison dribble out and Fatima knows that if this poison touches her, she will die . . .

She awakes suddenly, startled, but the singing continues. Sitting up, she sees that it is the Maulana; incredibly, he is singing, he is singing a quotation from the Prophet. He is singing that your wife is like your field, and you may go into your field as you wish. This verse, chanted softly to himself by the Maulana in his toady voice, is having a pleasantly soothing effect on him, making him—now that he has truly resolved to take Fatima as his wife—feel much better about himself and what he has done.

Mushahed, too, would be quite pleased with this particular religious verse. Yes, he would like that analogy. Women, and land. Fatima, and Pakistan. Land is eternal; how insolent, to want to own it. Religion and feudalism, how perfectly they reveal their obscene alliance, in this verse. The Maulana and the landowner, both of them thieves, rapists . . . both of them deserving of death, for their crimes and their arrogance.

Day Two in the Pakistani desert. Iqbal is still in Islamabad, just being briefed on the dead American his superiors want him to find the body and the killers of. The dead American is alive, as it happens, but he is not happy. He cannot believe that he is out here, in the middle of a forsaken expanse of shrubbery and dust, and will be here for at least another week. A week seems incomprehensible to Malone. He eats, he sleeps, he paces. Other than that, the day has only two pivotal events: the two times when Malone simply must leave his shelter, simply must step outside. Each excursion is preceded by as much reconnaissance as Malone, with only two windows to look out of, can manage. Look out into the desert, see nothing, see no one, dash outside, dash back in. Pace. Eat a cracker. Drink bottled water. Shake out the blanket. Turn over the socks, which have been washed in Vichy water and are airing across the chair back. Pace.

Time blurs; space contracts. Is there a world beyond this hut? Micky can barely remember. He is discovering what more experienced transcontinental travelers already know: that distance is actually harder to conquer mentally than physically, though intuitively you might expect the opposite. It is a well-guarded secret of business travelers that, though you have sworn to your spouse or lover that you will be missing them unceasingly, in fact you will not miss them one bit, and will barely even think about them. The time difference and other such impediments are not the real reason why they will not be hearing from you more frequently. The truth is that you are quickly absorbed into your new reality, engulfed by it, while home is by comparison much more abstract and, well, more distant.

Micky is a good illustration for this law of the geography of attachment. He is expending far less thought on home than home is expending on him.

Surveying the scruffy vista surrounding his desert refuge, Micky is a bundle of nerves and worry, but surprisingly, he is not homesick. Home seems unthinkably far away, like one's childhood—real, of course, but unreachable. I am sorry to tell you that the probable anxiety and worry of his boss and co-workers, not to mention the possible professional consequences of just disappearing into thin air in the middle of an important work assignment, barely cross Micky's mind. It is just before Mara's first visit that it suddenly hits him: his enemies do not know where he is, he hopes, but neither do his friends and his superiors. The solution he comes up with is this: Mara is to phone West-Fab. She can call collect! She is to ask for Josefina Chavez, the boss's secretary. Then she is to say that Micky has had to go, let's see, to the countryside to view a warehouse. No, that's too close to the truth. That things have been delayed by a few days but he is taking personal leave and will not charge a per diem, and he's fine. Or no, that he's got a second potential contract and has had to go back to Islamabad, near Islamabad, to look at their warehouses. He tried to call, but he couldn't get through, and he's afraid there won't be an opportunity to phone out there in the countryside around Islamabad, and so he's asked her to relay this message. Yes, that's good. It doesn't have to hold water, it only has to calm everybody down for a week or so. If they ask for details, Mara can say that this is all she knows, she's just a, let's see, a hotel acquaintance, yes, who has agreed to pass this message on. So they will know he is fine, and won't worry.

Day Three. Malone paces to the window, expecting to see nothing. There is a movement outside. Malone draws back, then advances cautiously. He sees a small figure, jumping across the sandy plain. Malone moves all the way up to the window. The small figure is wearing brown and throwing a stick. It is a boy, a boy of perhaps seven. The boy throws his stick, runs a few steps, crouches—it appears to be some sort of a game. He runs, jumps, crouches. Then he turns, looks up, and looks at the window of the shack. He sees Malone. The boy frowns and comes closer. Malone jumps back and flattens himself against the wall. He stays there, for a very long time. He counts to one hundred, then counts backwards to zero. His heart is beating, thudding. When he carefully, ever so carefully looks out the window again, the boy has gone.

In the afternoon, the boy is back. This time, he is not playing. He is standing directly in front of the window, at a distance of twenty feet, staring right into the glass. Malone collapses onto his mattress and despairs. He is discovered. Something dreadful will happen to him, probably. There is nothing he can do, nowhere he can go. Next time, the boy will bring his father, his fifteen uncles, and all the other warriors within a ten-mile radius, and Malone will be dragged out and speared. When he opens his eyes again, a count of two hundred later, no one is there.

In the late afternoon, Malone finally steps outside for his furtive visit behind the bushes. He has considered alternatives, but his upbringing is too conventional to depart very far from familiar habits of hygiene. He has waited as long as he could, hoping to delay things until nightfall, but this appears impossible.

Malone opens the door. He looks carefully in all directions. He moves with stealth and grace or the closest approximation of these that he can manage. He dashes behind the bushes, completes his task, and is on his way back to shelter when a small brown figure, his nemesis, materializing seemingly out of nowhere, steps right in front of him. Steps right between him and the door.

Malone looks at the boy. He sees an extremely dirty face with lively, liquid brown eyes and a nose that has needed wiping for some time now. He sees a baggy tan outfit, the drabness of which is effectively compensated for by two striking accessories. A brightly decorated, embroidered cap sits firmly on the boy's head, and his feet boast a pair of shiny, white patent leather shoes with bows on the front, shoes such as little girls in middle America wear to parties. And indeed, if we were to research the provenance of these shoes, we would discover that their former owner was in fact just such a girl. She outgrew her shoes. Her mother donated them to the Red Cross. They were flown to Pakistan and distributed to the refugees, who accept any pair of children's shoes with approval and give them to their sons, even if they are pink, even if they have bows, because sons are supposed to run and play and therefore need shoes, while girls are supposed to stay in the tent with their mothers and work and mind the babies, and therefore don't. Malone, ignorant of all this, wonders briefly about his new acquaintance's footwear.

The boy looks at Malone. He sees a pale, overweight man with bad posture. He sees an exotic person, a person who has blue eyes and light hair, a person who wears his shirt tucked into his pants, not flapping loose and long over them. But those are just the externals. The boy sees much, much more. He sees a person who appears to be an outsider, living here all alone, apparently abandoned by clan and kin, in a shack in the wilderness. He sees a person who, though male and large, has not yelled at him or smacked him for his impertinence or chased him away, but who stands non-pugnaciously, indeed nervously, looking at him. He sees a man who must, although he is white, be a refugee, too, of a sort. Who must have a refugee ration card. Who has no woman or other dependents with him. Who therefore might, just possibly, be induced to share his rations with a small, scraggly, permanently hungry boy and his mother.

To this end, the boy—whose name, by the way, is Hamid—attempts a charming, ingratiating smile.

When Mara arrives, late that night, she finds Malone in a strangely buoyant mood. True, he has barricaded the door with all available items, even jamming his mattress up against it. True, he is expecting a slaughter party to arrive at any moment. And yet . . . though fearful, Malone is not unhappy. The meeting with the boy gave him something to think about. Will the boy visit him again, tomorrow? Shall he give him some biscuits, if he comes?

Mara has brought a large bag, filled with things to ease Malone's confinement. She has brought a lot of food, in cans and boxes, and clean clothes. She has brought magazines, books, and stationery. The story of Malone's social encounter does not alarm her. The refugee boys are very independent. They run around all day just as they please. The shed belongs to the aid organization, and drivers or aid workers often sleep there.

Even if the boy tells his parents about Malone, they will not be concerned. "You're not on the moon here, you know," she snaps. "Just because this isn't Bethesda doesn't mean it's *Stranger in a Strange Land*," she finds herself saying. "Just act normal. The only people you really have to worry about are your buddies from the city, and they certainly won't look for you here."

Mara is very snippy and abrupt with Malone, just to make sure that he doesn't get any romantic ideas. This whole mess isn't his fault, she knows that, but all the same she deeply regrets ever having returned his phone call, having agreed to meet him for dinner, having spent the evening with him, and, most of all, having slept with him. He needs to understand that all of this means nothing, absolutely nothing. That she is helping him out of the goodness of her heart, and because he is a fellow American in distress, that's all.

As to his newfound friend, yes, it's possible that the boy is hungry. The refugees get enough food, in theory, but in practice it is distributed only to adult males. If the boy is an orphan, let's say, or the child of an unloved first wife, if he has no direct claim on adult male affection, then it's possible that he receives a bare charitable minimum. If he were a girl, he might be far worse off still, but of course Malone will not have the chance to develop any empathy for the girls, since they are locked up in their compounds and he will never see them, scrawny, half-starved, or otherwise, she adds. With that thought, she stalks off into the night, leaving behind a baffled Malone. Why is she angry? Why is she angry at him? Can she seriously be holding him responsible for the fate of Afghan girls and women?

Abandoning these fruitless musings, Malone selects a novel from his gift bag and immerses himself instead in the good old familiar world of international nuclear espionage. Just before falling asleep, he remembers that he didn't ask Mara to call West-Fab.

B y local standards, Fatima is an utterly worldly, irredeemably depraved person, an assessment she would not dispute. She thinks she has seen it all, done it all. Actually, though, she is still extremely innocent. For example, she considers the Belly-Gram to be the worst, most humiliating experience she has yet endured. Whereas there are, in her line of work, quite a few games that are considerably worse.

Ali Hakim knows and likes several of these, as Fatima discovers when she is sent to visit him.

Khan considers the Afghan lawyer to be impertinent and uppity, but smart. I, on the contrary, think that he is stupid, to inflict potentially injurious treatment on a girl belonging to, and liked by, someone as important as Khan. Won't she complain? Well, perhaps not—such a meek, scared little nothing of a person. So perhaps Ali Hakim, when he allows himself all sorts of excesses with this docile girl, is smart, after all.

Fatima has only recently arrived in Ali Hakim's office when she concludes in terror that he evidently intends to kill her. Why else would he blindfold her and wrap something around her neck?

Ironically, though, his hateful game ends up saving her life. When the door to his office bursts open and voices start screaming in Pashtu that he has betrayed his countrypeople, has sold them out to Pakistani politicians, has pocketed over 30 percent of the money intended for the holy war, when he shrieks something or other in denial, when thuds and pounds indicate that a scuffle is going on, Fatima can hear it all but she cannot see anything. Theoretically, she could pull the dupatta off her eyes, but thankfully, she is too frightened to move. In paralyzed silence she follows the debate, in Pashtu, over whether she, too, should be killed, and then she hears the voice interceding on her behalf, amiably pointing out that she is not really much of a witness to worry about, since she has not seen any of their faces. The amiable voice further argues that she looks very young, and that there are bloody marks on her arms where this human piece of slime Hakim has evidently injured her, that given the embarrassing circumstances of her presence here, she probably will not go rushing to the police with her testimony, and that in his opinion, she ought to be let go. Then she is grabbed by the shoulders and pushed somewhere, and the voice tells her to say her namaz prayer five times before taking the blindfold off. Huddled against a wall, she whispers it the commanded five times, and then one extra time in blessing of her amiable-voiced savior, before gingerly unwrapping the cloth over her eyes. When she still can't see, she panics for a moment, until a thin strip of light along the edge of the floor tells her she is in a closet. Fumbling open the door and peering out very carefully, she comes upon the grisly scene of a very bloody Ali. He might be dead already, or not, an ambulance might still save him, but probably not; at any rate it does not occur to Fatima to call for help. She assumes that he is dead. With a soft shriek, she escapes to a corner of the room, sheltering herself behind Hakim's desk. She eyes the door. Has she waited long enough? Will the men really be completely gone, is it safe to run away now? She decides to say the namaz five more times, just to be sure, but her eyes keep fluttering involuntarily to the bloody spectacle on the floor, liquid spilling more slowly now out of a cut on the neck. She is amazed to see that one can kill a person, such a big violent person, in much the same way as one kills a little rabbit. Ought she to pray for him, she wonders. But she can find no regret in herself that he is gone. It doesn't seem wrong, not really. He was a bad person, the avenging voices said so and she knows it, too. The voice that saved her, by contrast, clearly belonged to a good person. She would like to say something to that person, but of course she can't. Instead, she scrawls something on a piece of paper and drops it on the floor next to Hakim. Then she gathers up her courage and dashes out the door.

I qbal cannot believe it. He sits at his borrowed desk with the newspaper in front of him, staring at the printed page, and cannot believe it, does not want to believe it. "Who did this?" he asks, almost too amazed to be angry. "How is this possible?"

Toufiq looks away, clearly embarrassed.

"The 'signature.' Our ace in the hole," Iqbal says, incredulously. "Our way of telling whether we've got the right guy. Our way of weeding out the copycats. Right here, on page one, for the whole world to see."

Toufiq shakes his head discreetly to signify that he, too, is upset by this development, but continues to avoid Iqbal's eyes.

"The text of the messages," Iqbal goes on. "The killer's messages, right here in the newspaper. How could this happen?"

"We work closely with the press," Toufiq finally mumbles out, in answer. Then he inclines his head meaningfully toward the office of his superior. "We have, one could say, an almost brotherly relationship with the press."

There is silence while Iqbal absorbs this unsavory bit of Frontier nepotism. A boss who leaks information to relatives in the media, great.

10

The Maulana is at peace with the world. He is a changed man; everyone remarks on it. He smiles often; his voice has taken on a milder, gentler cast. Even his physical appearance is different. Where formerly his well-padded body gave off an aura of imposing bulk, he now seems merely rotund, as one who has finished off many platters of pullau topped by raisins and generously dribbled with lard. The news of his impending marriage elicits sighs of admiration, and his version of the event spreads quickly within the community. The Maulana is marrying, out of charity, a destitute young girl, daughter of a distant kinsman, following thereby in the footsteps of the Prophet himself, may-peace-be-upon-him, who married often and gladly and accumulated in this way—as one of his wives rather acerbically noted—a good deal more than the four women allowed to Muslims by God, thanks to special dispensations that always managed, fortuitously, to arrive in the nick of time whenever his eye or his strategic brain came to rest upon a desirable new candidate.

To the unanimous chorus of approval and admiration that greets the news of the Maulana's saintly plan, two dissonant voices offer a counterpoint. Mushahed, cursing, and then laughing, and then cursing again, as the absurdity of this new development slowly penetrates his thoughts. Fatima, herself, vowing that she will not marry the Maulana, she will not marry him, she will not be his wife.

"Of course you will not marry that disgusting swine," proclaims Mushahed. "You will marry me."

Shabnam, witness to this conversation, avoids Fatima's eyes, fearing that she will see there awful vulnerabilities of hope and belief. Words, words, words: can Fatima, who should know everything there is to be known about men and appears instead to know nearly nothing, believe in such words?

On Friday, the Maulana's fans are surprised and somewhat disappointed. Instead of the usual talk of God's punishment and rage, the Maulana is intoning suras about God's forgiveness and tolerance for the weakness of men. Instead of the quasi-pornographic warnings that many of his followers spend their week in quiveringly lubricious anticipation of, he is quoting the Prophet's admonitions about being kind to, and indulgent of, women.

Heaven lies under the feet of mothers, he quotes the Prophet. Women rear children; they are their first teachers, and hence do the work of prophets. A wife must not be treated like a servant.

Goodness me! So many kindly, loving sayings, from the formerly frothing mouth of our Maulana! His followers are first astonished, then disappointed, then slowly lulled into his contagious state of benevolent placidity. Several hundred women, on this Friday afternoon, will shake their heads in wonderment as they receive pats of kindly affection from husbands who usually return from the mosque puffed up with self-importance and masculine contempt.

Perhaps Fatima, if only she understood all of this, could find meaning in devoting her life to the pacification of militant Islam. Yes, Fatima could dedicate herself to the exorcism of the Maulana's demons, and, who knows, the entire development of radical Islam in Pakistan might take another, more benign course. But Fatima, a weak and ignorant woman, cannot grasp such abstractions. She knows only that if that fat and horrible Maulana heaves himself on top of her one more time, she will not be able to bear it, she will simply not be able to bear it.

As I told you, Fatima has a number of exceptional, dangerous traits. There is one I forgot to mention. She has, apparently, the ability to arouse feelings. She has gotten the Maulana to love her. Even the jaded Walid Khan has grown fond of her, in his own way. Mushahed feels a lot, but I suppose we shouldn't count him; he always feels a lot, about nearly everything. Jamila feels nothing, it is true, except gratification at this especially lucrative little fly caught in the web of the Maulana, but then Jamila never feels more than that. Jamila is a fly seeking to be on the side of the spiders, and if that is your goal, it is best not to let feelings get in your way.

Michael Malone felt fear. Even after she had taken off the chaddri, even after he understood what this was all about, even after she had left his room without having been touched by the paranoid, the fearful-of-diseases, and the suspicious-about-blackmail Micky Malone, even as he hastened to the ice cube dispenser to fix himself a stiff drink after this shock, he retained the image, not of her body emerging startlingly pale and naked from the absinthe-green chaddri, but of her face.

Iqbal knows about Fatima, in case you are wondering. He knows that Walid Khan includes among his personal business assets a Lebanese dancer, a Palestinian manicurist, an Austrian masseuse, and a whole inventory of destitute girls who do his bidding. In this group, Fatima does not stand out. There is no reason to take particular note of her.

Isa becomes his sister's shadow, but he has a handicap. It's not as if she has a nine-to-five job. Her routine is anything but regular. Some days she leaves the house early, other days late; some days she doesn't go out at all. There are times when he ends up following Jamila, who is about the same height. Not until he hears her haggling over the price of carrots does he realize that this shrewish voice is not that of his sister, and abandon the pursuit in disgust. Later he is annoyed with himself; why didn't he follow her back home, studying her gait very carefully to avoid future confusions! Stupid!

Other times, because she carries a large shopping net, he dismisses Fatima as Jamila and stays at his post instead of going after her. And one awful time, he is sure it is Fatima, swaying gracefully down the street in front of him, so on an impulse he sidles up very close, nudges her, and hisses, "Sister, it's me, Isa, I've come to help you." But the woman, who is Jamila's young niece, starts shrieking that someone is molesting her, and Isa has to run to escape the outraged passersby.

But finally all conditions are favorable and he manages to track Fatima all the way to the office of Khan. After that, his quest for information gets easier. Everybody knows a story or two about Khan. He's rich, he's mighty. He owns a large chunk of the property of the province, and a goodly percentage of the souls of its inhabitants. He has villas and houses in the hills. He has powerful cars. He has beautiful girls. He throws decadent parties. The beautiful girls entertain at the decadent parties.

Fatima, a beautiful girl, is visiting Khan. The Maulana, it seems, is allowing, perhaps even commanding it. Easily transiting from supposition to knowledge, from hypothesis to fact, Isa scowls in disgust.

Fatima, meanwhile, is not doing anything worthy of special attention. Life goes on, business prospers, except for the time when Mushahed makes a scene. It's an ordinary afternoon, five o'clock. Mushahed is lounging about in his uncle's antechamber, already displaying, were anyone looking, signs of restless discontent. He fidgets, he gets up, he looks angrily out the window, he sits, he fidgets. Fatima enters the waiting room. The secretary looks up indifferently, nods, and signals to Mushahed. Fine, here she is, and Mushahed is to take her to the Inter-Continental. She's been told the correct room number already, so just drop her off at the main entrance and wait there for her to come out again. *If* she comes out again, the secretary adds, chuckling. For this is no ordinary assignment! Today, she's going to see a famous actor. If she's star-struck like most women, she probably won't be back!

So now even his uncle's flunkies are taunting him! Something snaps in Mushahed. He grabs the man by the collar and shoves him against the wall. "One more word and I'll smash your face in," he screams. "And you can tell my uncle to send *your* wife to the hotel, and *you* can drive her there yourself, slave!" he screeches. Then he stomps out of the office, yelling imperiously at Fatima to follow, because he is taking her home!

The secretary watches him leave, shaking his head. What a hothead! Shall he inform Khan? No, better not disturb him. This is a problem he can solve on his own. After all, this isn't the first time this has happened. Fatima is a levelheaded girl. After Mushahed has taken her home, she will undoubtedly return to the office for new instructions. But to speed things up, he will send Ahmed after her. Ahmed can wait for her by her house and take her straight to the hotel.

Once out of the office, Mushahed grabs Fatima by the arm. He pulls her down the back staircase and bundles her into the car.

"Mushahed, I have to go to the Inter-Continental," Fatima pleads, trying to appeal to his reason. Mushahed says nothing, just drives on. "Mushahed," Fatima repeats, timidly. "I don't care about that actor, you know that. You shouldn't pay attention to what that stupid Munir says. He was just making a joke. Please take me to the hotel now. Don't do this again. You'll only get me in trouble."

Mushahed keeps driving. Fatima begins to cry.

Mushahed is silent, silent but angry. To the accompaniment of loud, very loud cassette music, he drives indignantly, blindly through the streets.

Ahmed has been told to wait for the woman on the corner near her house and to take her to the Inter-Continental Hotel. She might be trying to get a scooter cab, Munir has warned him. Since she is not expecting him, she might not notice him right away, so he should watch carefully and attract her attention when she emerges from the house. Then he should drive her to the hotel. Once there, she is to go right on up to room number 136. A suite.

So Ahmed drives to the corner and waits. He waits for quite a while. Actually, he is starting to get annoyed. But what can he do? He can't very well knock on the Maulana's door, demanding the girl.

Almost twenty minutes later, his passenger finally appears. Maybe his attention had lapsed, or maybe she came out of a side entrance; at any rate, Ahmed doesn't actually see her come out of the door. She just appears suddenly beside the gate in her green chaddri. She seems to glance at his car, but instead of coming toward him, she heads down the street. "Over here," Ahmed shouts. "I'm driving you." There is no response; she just keeps walking. Ahmed is furious. Where the hell is she going? He doesn't understand why his boss puts up with it. A no-good slut, too stupid even to make a decent whore! Nothing but trouble with this one! He jumps out of the car and runs after her, shouting, "Here, here, the car is right here!" He actually has to catch up with her and grab her by the pleated material of her draperies. "Fatima?" he asks, just to be sure, and the figure gives a slight nod and allows herself to be guided into the backseat. He'd better not drop her off in front of the hotel, though that's all he's been told to do. No, he doesn't trust her to get it right. He'd better take her right on up to the room, to make sure she finds her way and doesn't try to chicken out like last time. Murmuring threats and gripping a handful of green fabric, he pushes her into the lobby; a good thing, too, because

CHERYL BENARD

some sort of reception is going on and there are hundreds of people everywhere, she'd be sure to get lost in the crush, slow-witted as she is. Room 136: he marches her straight to the door, knocks, steps back, and nudges her impatiently inside.

11

Lilly is annoyed. She lacks perspective; she still believes in journalism. It's an honest mistake to make, if you live in a country where journalists are occasionally flogged in public for publishing a dissenting view. At any rate, she regards herself as a serious political author and is deeply offended to be asked, by her newspaper, to interview Babu Subramaniam, idol of the Indian silver screen, heartthrob of the neighboring millions, who has chosen to grace unworthy Peshawar with his radiant presence for a few brief days. Lilly considers herself demeaned by such a request. "I'm not a society columnist," she rages. On the telephone, negotiating a time for the interview, she is curt, almost offensive. Subramaniam must be a very tolerant individual, or else he must be really desperate for publicity, to grant an interview to someone so rude and condescending. "These people will do anything to see their name in print," Lilly snaps when Sonia points this virtue out to her.

When she returns from the meeting, Sonia and Gul are waiting anxiously for her report; the servants hover in the background, hoping for a gossipy tidbit about the star. Lilly accommodates none of them. "Fat" is her only comment to their queries. "Obese" is all she will say when they persist in their curiosity. "Hung-over," she says with absolute finality, before retreating to the desk in Sonia's study to pound out, angrily, the story her newspaper is demanding.

Julia happens to be in the bazaar at the time of the next murder. She is on her way back to the hotel from a visit to the U.S. consulate.

Initially, as you will recall, the trip to Pakistan was a sentimental journey, but Julia can't help herself. She's just not a sentimental sort of person. She's a restless, troublemaking, question-asking kind of person. So she decides to go to the U.S. consulate. Her intention is to raise hell. The whole story with Micky is starting to strike her as quite fishy. Iqbal is nice, but what good is nice? He obviously has no clue to her brother's fate, and with the additional more recent murders to occupy his attention has basically written him off. She can't get any real information about Micky's Pakistani business partners, and his mysterious girlfriend is unavailable. There seems no other ready outlet for her feelings but to raise hell in the U.S. consulate, but, storming into the building, Julia finds it practically abandoned. Except for an elderly secretary who calls her "dear" and radiates sympathy for her and "your poor, dear" brother, there is nobody there to throw her tantrum for. The consul is gone, and so are his assistant and his personal secretary, leaving only the warmhearted Emily, a couple of Marine guards, and the local staff—not a satisfactory audience.

The most Julia can do is summon up a stern tone of voice and tell the sympathetically clucking Emily that she expects to be contacted very, very soon by someone of *authority* who is prepared to give her some *answers*. Then she retreats.

She decides to visit the archives of the local newspaper. Lilly has given her the address and a name, and she wants to look through its files.

She decides to walk through the bazaar, to give herself time to calm down.

She starts walking past the shops very briskly, but comes to a stop at the Kashmiri tea stall. It's a stiflingly hot day, and the marketplace is so loud. It's kind of like being in hell, Julia reflects, except that there is probably nothing as delicious as Kashmiri tea brewing in hell. Here, though, it boils and boils in huge vats, right out in the open, the special leaves from the Kashmiri mountains and the milk and the cardamom pods and the nuts, all simmering together for many hours until they reach the perfect, creamy consistency. You drink it with sugar or, if you are a local and it is summer, with salt, which by the way makes excellent medical sense and helps you avoid dehydration, but is an acquired taste that foreigners rarely develop.

Julia stands by the vats for a while, watching the steam from the giant tubs rush up to meet the steam of the hot Peshawar summer, steam on steam; people are yelling and cursing and haggling, but the noise and the heat mesh together into a dreamlike blur. The effect is oddly soporific. It all seems so unreal Julia finds herself drifting into a trance-like state of watching, from which she finally pulls herself with difficulty. Turning to go, she finds herself abruptly face-to-face with a woman in a shrill, sickeningly pink sari, her face distorted by terror, her mouth opened to scream, her slim braceleted

151

hand raised defensively above her, dripping blood. Less than a fraction of a second later, as quickly as one awakes and realizes that one was dreaming, Julia recognizes that she is face-to-face with a movie poster. Just a poster for one of those gory, hysterical Indian films. But just for that initial fraction of a second, the actress's look of horror had gripped her, jolting a stab of fear through her body.

So it seems a bit creepy, later, to realize that a different Indian actor, Babu Subramaniam, must have died, might have screamed for real, at right about that moment.

Babu Subramaniam, the fourth victim—to Iqbal's count, for even he by now has firmly placed Malone in the realm of the dead. BRING YOUR ENEMIES TO FALL, the note says. The fact that the message for the first time duplicates a previous note inspires a lot of speculation. It also calls forth a rare burst of humor in Toufiq. The murderer, he hypothesizes, could be an amateur film critic who is making a cruel comment on the lack of originality in Indian film. If they continually recycle their plots, he is probably saying, why shouldn't he recycle his message.

Iqbal smiles politely; they all know the situation isn't funny. When a popular Indian is killed in Pakistan, there is nothing comical about it.

"India . . ." Lilly murmurs, very thoughtfully, but when her friends ask her what she is thinking about, she just shakes her head impatiently.

Iqbal requisitions videos of Babu's most successful movies in order to do some posthumous research. Randomly selecting one, he stays home to watch.

A wild and stormy night. In a pitiful little shack, trembling in the rough wind, a young woman is giving birth to a child. Clutching her newborn infant, a girl, she falls back exhausted onto the straw mat. A pounding noise outside, the door opens, a rough and evil-looking, enormous man comes crashing in. It is the young woman's husband. He lifts up the infant, sees with a growl of disgust that it is a girl, grabs the child, and runs away with it as the mother, frantic and hysterical, stumbles pleadingly after him into the fierce rain and then collapses onto the muddy ground.

A few days later. The husband, who is the leader of a gang of bandits, breaks into the villa of a rich man. The wife has just given birth to an infant son. The bandit kidnaps the child, takes him home, and orders his wife to tell everyone this boy is the child she has given birth to, and to raise it as her own. The woman weeps for her daughter and protests, her husband beats and curses her, she still resists, then she looks down at the little boy her husband has thrust into her arms and her heart melts with love for the child. She presses him close to her and her husband marches away, satisfied that she will obey his orders.

Meanwhile, the rich family is desperate over the loss of its son. For days they wait for communication from the kidnappers. The father paces up and down in his lush marble foyer, swearing that he will pay any ransom, that he will give his last rupee for the return of his son. But no message comes. The wife falls into a state of despondency; a doctor examines her and announces that unless her depression lifts, she will die, die of a broken heart. Her husband is frantic. The wife weeps and moans and slips slowly closer to death. Just then, a bundle is found on the back stairs by one of the maids. In the bundle is an infant girl.

From her upstairs bedroom, the wife hears the sound of an infant crying and totters down the staircase. She does not care that it is a girl; she does not mind that it is not her own son. Clutching the baby to her, she declares that the gods have sent her this child to replace her own, and that she will keep it. For the sake of his wife's happiness, the rich man agrees to raise the girl like his own daughter. The girl, of course, is the bandit's child.

Years pass. The boy grows into an adolescent and finally into a young man; into, in fact, Babu Subramaniam. He is a virtuous and gentle fellow, constantly at odds with his father, constantly defending his mother against his attacks, bookish and well mannered. Finally, the bandit gives up on the idea of ever turning this little Caspar Milquetoast into a son after his own heart. Instead, he devises a diabolical plan. He will kidnap the girl—his own daughter—who has grown into a buxom and lovely young woman, and take her to a deserted hut. Then he will pump his son—really the rich man's son —full of drugs and alcohol, and tell him that the girl is a prostitute. In his drug-crazed state, the young man will rape the girl. The bandit will arrange to have the rich man arrive on the scene, where he will reveal to him the true identities of those involved. Heartbroken, miserable, and ashamed, the rich man will have no choice but to agree to an immediate marriage between his adoptive daughter and his flesh-and-blood son; a marriage in which the girl's dowry will include a fat monthly payment to the bandit, her biological father.

The plan proceeds. The young man is first injected with an unnamed drug that has the effect of transporting him to a state of erotic frenzy, and is then plied with whiskey. Panting with chemical lust and inebriated beyond sensible thought, he is taken to the deserted hut. The kidnapped girl, meanwhile, has been forced at gunpoint to don seductive Western apparel and to paint her face; then she is thrown into the hut with the young man. He sees the girl; he growls in ferocious anticipation and heaves himself at her recoiling figure. He grabs *her, laughing, and is about to do the dastardly deed when, glancing down at her face, he sees that tears of outraged virtue are streaking her garish makeup. The realization that this girl is unwilling stuns him out of his drug-induced trance and he ceases and desists with an enormous physical effort that the camera records in exhaustive detail, each agonized second of his monumental struggle shown at close range. Panting with exhaustion, he falls back onto the bed.*

The girl, terrified at first but realizing that he does not intend to harm her, brings wet towels from the bathroom and bathes his sweating brow. The bandit and the rich man, arriving in anticipation of finding the two in an explicit and disgraceful situation, instead find them sitting peacefully at the kitchen table sipping tea. In the climactic final scene, the young man learns of the evil scheme that has been thwarted, and learns, too, that the bandit is not his father. A scuffle ensues in which the bandit, trying to strangle the young man, slips and hits his head against the stove, and conveniently dies.

The young man and the young woman, brought together by the horrendous experience, fall in love and marry, and go off to live in the villa of the rich man; happy end.

This plot is absolutely typical for a Babu Subramaniam film, and typical of popular Indian films in general. Invariably there are bandits and rich men, babies switched at birth, heroes and heroines who are killed and then reawakened to life by one of India's popular plot twists (they weren't really dead, just drugged to seem dead; they had an evil twin who was killed in their place, etc.).

Iqbal has seen Babu's movies before, of course. Hostilities between Pakistan and India scrupulously except the entertainment industry, and in fact, if Indian strategists were just a little bit more innovative, they could bring their South Asian enemies to their knees by withholding entertainment from them. A few unremitting years of nothing but the *Ladies' Prayer Hour*, combined with the censored *Horsemen*, and the Pakistanis would surrender unconditionally.

The Khyber Inter-Continental is not pleased; two deaths in its hotel: that is not good publicity. The manager lowers the price of the Moghul Buffet by a dollar.

A dead Indian movie star; Islamabad is not pleased. Lilly's editor is probably the only person actually happy about the event; he publishes, exclusively, the star's last interview. Lilly wants to take out some of the nasty bits, feeling guilty, but it has already gone into print.

The Indian connection gives new vigor to the investigation. Iqbal is on the chase again. Could militant Sikhs be behind it? Islamic fundamentalists perhaps? Or is it an internal Indian affair? The possibilities are many. India, India, why India? Iqbal chases many leads, pursuing them eagerly into many dead ends.

B abu Subramaniam, heartthrob of millions in a country where the silver screen is undimmed in its glory. A few rupees, and you are transported to the world of the rich, the beautiful, the in-love, and can forget your arranged-marriage husband, the mother-in-law who torments you, the dust of the streets you sweep, your hunger. The stars of the movies are not hungry; even when they play abused and starving heroes, their faces are round and their bodies soft from the greasy delicacies of well-stocked tables. To be rich and beautiful, in India, still means to be fat, especially if you are a man.

The female stars aspire to Western ideas of beauty, and struggle to attain the emaciation that comes so naturally to their audiences, but the men still adhere to the former national beauty ideal of boyish, pre-puberty, round-cheeked baby-faced fat.

Babu hovers, with some effort, right on the brink. He is well proportioned enough to be considered handsome in the West, but no one would call him angular. His downfall is alcohol, alcohol and sweets. And laziness. The slow smile and languid courting behavior that make all those millions of female Indian hearts beat faster are not just an act; this fellow is lazy. Girls admitted to his bedchamber, excited but apprehensive about the sophisticated techniques their debonair lover will expect, are often taken aback to find a sluggish, drowsy individual who wants to be massaged for hours and often falls asleep under these ministrations before anything else happens.

In fact, his cavalier treatment of these ladies is due not only to laziness but also to his personal inclinations, which tend, to Babu's own regret, in the opposite direction. Babu is lazy and sluggish, but there is a hot-blooded side to him, too. Innumerable are the fistfights and scandalous altercations he has been involved in. What Babu really likes is to go to bed with muscular, lean, and somewhat disreputable boys, and to get into a fight with them shortly thereafter and throw them out, or have them thrown out by his bodyguard.

Fortunately, he has found a congenial and helpful friend in Devi, his female counterpart in Indian cinematic stardom, his soul mate, and his perfect bride in all ways but one. Devi, whose promiscuity is remarkable, needs a photogenic, tolerant husband just as much as Babu needs a media-proof but maritally undemanding wife. And the studio needs for each of them to have a glamorous, highly visible spouse, in order to preemptively silence the nasty gossip.

What an inspired moment that was, when the harried Indian studio executive hit upon this brilliant solution: to take his two worst headaches, his two scandal bombs just waiting to go off, the sweet leading lady who is really a nympho and the dashing leading man who is actually a faggot, and marry them to each other in a spectacular media blitz! It's perfect, an arranged marriage made in heaven. Everyone is happy. The studio has lots of glossy pictures of the loving couple, and the bride and groom have their freedom and, as an unexpected marvelous bonus, a genuine friendship as well.

So things are swell with Babu. He is famous. He is rich. He has his boys and he has Devi for camouflage. Life is good, though not right now: why did he agree to come to this godforsaken dumpy corner of a lousy country? What a stupid PR stunt. Research, right! "Locations" . . . it's a cruel joke even to use a term like "location" to describe this miserable place. Pakistan is a pain, pure and simple. A colossal, Islamic pain. The alcohol in the hotel costs a fortune, forty-five dollars a bottle, which Babu can readily afford but is annoyed about, on principle. And you have to go to a special little room to get it, passing under a sign that says: FOR NON-MUSLIM FOREIGN PASSPORT HOLDERS ONLY, which Babu considers a monumental bit of self-righteousness. "Abandon hope, all ye who enter here" . . . the nerve!

What a bunch of sanctimonious assholes they are, these Pakis. Bugger them all! Babu laughs; actually, he wouldn't mind doing just that. They're not bad-looking, and there's something kind of sexy about their grim faces and their angry demeanor. And he's sure they're all fags, you can tell that much just by the way they treat women. But they'll never admit it, will they. No, it's not worth taking any chances, not in his place. One wrong move, and the religious fruitcakes will be after him; no, better not take any risks. Babu sips his whiskey glumly and averts his eyes from temptation when the room boy arrives with more towels. No, it isn't worth it, not even with that skinny muscular little devil sending out what Babu knows are clear invitations.

Babu has drunk twenty-five dollars' worth of whiskey and is only just beginning to relax a little. What a bore. What a stupid PR stunt, bringing him here. There is a knock on the door, but his irritable shout receives no response. Babu heaves himself sluggishly from the bed, spilling two dollars' worth of whiskey. He opens the door; a bizarre apparition faces him.

For a moment he thinks the whiskey must be more potent than he had believed, but no, it's just a woman, a Muslim non-foreign female in one of those dirty little potato bags they wear. "Aren't you sorry that's not a sari, honey," he says, before becoming aware, with a stab of alarm, of the male standing behind her. No sense of humor in this miserable country, he knows. But it seems to be okay, no offense taken. Instead, the man gives the female potato sack a rough shove that throws her up against Subramaniam. Babu steps back, the female lump stumbles in after him, the door is slammed shut from the outside. Babu shakes his head to clear it and says, "Honey, I think you've got the wrong room."

There is no reaction. Babu's alcohol-befuddled brain works hard and comes up at last with an explanation: a joke. This is a joke, played on him by Devi. In fact, this probably *is* Devi, Devi pretending to be a local belle. Well, okay, then! Babu is always ready to go along with a good joke. "Hey, sweetheart," he says, "want to be in the movies? Let's have a look at the legs." Certain now that he will find Devi underneath the bag, Babu grabs the woman confidently and yanks up the chador.

Knobby knees and hairy, muscular thighs emerge, leading up to boxer shorts. No, this isn't Devi. Startled at this turn of events, Babu pauses, but his mystery guest continues the motion, wresting the chador off and standing before him in a white shirt and underpants, hissing angrily as he struggles to untangle the green cloth from his head and arms.

Babu recovers quickly. Wonderful! Devi, that marvelous Devi, who knows him better than anyone else, has rented him some entertainment and sent it to his room, gift-wrapped. He laughs delightedly. "Welcome!" he booms. "Welcome, my Pakistani friend!" It occurs to him that his visitor is looking a bit wild-eyed, even for a Frontiersman, but hey, there's nothing wrong with wild-eyed.

"My friend," he suggests, though, to mellow the guy out a little, "help yourself to some non-Muslim foreign passport holder refreshment. I won't tell!" And seeing his guest reach for the bottle, he starts searching for the remote control to turn off the television. No need for censored entertainment when you have some uncensored activities in store. He is still laughing when the whiskey bottle first strikes the back of his head. The second time he moans, and by the tenth time he is no longer moving at all, just lying motionless in a puddle of whiskey and blood.

And now, sadly demised, the spirit of Babu is dependent on the law enforcement officers of an enemy state to bring his killer to justice. The enemy law enforcement officer, let it be said, is doing his best.

Babu Subramaniam, wed to the lovely Devi only last September, still radiates all that charm and appeal that make the heart of lady cinema viewers everywhere beat faster. Rumors of a visit from the stork to the contrary, Devi and Babu plan a joint screen venture "sometime soon," Babu promised with his famous smile. And what brings him to Pakistan? "Just trying to collect some local color," he explains, suddenly serious. "I always research my parts very carefully, almost scientifically, and this one is especially important to me." And what part is this? "I can't say too much just now," he teases. "But it will deal with the fate of our two countries since Partition."

Iqbal sighs and shakes his head. Before him, mountains of movie magazines, press clippings, and photographs simper on about the charm, the virility, the liquid brown eyes, the lavish society wedding of the handsome, the gorgeous—the, to Iqbal's dispassionate eye, merely pudgy—star of film and screen Babu Subramaniam.

There is nothing in the clippings, as far as Iqbal can make out, to explain why the room boy of the Inter-Continental, entering with a passkey at 11:30 a.m. to make up the room, should have found the Indian collapsed across the bed with his skull smashed in by a whiskey bottle. Or why there should have been one of the ubiquitous notes shoved into his left hand. Throwing the magazines aside in disgust, Iqbal gets up to pace the floor some more.

"Nothing," he says, "I have accomplished nothing."

"Oh, for God's sake, Iqbal," Lilly says, and Gul murmurs, "Darling, sit down."

"Ignore me," Iqbal replies, as everyone sighs in exasperation and exchanges annoyed looks: how can one ignore him, when he is prancing up and down grimacing with despair and moaning dark threats and predictions.

"You are the dust, *ha*! I am the dust, dust under the feet of those fools in Islamabad," he mumbles.

"Why don't you sit down, and calmly go over everything you know," Aunt Sonia suggests. "Quietly, or out loud, however you wish. Or else have a drink and go to bed. You're just driving everyone mad with your pacing."

With a theatrical sigh, Iqbal marches off to pour himself a drink.

"Come on, tell us those verses again," Sonia says, calmingly. "There must be some clue to be found there."

"Yes, Miss Marple," Iqbal says, raising his glass to her, but he pulls up a chair, sits down facing his ladies, and thinks for a minute.

"So as you know," he begins, "the first message only said: YOU ARE, we suppose because the murderer was interrupted, or maybe because he deliberately intended to build up the suspense as he went along. The second one said: YOU ARE THE DUST. The third one was a little different. It said: BRING YOUR ENEMIES TO FALL. Still, the handwriting was the same, the lab says, though one can't be entirely sure. The first message, after all, was smeared in blood with a finger, the second was in capital letters, the third in handwriting. Then the fourth message was the same as the third, which was the first time there was a duplication."

As Iqbal speaks, Lilly sits up tensely.

"Iqbal," she says, in a ghostly voice.

He looks at her.

"Iqbal," she says, in a voice quite unlike her. "I've

heard that somewhere before. You can find that. It must be published, somewhere. I know I've heard it before, I really have."

It takes her fifteen minutes to convince him that this is not a cruel joke intended to drive a miserable man over the brink and to make her very own best friend a widow. Even at breakfast the next morning, before undertaking any action on this score, Iqbal makes Lilly swear a variety of oaths concerning her earnestness. And, of course, he tries to coax, badger, and trick further details out of her. "Think," he implores her one minute, only to instruct her to forget all about it and let her subconscious ease it gently to the surface. Neither tactic brings results. Lilly cannot, she simply cannot remember where she has heard this verse before. She cannot even remember whether she read it in a magazine or a novel, heard it on the radio, or saw it on television.

Iqbal puts all sorts of unlikely bloodhounds on the track of the verse, of course; researchers, librarians, English teachers, poets. With his characteristic energy, Iqbal is constantly on the phone, harassing and hounding them and cheering them on, his own little private search party in the swamp of words.

Even though she assesses this endeavor as pretty hopeless, Julia wants to help. She uses a press club computer to look up the key words, she accesses *Bartlett's Familiar Quotations*. She is not surprised when nothing promising turns up.

Julia calls her aunt. Then she decides to check in with West-Fab, where an excited secretary puts her right through to Mr. Hamish, who answers the phone breathlessly, verbally enfolding Julia in a huge corporate embrace. He wants to post a reward for information regarding "Micky's whereabouts, and I want you to know, Julia, that all of us here at West-Fab believe he will return, we are waiting for him to return, and we are confident that he will return!"

On the way back to the hotel, she finds herself drifting into the bazaar once again. Passing aimlessly through the labyrinthine path of shops, she ends up in the textiles and clothing section, and she sees a stack of burqas and chaddris. Out of the mass of fabric she pulls a green Afghan chaddri, and, on an impulse, she buys it.

The shopkeeper wraps it in brown paper. She takes the package to her hotel room and dumps it on the chair, but then she is curious. She wants to know how it feels, what the world looks like through a grid. Is the chaddri heavy? Is it very hot?

She unwraps the package and pulls the mass of fabric over her head. To her surprise, she can see better than expected—but only while standing still. Taking a few tentative steps, she finds that when you move, the grid —which, after all, is not attached to your head in any way, is not even anchored to your ears as a pair of sunglasses would be—begins to shift, so that little black squares constantly cross your field of vision. And you can look only directly forward, not sideways and not down, which has to be a real handicap on uneven and unpaved roads.

Next, Julia wants to see herself in this exotic garment. Remembering that there is a mirror above the sink, she walks toward the bathroom. She hasn't figured out how to use her hands under this thing, so she nudges the door with her foot.

It opens.

She screams.

Well, of course, it's just her own reflection, her unrecognizable self in the full-length mirror she has forgotten was there, on the inside of the bathroom door. She has forgotten the mirror, and she was not prepared for the fact that, for the first time in her life, she will look into a mirror and not see her face.

Julia takes a breath and a step back, but then she advances again and studies herself more closely. The chaddri is brand-new, not yet dusty; the creases are crisp and perfect, the color poisonously vivid. She expected to see a peasant woman in the mirror, to see herself, looking like a peasant woman. Instead she finds herself face-to-face with a science-fiction apparition. She expected to see someone downtrodden and restricted, but instead this faceless figure looks regal, forbidding. Of course her thoughts are colored by all that has happened, and her nerves are strained. But in that first instance in which she glimpses herself, unrelenting and without a possibility of human expression, she realizes that for all her cosmopolitan illusions she is in a very foreign place.

The veil is a walking prison, yes, a constant sensory deprivation, a symbol of servitude. But you are distant in it, too, untouchable, like a god too powerful to have a name. Too frightening for anyone to dare to look upon his face.

Fatima has gone to the bazaar today, too; for her, though, for once, it is a lighthearted mission, a mission to bring pleasure to herself. She is off to buy some bangles.

Mushahed is taking her, and she is wearing the chaddri. It's easier to take a rickshaw cab, so they leave their car behind. Mushahed sits beside her on the hard red plastic. If we could look under the chaddri, would we see a mischievous smile on Fatima's face as she angles her shoulder ever so coincidentally in behind his, bring-

ing a soft breast into contact with his arm? On the
curves, does she fall against Mushahed for balance just
a little harder than traffic conditions warrant? Is Mushahed breathing just a little faster than the heat of the
day can explain, when they descend from the cab a few
minutes later and move into the crowded bazaar?

At any rate, they soon make their way to the lane
where the bangles are sold, stall after stall of the gleaming gold-flecked ornaments. So many colors! Box after
box, red and green, amber and pink, turquoise and yellow . . . Fatima stands transfixed, as greedy and as hypnotized as she was when her brother Isa bought her first
bangles for her. They were purple, and they were glass,
and purple was not an appropriate color for a child's
bangles, and children, besides, were supposed to wear
the newfangled plastic bangles, which can't break and
cut them. Her mother shook her head disapprovingly
when she came home with her purchase, but Isa just
laughed.

Today Fatima hesitates over the pale blue ones, then
her hand hovers undecidedly over the sea-green. Pastel
colors are brand-new this season, and tempting. All
around her, nudged and advised by their friends,
women in burqas and chaddris study the offerings.
Then, decision made, an arm will suddenly shoot out
from the huddled cloth and stretch demandingly toward
the bangle vendor. With an indifferently professional
air, he seizes the hand, assesses it for a moment, selects
the smallest possible bangle size in the chosen color, and
compresses the hand tightly at the level of the knuckles.
When the bones have been pressed into their most com-
pact form, he begins forcing the bangles over them, five
or six at a time. This is an amazingly intimate act, when
you think about it, for a society like this one, but no one

seems bothered. Clearly, the bangle vendor, like the medical doctor, operates under a special dispensation, a somber professional permitted to touch women.

Remembering Isa and that long-ago visit for her first bangles, Fatima's lighthearted mood fades as she starts to feel nostalgic for what now strikes her as the lost innocence and happiness of her childhood. With the chaddri to conceal the tears that brim in her eyes, she gives herself up to self-pity for a moment. Then, still in the grip of that sentiment, she points to the purple bangles and extends a pale arm. For these slender fingers, the vendor chooses his smallest size. A quick grip, and the hand is squeezed into the shape of a little bird's claw; a professional twist of the bangles, and they clear the hurdle and click into place on her wrist. Snap—a bangle breaks and is carelessly brushed aside by the vendor. That's his liability. Four go on, eight go on. Snap—another one breaks, the razor edge of the glass leaving a bracelet of tiny blood drops on Fatima's wrist.

Mushahed frowns, but Fatima is undisturbed. This is part of buying bangles. A little pain, a little blood; if Fatima were philosophically inclined, she might find here a metaphor for a woman's transit through the major events of her life. She isn't, though.

On the ride back, in the privacy of the curtained rickshaw cab, she extends her abused hand to Mushahed, who takes it gently and traces the nearly invisible cuts with a reverent finger, and, with this medical dispensation, allows himself to kiss her wrist.

Fashion seems to be on everyone's mind, this day. At Sonia's house, Lilly is in a tizzy, having received by messenger, in a bright yellow envelope with the letter "M" embossed on it in gold, an invitation to a soiree. And not just any soiree. The sender is Shabnam Mansuri, a rising star in local politics, a feudal princess, and, as Lilly euphorically hopes, her entrée to the jet set of the North-West Frontier.

She is anxious about what she should wear. Something debonair, something casual but striking, something to knock dead all those fabulous important people who will undoubtedly be there. Hatefully, Iqbal suggests a chaddri. That way, he says, she can do undercover journalism. She can reveal cover-ups. She can uncover scandals.

His jokes get successively worse, until Sonia raises the intellectual level by starting a discussion of veiling. Its anthropological significance. How her grandmother, who was in purdah for her entire life, felt about that. What the stirring young Egyptian nationalists of earlier decades, whose writings she remembers thrilling over as a young woman, had to say about it.

When she retires for the night, the young people remain engrossed in the subject. Sonia allows wine with dinner, but when she departs, more serious refreshments emerge from the cupboards. After quite a bit of vodka, the evening culminates in a Muslim Ladies' Ping-Pong Championship. There is a Ping-Pong table in Sonia's garden, and there the assembled group plays doubles, Gul and Lilly against Iqbal, who, as Lilly points out when he protests the arrangement, as a man counts double in Islamic law. They wear sheets from Sonia's linen closet; Iqbal has to wear an improvised chador, too, to keep things fair and to meet the Maulana's requirements for avoiding the arousal of lust by male athletes. Since he is even less used to constraining garments than his two modern women, Lilly and Gul beat him easily.

The heels of the women's shoes get caught on the soft lawn, until they kick them off to play barefoot. The scent of jasmine and roses hangs heavily in the night air, along with a faint aura of sadness and failure. The players collapse onto the grass and Lilly begins reciting poems about the veil. There are many of them, authored by turn-of-the-century Arab reformers and nationalists, and by women, too, of course. Many of them are poignant, some are funny, comparing veiled women to different kinds of vegetables, to eggplants, to onions. Iqbal likes the eggplant one, he turns it into a little song and sings it romantically, annoyingly into Gul's ear. Lilly smiles, then she suddenly lets out a small, stifled shriek.

"Iqbal!" she yells. "That's it! Your words, your messages! They're not from a poem," she gasps. "It's not a poem at all, I remember now, that's why it took me so long, I kept trying to think of a poem, but it's a song. It was a song, a song at the Asian Women's Conference in Delhi two years ago. It's a song, it's an Indian song."

Instantly, all of them are sober again. Iqbal lights up at the possibilities, but right away his face clouds over again at the thought of the consequences. India. Pakistan. Murders. Women. Somewhere, in that tangle, is his answer. But how to get the right grip on this? Finally, he falls back onto the lawn.

"Sex," he announces, nodding sagely. "I have made a mistake, a grave mistake, in my thinking. I have dismissed the idea of a serial killer, because we never had one in Pakistan before, and because I could not find anything linking these killings to a foreigner from a country that does have serial killers. And this was a mistake, as I now see. Women. Sex. *Cherchez la femme*. I have scorned the trite but true First Law of Criminal Investigation. After all, everything has to begin sometime, right? Technology, fashion, refugees, all sorts of things come into Pakistan from beyond our borders, isn't that right? So why not serial killing? And anyway I was wrong on two counts. Of course sex crimes are indigenous to Pakistan. Honor killings, we have them all the time. Yes, I'm quite sure I'm on the right track now, this is a sex crime all right. India, and sex," Iqbal shouts, pulling Gul to her feet and spinning her about. "I have to think about India and sex."

Lilly sleeps late the next morning, trying to rest up for the party at Shabnam's house. Then she tries on all of her clothes, some of Gul's and even some beautiful embroidered shalwar kameeses of Sonia's, trying to find the perfect thing to wear. "Oh, forget it," she keeps announcing, at intervals, as she tosses the discards onto the floor or the bed. "I'll just bowl them over with my wit and my intelligence. They won't even care what I'm wearing." This does not stop her from choosing, at last, the most beautiful garment available, a dress that Gul has had made out of an antique sari. "All the young men will fall in love with you," Sonia says with an approving smile. Lilly smiles back tolerantly. It's easy to impress the men. The person whose good opinion she really hopes for is Shabnam.

S habnam. Most names have a meaning in Asia. Gul, for example, means "rose." Lilly has Europeanized her name, which is actually Lala, meaning "poppy." Shabnam means "frost." It means "ice crystal," and it suits her.

It's easy to see, really, why everyone is so intimidated by her, men in particular. Shabnam's beauty is crisp and bitter, a little chilling. And yet she isn't hard. Cool as the early morning frost painting splintered flowers on the windowpanes, Shabnam is as feminine as a rose, a poppy, a gardenia, a daisy—a cold one, anyway, etched hard and frozen on glass by an artist, using acid.

Lovely Shabnam, whom no man has dared to cross, whose every wish and whim are fulfilled, who strikes fear into the hearts of the boldest men—nothing has ever gone wrong for Shabnam. Well, her father would have preferred a son, of course, as his eldest child. But it was just the merest little breath of a preference. Salman Mansuri is an enlightened man; he would not make his young wife or the arriving daughters pay for nature's caprices, and at his level of society, preoccupied with mergers and vast international deals and the fates of governments, one is not petty enough to be obsessed by the gender of infants. And very soon, he forms a special tie with this daughter.

As a little girl, Shabnam is delightful, to play with, to spoil, to carry around like a little clever trained monkey; a tiny, impertinent little female toy, and at the same time blood of his blood, a smaller, softer version of himself. Is there, in the deep bond between many an upper-class Muslim father and his daughter, a sense that this is his female counterpart—much more than his drowsy, elegant, expensive wife, a highly suitable, uninteresting woman chosen for him on dynastic grounds by his parents? His eldest daughter, by contrast, may be the first female person he has ever been really close to. If I had been born a woman, such a man might think to himself, I might have been like this. A tantalizing thought, perhaps, for a man in a culture that gives him few opportunities to meet women as personalities. When his little girl, so small, so graceful, so stubborn, sets her heart

CHERYL BENARD

on some goal and pursues it with the ruthless single-mindedness of a cobra, such a man may be fascinated by the contrast between the little wisp of a female body and the ironclad will that inhabits it, and smile to recognize her as a kindred spirit. All over the Muslim world, a certain class of very wealthy, very powerful, very terrifying men melt into syrupy little puddles of pride and adoration at the sight of their straight-backed, proud, hardheaded daughters. Shabnam has precisely this kind of father. She lives in one of his houses, alone (which means with a cook, a sweeper, a maid, a kitchen boy, and of course the chowkidar, the watchman who lives in the garage). She teaches history at the University of Islamabad. She travels to Europe, to America. She entertains friends, male and female, in her house. She is free, just as free as those mythical women in the stories of Isa. And—merely one paradox of many, in paradoxical Pakistan—her father rejoices in her freedom, while a father of somewhat lower class would instantly murder a daughter who even dreamed of such a life.

She even has lovers. "My flower of ice," they like to murmur, just at the moment when this frost is melting in their arms. "Mmmmh," says Shabnam. Sometimes she hums, afterward, or sings, combing her hair, taking a bath or a shower. She might sing a ghazal, or a disco hit, or the theme song from a new Indian movie. Or she might sing one of the political songs about the oppression of peasants, of ethnic minorities, or, and these are usually the most lyrical songs, of women.

She might, just to give you a for-instance, sing a song like this one:

You are less than the dust, my sister.
Rise up on the wind like dust then

172

And blind the eyes of your enemies.
Who can stop the dust?

You are less than an insect.
Crawl, then, like an insect,
Crawl like a termite,
Into the houses of your enemies
And bring them to fall.
Who can stop the insects?

There is a third verse, too. If her lovers were paying attention to the words, they might find the song distressing, but I'm not sure they listen. I suspect that they just hear her voice as a faint melodic hum and flatter themselves that they have made her happy. Anyway, the third verse goes like this:

You may as well be dead.
Wrapped in your shrouds, my sisters,
Be like death, then, to your enemies,
Seeing but unseen, in your shrouds.
Who can stop death?

I qbal's new theory about the nature of this crime has thrown him into a frenzy of activity. He plunders the libraries of the universities for literature on sex crimes. He holds clandestine meetings with informers who give him the names, beliefs, and sordid private practices of extremist fundamentalists in the area. He compiles case histories of honor killings. In between, he agonizes over the consequences of arresting a fundamentalist.

Lilly's lack of enthusiasm is a constant thorn in his

side. "I just don't know, Iqbal . . ." she begins, but he will not even let her finish. Nothing can stop him.

Soon he has fat packets of dossiers on dozens of known radicals whose politics have a sexual twist. He has twenty-four male students between the ages of sixteen and twenty-nine who have thrown acid on, ripped the clothes off, or otherwise assaulted female college students who failed to accede to the rules of Islamic dress. He has sixteen men between the ages of seventeen and sixty-five who have attempted to murder a female relative for a sexual misdemeanor within the last five years, and he has a dozen men who recently repudiated a bride for non-virginity. He has eight men who threatened to assassinate the head of television and radio unless women program announcers were removed from the air. He has 414 male subscribers to a magazine called *The Eternal Truth*, a fundamentalist journal specializing in graphic sexual denunciations of contemporary Pakistani decadence.

He is running all these names through computers in Islamabad according to a program of his own devising. He consults, long distance, an expert in Bangladesh who helps him design a psychological profile of the killer, something Iqbal has always scorned before. His certainty about being on a hot trail increases as his list of potential suspects grows longer, and certainly many of them sound like plausible candidates for nearly any act of lunacy. The list includes several of the staunchest followers of the Maulana and, as far as Iqbal is concerned—informers having hinted that all is perhaps not as it should be in the godly household of the saintly man—it includes the Maulana himself.

"But all these guys go after women," Lilly protests, "and your victims are all men! And okay, they all hate

India, but what does that say? We're in Pakistan, Iqbal, remember? *Everybody* here hates India."

But Iqbal just shakes his head in annoyance. A detail! Besides, it's not true. Men *do* get killed in honor crimes. For instance, if a married woman has an affair, her lover will often be killed right along with her. It is entirely possible that, for every male victim of his current investigation, a woman has been murdered, too—if the family doesn't report it, and the body isn't found, then who's to know? Besides, he instructs Lilly, it is entirely possible that the next victim, if there is a next victim, will indeed be female.

True, that is entirely possible.

But it doesn't happen that way. The next victim, as it happens, is Jamal Abbas, publisher of *The Green Banner* and very definitely a man, though not a very nice one.

Jamal Abbas. What a promising career lies before him, until it is so tragically cut off. A degree in education and political science from Columbia University, New York, N.Y. He did well there, too; with his dense black beard and his terrorist's eyes, and his contemptuous classroom commentaries, he aroused awe and fascination in classmates and professors, alike. He even got a scholarship.

Academic masochism in America: a topic worth looking into, though not our topic today. One of his professors almost got divorced over Jamal Abbas. His wife was a feminist who, at ten o'clock in the morning, happened to encounter Abbas's wife in a grocery store on Broadway. It was a muggy June day, but Mrs. Abbas was properly dressed as always. She wasn't even wearing the Pakistani burqa, no, she was clad in a superfundamentalist concoction consisting of a heavy, gray Egyptian coat; a thin veil covered, from the eyes down, by yet another, thicker veil; gray cotton stockings; and then, to complete the ensemble and conceal her lascivious fingers, white cotton gloves. Lucy had seen Mrs. Abbas many times before, but today she watched in fascination as the swaddled woman attempted to purchase an eggplant; it reminded her of the game her mother used to organize at children's birthdays, where you make the kids wear mittens and try to eat a chocolate bar with a knife and fork.

Still in the grip of this image, Lucy came home to hear her husband exultantly inform a colleague, on the phone, that he had asserted himself at the meeting and gotten the scholarship for that clever fellow Abbas, instead of that boring and unimaginative little Korean girl the department had initially favored. Hanging up the phone and turning innocently around, he came face-to-face with the enraged, Medusa-like countenance of his wife—but that's another story.

Jamal Abbas, at any rate, returns to Pakistan in triumph to become the editor of *The Green Banner*, a fundamentalist publication relentless in its condemnation of the Great Satan U.S.A. and its campaign of cultural imperialism; a journal reportedly funded by—it depends on whom you ask—either Saudi Arabia or the CIA, or both.

In Peshawar, Abbas meets with the Maulana, and with a number of other religious and community leaders. He has a specific project in mind. He wants to restructure the educational system of the North-West Frontier Province, and subsequently of all of Pakistan.

He is qualified for such an ambitious project, after all. Doesn't he have a degree in political science and education from one of the Western world's better-regarded universities? The Western world—what a civilization! New York—what a place! Education—what a wonderful thing! And he is only one of Columbia University's remarkable Third World alumni.

For example, take Hafizullah Amin. He was in the Education Department of Columbia University, too, just like Abbas. Then he went home to his native Afghanistan and pursued a career in politics. Murdering his predecessor, he made himself head of state. You may not have heard of him, but he's famous on his continent. It is reported there that he used to have his opponents buried alive, and then run bulldozers over the spot. People who disagreed with his plans for the country, it is said, were thrown into septic tanks to drown. When news of his rather drastic didactic measures reached the United States, several embarrassed former professors were interviewed about their erstwhile pupil. They just couldn't understand it, they said. He was such a bright fellow. His grades were excellent. He was perfectly friendly and nice when invited to a Thanksgiving dinner, and enjoyed the cranberry sauce.

Now, it would hardly be fair to blame Columbia University for his later excesses. But it does make you think. Isn't education supposed to, you know, form you? If you educate someone for six years, in a spirit of freedom of thought and openness of mind, and then that person goes home and dumps everybody who disagrees with him into a vat of shit, then does that say something about your educational effort, or doesn't it?

Scholarships are granted on the basis of intelligence, Professor Gutenbach informs his wife, the abovementioned, very angry Lucy. And not on the basis of— with a pitying smile, he gropes for the term that best characterizes his wife's naïve view—the "character is-sue" or political correctness.

Oh, is that so? Lucy replies. So character is ridiculous, too, now, is it? So, along with morals and equity, char-acter, too, has been assigned to the rubbish heap? Whereas it is entirely appropriate and ever so modern and enlightened and value-free to give American schol-arships to fundamentalist, sexist, anti-American psycho-paths.

With a deeply dramatic sigh, Larry Gutenbach reit-erates that scholarships are given out on the basis of academic merit, period. And Jamal Abbas is extremely intelligent, whether one approves of his marital life or not.

Oh! Lucy replies. Of course! How perfectly reason-able! And Hitler built great freeways! Too bad Columbia didn't have the opportunity to give him a scholarship, on the basis of his highly intelligent Autobahn network!

Larry Gutenbach grabs his papers and stomps off to his afternoon meeting, which with any luck will last well into the evening.

Jamal Abbas gets the scholarship, he applies himself to his studies, he graduates, and then he goes home so that his native country may benefit from his finely honed American education.

Jamal Abbas most definitely has a social conscience. His mission is to improve the education system of the North-West Frontier Province. And he knows just how to do it. First, all the girls and women have to be re-moved from school. Kick out the female teaching staff, throw out the female students, and let Islamic science begin! He has a plan for the women, too. For them, he proposes setting up women's colleges, where subjects appropriate to an Islamic woman's role in society will be taught. You can take courses in how to pick a good grapefruit while blindfolded and bagged in a chador, I imagine.

And Jamal's plans go still further than that. For example, he plans to gain control of the Peshawar University Medical School, throw out the imperialist stooges who staff it, and replace them with a dedicated corps of Islamic doctors. Once this has been achieved, the implementation of Islamic justice can finally commence: such as cutting off the hands of those convicted of stealing, a sentence presently imposed but not carried out, since none of the culturally alienated, decadent pro-Western Pakistani doctors will agree to perform this surgery.

The Maulana wholeheartedly endorses all of these God-inspired plans. When Abbas comes to pay his respects, he kisses the young man. Kiss, kiss, kiss, once on each cheek and then once more. Yes, it's love at first sight between the Maulana and Abbas.

Abbas is connected to Fatima, too, indirectly. The Maulana, filled with happiness and pride at the sight of this young warrior of Islam, does him the great honor of inviting him to his wedding.

And Abbas is connected to Shabnam, in a way. She will be the first to go, I can promise you, if Jamal Abbas is put in charge of revamping the colleges and universities. I don't think she will like it at the Islamic Women's Domestic Science Institute.

As it happens, though, Jamal Abbas will not be attending the wedding. Nor will he be assigned the job of re-Islamicizing Pakistan's education system. He will, very shortly, be dead. It looks like a straightforward robbery, this time. His wallet is gone, and someone has even taken his Adidas shoes. But there's a note in his pocket. The note is strange. Iqbal doesn't even believe it really is a note, at first, but graphologists in Islamabad insist that it belongs with the others—with the handwritten ones, at any rate.

"DEATH TO YOUR ENEMIES, MY SISTERS," the note reads.

Sisters? Brothers would make some sense, as in: Muslim Brotherhood. In liberation, in politics, in revolution you often have brothers. You never have sisters.

Iqbal does not have much leisure to pursue his musings concerning the gender of solidarity. The fundamentalists are on his back, and the government isn't too happy either. Who could have killed Jamal?

"I could have," Lilly says.

Iqbal is not in the mood for humor. Sisters, sisters, what on earth does that mean? He is inclined to see it as a verification of his current hypothesis regarding crime, women, and sex. Has Abbas somehow injured or dishonored someone's sister? Is his family involved in a feud with another family, in which case the woman in question could easily be someone's wrongfully deflowered great-great-great-great-great-grandmother?

What about the New York connection? Both Abbas and Malone were students in New York.

What about Babu? Has he ever been to New York, maybe for a film festival? Does Abbas perhaps have a link to Indian extremists?

Iqbal and Toufiq are working like madmen. Slothful bureaucrats? Not these two. So it really does seem a bit unfair, when the most pertinent bit of information comes from elsewhere; worse yet, from across the border. The idea surfaces in India, where somebody evidently pieces together the message fragments and recognizes the Indian song. It hits the British press before arriving in Pakistan, which is particularly galling for Iqbal's superiors. Iqbal comes home that afternoon in a terrible huff.

"Feminist killer in Pakistan," he spits, and slams the faxed copy of the British newspaper article down on the coffee table. "Thank you very much, Lilly," he says, through clenched teeth. Expelling a lot of air from between compressed lips, he drops onto the sofa, grabbing the article again.

" 'An Indian feminist song is the leitmotif for a serial killer currently stalking Pakistan's North-West Frontier Province,' " he reads, shooting murderous glances at Lilly. There is a brief silence.

"Oh, what the hell," he says. "The story was too good not to hit the international press, whether we had known it first or not."

The killer—a feminist? A woman? It certainly seems highly improbable. On the other hand, there is the ubiquitous woman-in-the-green-chaddri invariably mentioned by witnesses as having been noticed at or near the scenes of the crimes. Iqbal and Toufiq have been inclined to dismiss that particular clue as irrelevant, since women in green chaddris, make up roughly one fourth of those women in Peshawar who wear chaddris, making it statistically unsurprising that the woman closest to the victim always happened to wear green.

Even now, they hate to reassess that decision, since its reassessment leads nowhere: as a clue, the green chaddri is absolutely worthless. If you suspect all women in green chaddris, where will it get you? Might the killer be a woman? Iqbal shrugs his shoulders and sighs.

Islamabad has instructed him that the possibility must be very seriously considered. " 'We have female terrorists, female politicians who want to overthrow the government, and the last time a Pakistani government fell, women made up the overwhelming majority of the demonstrators in the streets. So why not a female killer?' " he quotes from what apparently was a highly annoying telephone conversation with his superiors. " 'A criminal investigator must keep an open mind, Iqbal,' " he mimics. " 'You are behind the times, Iqbal. Why not a woman, after all? We've left you in Peshawar too long, you're starting to go native. Don't turn into a Pathan on us, Iqbal, remember you're a Punjabi.' "

In India, a quickly produced commercial recording of "Dust Rising" becomes a smash success, rushing right to the top of the charts. The popular version is sung by a male Indian pop star who croons it out throatily and somehow manages, when interviewed on the subject of women and feminism, to turn the conversation to his racehorses instead.

12

Pakistan has an unusual approach to the woman question. It's probably one of the most horrible places on this earth to live, if you are a woman. On the other hand, women's rights are at least considered to be a genuine political matter, not something trivial, ridiculous, or stemming only from the frustrated brains of deluded feminists. Pakistani politicians often have themselves photographed for the newspapers receiving delegations from militant women's groups. Everyone looks very solemn; the women wear little scarves so that they can be photographed for the newspaper and appear to be lecturing their host sternly while he listens, head slanted, their attentive pupil.

"A hollow gesture," Lilly says, contemptuously, and I'm sure she's right. Still, a hollow gesture is better than a slap in the face.

In the Pakistani Parliament, a number of seats are permanently allotted to women. These are unrelated to the outcome of elections, and additional to any women that may be chosen on their own merits, thus giving women better statistical representation than they have anywhere in the West, including the United States. The women all sit together, in little rows, two-by-two like schoolgirls in early rural America, heads covered with scarves. Around them swells the crowd of men, an ocean of suits, turbans, Gucci shoes, and tribal dress, depending on the constituency that has sent them here. Viewed from the visitors' gallery, this Parliament looks very much like an episode of *Star Trek*; looks like an intergalactic symposium. And the women, a grimly assertive and puritanical little island in that sea of male diversity, clearly come from the most distant planet.

The Pakistani women's movement, meanwhile, is the best-dressed one in the world, since it is replete with elegant upper-class ladies. While this initially seems surprising, it's actually quite logical; who else has the leisure, the freedom, and the education to act up? Often, an upper-class daughter discovers feminism at the university and brings it home to Mother. That is how you usually see them at rallies and demonstrations: the young, rebellious girl with the androgynous haircut and the determined look on her face, marching beside an elegant lady with a pearl necklace and a silk suit. The driver is probably parked around the corner, in case his mistresses get tired or run into difficulties, and the sidewalk is lined with gallant young male students, ready to defend the ladies against rowdies or the police.

Upper-class men, too, find women's emancipation clever and trendy and follow its progress with a mix of absorption and amusement. They think their daughters and wives look just too sweet and adorable when, all stirred up and earnest, they rush off to some meeting or protest. They read the petitions very solemnly, frowning in agreement over particularly stirring passages, and joke to one another about the personal discomforts and deprivations they are suffering because of their women's feminism, the personal contributions they are making in terms of donated office space, Xerox machines, and the like. "My wife is in the Women's Action Forum, now," a wealthy industrialist will say to his friend, beaming broadly with a mixture of amusement and pride. "I'm giving them a small building, actually, to hold their meetings."

"Acha," his friend will joke in typical Pakistani exclamation, "you are a wise fellow, they're going to take power soon, and then you'll be on their good side."

You may agree with Lilly and find this condescending, but in my opinion, ladies, it could be worse.

What I particularly like is that you will never run into a Pakistani woman who, eyes coyly slanted at whatever men are within range of her simpery little voice, declares that she just cannot understand what these feminists *want*, anyway. *She* never has any problems. Not even the most reactionary dunce would deny that women, in Pakistan, have plenty to complain about.

It comes as no surprise that, when gender appears to be an issue in the murders, Islamabad dispatches the head of its Women's Bureau to check the situation out.

Iqbal is apprehensive about the arrival of Rabia Naqvi, the Bureau's director. Lilly knows her, but refuses to reveal more about her than to comment, gleefully, that Iqbal is sure to find her "stimulating."

"Ms. Naqvi says that every third woman in Pakistan has clear homicidal inclinations," he announces, upon returning home that afternoon. Allowing his eyes surreptitiously to sweep the room, he counts the heads of the females present and shudders to discover that there are three.

"What was she wearing?" Lilly inquires hopefully.

"Wearing? Well, as a matter of fact she was wearing a tiger-striped shirt and safari pants and a silver turban, and high heels," he says, cracking open some pumpkin seeds with his teeth.

"She says it's likely to be a whole group of women, acting in complicity," he says, taking a large gulp of pomegranate juice. "She brought her own eunuch," he says, of her male secretary. "When she claps her hands, he brings her a freshly sharpened pencil. Two claps, he brings tea. She made us clear out two offices for her, and said she was setting up headquarters here for the duration," he reports, fanning himself with a folded newspaper.

Lilly, who knows Rabia quite well from many previous encounters, follows his narration with a sleek and very nasty smile.

"She weighs 180 pounds, and had the kebabs sent back three times at lunch because they were overdone, and didn't eat them until they brought them to her raw and bloody," he says. "A fabulous woman, really," he concludes with honest awe.

Lilly murmurs something about male masochism, but Iqbal forestalls her further contemplations.

"Maybe the Maulana was right," he says, reaching thoughtfully for his green tea. "Maybe you feminine persons are dangerous. Maybe it is better to lock you all up."

If you have the disposition of an informer, in Pakistan, you do not necessarily go to the police. Actually, the police is probably the last place you should go. At the police, either you will have the misfortune of dealing with a zealous, idealistic officer who thinks you are a

186

sleazy piece of garbage and locks you up to make sure you divulge absolutely all of your sleazy information, or you might happen upon a corrupt individual who will steal your knowledge, toss you out on the street, and then barter it around himself.

Iqbal had diligently addressed himself to the staff of the Inter-Continental Hotel. He had appealed to them to come forward with anything they may have noticed, anything at all, however slight. Mohammad, who has the disposition of an informer, did not respond to this call.

He had noticed something all right. He saw the victim, in fact. He saw him running down the stairway behind a tall American woman. There was a large plastic laundry bag clutched in his hand, he acted nervous, and his movements were hasty, as though a devil were pursuing him. It was an extraordinary sight, and Mohammad remembers it vividly. But he didn't say a word to the police when they showed up at the hotel asking questions.

Instead, he has been biding his time. Discreetly, he has ascertained by casual chatting with his hotel colleagues that the man he saw indeed matched the description of this fellow Malone. He was careful not to betray too much interest, but he figures that a certain amount of curiosity about something as exciting as a murder, right in their own hotel, is certainly allowable. He took care never to be the first one to raise the topic, but when it came up, he seized the opportunity to get in a few questions of his own.

When he learned that Malone had been here to do deals with the mighty Khan, his way seemed clear. Still, he hesitated. It would be wonderful to have something of value to offer Khan. But there is a risk, an enormous risk. What if, for some reason, Khan is the one who "disappeared" the American? How would Khan feel about somebody who knew that the purported murder victim was not dragged bleeding and half-dead from the premises but was seen walking out of the hotel of his own apparent volition, nervous but hale?

Still, as Mohammad replays the scene in his memory, the American's departure from the hotel seemed far more like an escape than an abduction. So it seems likely that Khan might be interested to hear about it.

It takes time to reach this conclusion and then to mentally review and recheck it. It takes time to persuade Khan's secretary, without giving away too much, that he has a message for Khan's ears only. It is surprising how terror grips him once he is in the actual presence of this mighty man. But Khan deals with him gently. He cannot actually say, afterward, whether he has told Khan something new, something useful, or not. He leaves the office on a cloud, nonetheless. Khan, while receiving the news concerning his American partner with indifference, expresses pleasure over the act of fealty his visit implies. There is always a need for attentive, reliable men, he murmurs. No money is offered, but the informant leaves with a feeling of reward. The secretary has been instructed to take note of his name. One will contact him soon, to discuss how he can be of further service. The door is open!

After this visit, Khan conducts his remaining business as usual, but when he is finished, he remains seated behind his desk in the darkening room and reflects on this new development. Later today, some of his men will visit the informant. By then they will know everything there is to know about him, know every possible way to hurt him. They will test him a bit, mentally and physically, and in the end they will know whether he is what he appears to be, or whether this is a trick. If it turns out to be true, one can give him some money, Khan muses aloud, and his assistant notes the instruction with an obedient nod. The Inter-Cont. is not a bad place to have a news source. If he was lying, of course, one will eliminate him.

But that is a minor side issue. The heart of the matter is more disturbing. Suppose this pathetic little opportunist was telling the truth. Suppose Malone is not dead at all. Then where is he? He can't have gone home, or the authorities would no longer be searching for his body, and the sister would not be moping around Peshawar. If he didn't go home, though, then where is he? He may still be here. If he is still here, and he has not revealed himself to the Pakistani or the American authorities, and even the sister does not know his whereabouts, then there is only one explanation. The CIA. So. Malone is, as Khan had feared, an agent of the CIA. He is on the prowl, collecting more evidence against Khan, or doing who-knows-what secretive thing to destroy Khan.

But this is not Virginia, not America; this is Khan's turf, and he will not be brought down so easily.

If the informant strikes his assistants as believable, Khan decides, then he will dispatch one of his squads to seek the American agent out, to find him, and to make him what he has sneakily tried to deceive everyone into thinking he already is.

Dead.

Each passing hour makes Mara more nervous. Who would ever have supposed, when she answered her personal 911 call from Malone, that things would get so out of hand? She has assured Malone condescendingly that everything is perfectly okay, but in truth she is worried, very worried.

And the worst part is this feeling of being utterly alone. Can it be a coincidence that some serial killer started his spree right after Malone had his weird little scare in the hotel and got spooked and ran? Or are some very nasty killers really after him? How long will it take before someone comes after Mara in a truly serious way?

After all, this has become a big deal, a really big deal. Even the large daily international papers are picking up the story, glad at this change from the usual news emerging from Pakistan: bombings in Karachi, mines along the border still making farming impossible, riots over the Kashmir issue, tedious things like that. A female avenger on the prowl in Peshawar, you can see how this delights correspondents languishing in Islamabad or Delhi. Murder and passion behind the chador. Mysterious notes. The war of the sexes, Islam style. Anthropologists, sociologists, feminists, historians—everyone has something to say.

Lilly is quite annoyed. "A couple of unnecessary fat old fools get themselves knocked off, and suddenly the newspapers are full of women's issues," she snaps. Several of those articles are her own, which does nothing to appease her.

Iqbal, meanwhile, goes for feminism in his usual total-immersion style. He becomes, for a brief exasperating time, the household's resident expert on women's affairs.

He does not immediately realize that this is not purely an ideological and intellectual problem, and that it is more than merely interesting. Not only is he supposed to develop a personal opinion on whether a woman could have, might have, should have committed these murders; he is also supposed to find the woman.

This realization, when at last it penetrates, fills Iqbal with a peculiar light-headedness. "All I need to do," he says with a chuckle that evening, rubbing his hands enthusiastically, "is to find a Pakistani woman with a motive to hate men. Why, that narrows it down to about forty million suspects, right, Lilly? Hey, ladies," he shouts, "why don't you just tell me very frankly if it was one of you or not; then if it wasn't, that'll cut it down by three already. That's only 39,999,997 left to go! But then," Iqbal goes on, voice teetering alarmingly between hysteria and hilarity, "83 percent of them are illiterate, aren't they, so they couldn't have written the notes!"

It is not very difficult to sympathize with Iqbal's state of mind. Veiled women, women about whom inquiries cannot be made without the entire clan's being up in arms at this invasion of honor and privacy: Iqbal certainly has little cause to feel optimistic. On the other hand, it really seems inconceivable that one of those traditional women had anything to do with it. It had to be either a foreign woman, or a very politicized one, or a psychopathic one with a good education; if it was a woman at all.

"An insane female killer is stalking Peshawar in a chaddri executing important men, and I have not the slightest clue to who she might be" is how he sums it up.

"Your work is certainly very difficult," Gul comments softly, in empathy.

"Oh, Gul, my lovely rose," he sings to her in response.

M alone and Hamid are pals now, just about. They sit on the stoop in front of the shack. The boy examines Malone's property, his books, his clothes. They spend a lot of time together. Even when they are not together, they think about each other. Malone worries about Hamid. The kid is too dirty and too skinny. Just as Hamid has dreamed, he gives him food. The kid always wraps part of this food up, very conscientiously, to take away with him—for his supper, Malone supposes.

But Hamid worries about Malone, too. Having gained entry to the shack, he has ascertained that Malone has no weapon, no weapon at all. A man without a weapon! This is unheard-of, really unthinkable. He concludes that his odd white friend is in some kind of very exceptional circumstance, but he cannot figure out what it might be. If he had done something really bad, he would not have been exiled, he would have been killed.

In the back of his mind, Hamid has a suspicion that he knows what it is. His new friend, he suspects, is timid. A timid little rabbit in a big body. That explains why he never explodes in violent annoyance, the way all the other men he knows frequently do. It explains why he has no weapon. It explains why he is here. He has run away from the fighting, run away from being a fighter. This burgeoning theory causes a great dilemma for Hamid. Nothing is worse, is more disgusting, than a cowardly man. Nothing is more unmanly than running away from a fight.

And yet, somewhere inside of himself, Hamid can sympathize. Even boys his age are expected to do their part for the holy war. The men take them away when they are seven or eight; they take them to special training camps. Sometimes, Hamid knows, they let them become martyrs. Sometimes these children are sent in advance of the fighters, to find the mines. When the mine explodes, the boy becomes a martyr, going directly to heaven. Fathers offer up their sons for this cause, without bad intent; everyone knows that children are particularly suited for this, because they have good instincts and because God loves them and protects them especially. Besides, the fathers themselves are ready to become martyrs, too, but before they become martyrs, they want a chance to fight, and they can't fight if a mine blows them up. Boys can't fight, but they can give the men a chance to fight.

Hamid knows all about this because he hears the women talking about it. The women are unimpressed by this brilliant military technique. When the fathers arrive to take the seven- or eight-year-old boys along, the women scream and weep. The mothers sob heart-rendingly. Clinging to their sons, they plead with their husbands. They invoke God and the saints and scream for the help of Fatima, the daughter of the Prophet. They throw themselves on the ground to block the way. Sometimes they even try to fight with their husbands, but they are easily brushed aside. Then the other women rush up to comfort them, and all the women weep and scream.

Women do not seem to like the idea of heaven as much as their men do, as far as Hamid can tell. They don't mind it for their husbands, but they don't want their sons to go.

Hamid has no father to come and take him away; no uncles, either. He thinks that he is relatively safe from heaven, and his mother thinks so, too. Taking him away would mean leaving her, a woman, all alone. This is unthinkable. A woman needs a male chaperon, even if he is only seven years old. If Hamid were gone, another family would have to take his mother in, but since she has no relatives, no one will do that. This is their great problem—no adult male relatives, no ration card. If you have no ration card, your food comes from charitable donations collected in the mosque, and these are skimpy.

To be fair, though, things aren't all bad. It isn't bad living alone with his mother; it's quite peaceful and nice, actually. And it isn't bad to stay away from the mine-fields, either. So when he concludes that Malone is probably a fainthearted, rabbity, unmasculine, cowardly runaway, not all of Hamid can wholeheartedly condemn him for these qualities.

Still: a man without a weapon, it offends Hamid's sensibilities. A man without a weapon, that's just impossible. Malone is taking care of Hamid and, unknowingly, of his mother. And Hamid will take care of Malone. Cautiously, stealthily, he makes his way to the camp arsenal. At prayer time, when he knows exactly where everyone will be, he slips into the arsenal and procures the basics of manhood for his friend Malone. A knife. A Kalashnikov. Ammunition.

There. Now his friend is respectably equipped once again.

Malone is appalled at this bounty. Lacking any other ideas, he hides everything under the mattress. Just to be on the safe side, he places the rifle gingerly with the barrel side on the foot end, pointing at the wall.

Mara comes to see Malone. The consul has not returned yet, but he is expected back any day now. So this, Mara explains, will be her last visit. She has brought another box of provisions, and the next time she comes, it will be to collect Malone and take him back. Then Hamid comes and, chatter chatter, he and Mara have a lot to say to each other. And Mara has a lot of information for Malone. She can tell him that Hamid is an orphan, fatherless. That he and his mother receive no rations. And then, since she is on the topic, she gives Malone the rest of the story. It is basically the same story that Lilly got. Malone hears about the Australian protein biscuits. He hears about the hysterical paralysis befalling women who are confined to the narrow space of a tent for years. He hears again and at greater length about the bodily functions that have to be controlled until night falls, because the latrines belong to the men.

All of this information is packed into wads of hostility, but Malone is oblivious to that. He is not only appalled to hear all of this; he feels a personal relevance. It took him exactly one day to go crazy in confinement. He tried to wait until nightfall, to go behind the bushes, but he hadn't been able to wait—and he wasn't even pregnant. Why aren't there any latrines for the women? Mara shrugs angrily. Because, she snaps, there is a hierarchy in refugee work. There are the "gunrunners," the exciting, macho guys who have a direct line to the resistance groups, who dress themselves up in stupid Afghan pants and pancake-shaped Afghan felt hats and go sneaking across the border to visit arms depots. And then there are the "blanket-runners," boring female do-gooders who take care of the boring women and children and old people and sick people.

Mara still trembles with rage when she remembers the meeting, only last week, during which the nice lady from Save the Children tried to explain how one can grind up the protein biscuits, mix them with boiled water and powdered milk, and use them for baby food. The men at the VOLAG—Voluntary Agencies—meeting rolled their eyes, sighed, groaned; they certainly didn't come all the way to exciting, dangerous, glamorous Peshawar to talk about baby food.

From this angry, garbled tale, Malone extracts one bit of pertinent information: Mara is vulnerable. Yes, the formidable, uppity, powerful Mara experiences defeat, pain, and humiliation. People mistreat her! She has feelings! She has needs! Malone senses an opportunity. He knows perfectly well that Mara thinks he is, well, a jerk. Not just male, which is bad enough, but a clumsy, timid, ideologically hopeless male jerk on top of it. Wouldn't it be great to change her opinion?

Besides, this problem seems totally within his scope. This is a technical problem, a problem of location and organization, a problem very much like the problems he solves each and every day in his job. Where should the warehouse go? How big should it be? What are the traffic patterns and access routes? This is Malone's daily bread, this is something he can do. Malone is radiant: a problem, a solution. What could be more American? There's a job to be done. He is going to build a second set of latrines for Hamid's mother and the other ladies in the camp, his fellow sufferers in restricted movement, boredom, and fear.

He insists that Mara should point out an appropriate location, based on her knowledge of the camp. Mara waves her hand impatiently in an eastward direction; she's thought about it, too, but she could never get the manpower, nor does she suppose for even one second that Malone is up to more than idle talk. Only Hamid takes the announcement seriously. Hamid is bouncing up and down with excitement, a project, a project. When can they start? Can they start right now? Then at least can they start tomorrow?

Perhaps I have incorrectly given you the impression that Malone is Hamid's only friend on earth. This is not so. In fact, there is a whole group of young men who have also taken notice of Hamid. No, don't worry, they don't want to recruit him as a human minesweeper. They think that is disgusting. They are disgusted, totally disgusted, by the way this holy war has been conducted. They are revolted by the corruption, the hypocrisy, the infighting. Their hearts hurt when they walk through the camp and see the filth, the desolation. Who are these young men? They are students. They are studying engineering, and medicine, and chemistry, and the rest of the time they are studying the Koran. The Koran is such an interesting book. It resembles a Rorschach inkblot, in a way. Five people can look at one and the same page, and see five different things. What you see depends on you, on the way you live, on the way you are. These men are idealistic, young, and angry. When they look at the Koran, they see fire, faith, and revolution. They live in student hostels, but they spend their free time in the camps. They volunteer to work as teachers. They pitch a tent, round up all the children, set the little girls and the little boys down in the sand in separate rows, tug the little girls' scarves firmly into place, and have them call out verses from the Koran, as loudly as their little voices can. They distribute money to the especially needy. They have read a little bit of Fanon, but not a word of Marx. They see themselves as the protectors of the weak.

Life would not be too wonderful for women like you or me if these young men were in charge of the world, but there would be some other women for whom it would improve. Widows would certainly receive rations, and there would definitely be health clinics and bathrooms for women, if these young men were in charge.

The powers-that-be, in the camp, ignore these young

men. Well, that's a mistake. A few years hence, these young men will be marching on Kabul, and the disenchanted followers of the other, older leaders will be rushing to join them, in droves. But that is in the future. At the moment, these young men are studying for their exams, reading the Koran, and fondly patting orphans like Hamid on the head.

M ara calls the consulate daily. Malone, too, is eager for the consul to return, but not as eager as Mara. Compared to Mara, Malone is blissfully ignorant, ignorantly blissful. For example, he doesn't even know about any of the murders. Consequently, he has privately concluded that he probably overdid his response to Khan, that he was probably in no danger at all. Mara, on the other hand, has come to the opposite conclusion.

Whereas at first she thought Malone was probably a nut, a sort of political hypochondriac, she now feels that he probably did very narrowly escape being murdered, somehow. And the responsibility of making sure that it stays that way, until she can hand him over to reliable American authorities, weighs on her terribly.

She thinks Malone is safe in the camp—probably. At the same time, he is a sitting duck. He doesn't have a phone, he doesn't have a car, he doesn't even have a lock on his door. If the killers find him, they'll pick him off like a little scared rabbit. The arrival of his sister has made things a hundred times worse. The temptation to tell her the truth is nearly irresistible, but Mara knows she must resist the impulse. It can do no good to tell her, since there is nothing Julia can contribute except a rash, impulsive action. For which no one could blame her. If it were *her* brother, and she had thought he was dead, and then she heard that he was alive, Mara would not be able to wait discreetly for the best moment to whisk him out of the country. She would insist on seeing him immediately. And Malone, with all of his paranoia, is right about one thing. In this city, intrigue, corruption, and betrayal rule the day. You can trust the American consul, and probably you can trust this fellow Jim, but that's about it. Mara decides that she will simply have to carry her burden alone a little bit longer.

When Julia finally meets Mara, she is of course unaware of the other woman's tortured considerations and guilty conscience. Though Mara's reluctance to see her seemed suspicious, Julia is willing to give her the benefit of the doubt.

So, although it really is more than obvious from the start that Mara is acting very peculiarly, Julia does not seem to notice, perhaps does not want to. She prefers to think the other woman is just very reserved, or maybe in shock. Mara receives Julia politely enough, but she is wary. She fails to express any grief or impart any con dolences. Instead she natters on about the annoying meeting she had yesterday and about how exasperating her ex-pat. colleagues are.

Then she speaks at length about the merits and faults of Green's vs. Dean's Hotel. Julia charitably supposes this is her way of being tactful. She is leaving it to the bereaved sister to set the pace for their conversation. As they chat senselessly, Julia studies her brother's lover. She is pretty, but her face is very serious and she appears very distracted; somewhat frenzied. Julia has so many questions for her, but she isn't sure, under the circumstances, how to broach them. She wants to know what kind of a mood her brother had been in, when

Mara last saw him. Had he seemed frightened or worried? Did she know that he had tried to reach Julia? Did she perhaps know, or could she guess, what he wanted to say to her? Had he told her about his business here?

Julia is accustomed to asking probing questions, but faced with the indeterminately bereaved maybe lover, or maybe just one-night stand of her murdered brother, she is at a loss. Mentally scanning her usual techniques, she finds none of them appropriate. She can't very well interrogate this woman, or confront her. On the other hand, the I-am-so-harmless-and-not-very-bright-so-you-can-just-relax-and-say-whatever-comes-into-your-mind approach to interviewing, one that Julia favors and often uses with great success on male politicians and military leaders, is not appropriate here either. Mara is closed-mouthed already. Julia doesn't want to turn her off entirely. So she is still groping for an entry point when Mara suddenly offers her one.

"Micky told me a lot about you," she says. "I don't have a brother. Were you always very close?"

It's pretty obvious that Mara just wants to distract her guest. She plans to find an abstract topic, safely in the remote past, so that she can chat for a decent amount of time before getting rid of her again. She doesn't want to have to answer any of the many questions that Micky's sister undoubtedly has. But Julia doesn't see this. She is grateful to be offered a fairly neutral, and yet personal, topic. She is hoping to get a little closer to Mara, to get her guard down.

Or so she thinks, but she is deceiving herself. The truth is that Julia is still very distraught. She is touched that someone is showing an interest in her brother's life. Finally, here is someone she can discuss him with. Julia jumps on the question with sentimental enthusiasm.

"No, we weren't always close," she says. "Not really. We were very different from each other. Well, you seem very different from him, too."

There, now she has blurted out what she has been thinking since first setting eyes on Mara. Did this formidable, earnest woman even take her brother seriously?

"You know," Julia goes on, taking the bull by the horns, "Micky might have seemed a little superficial to you, you're so committed and obviously political, but he really was a much deeper person than it seemed. I don't know if you had the chance to discover that."

She gives Mara a moment to answer, but there is only silence, so she rushes defensively on.

"He was not only the kindest person I know, he was also very brave. He had so much to overcome. Later he was a big, strong guy, but as a child he was so little, so weak. He was this pale little thing with a face like a doll, and unfortunately he had a lot of physical problems. He had to wear his leg in a brace. One of his eyes was much weaker than the other, and he was supposed to wear a patch over the better one so the weaker one would be exercised. Elementary school was a nightmare for him. The other boys were brutal. They didn't have any peer mediation programs then, I can assure you. It was pure Darwinism. If you were a weak little puppy, the wolves tried to bite you to death. They pushed him, they kicked him, they made fun of him. They threw his schoolbooks and his homework in the mud. On the way home they chased him . . ."

She stops, lost in thought, remembering that little blond boy. As long as they went to the same school, things were a little better. At least she could go home with him, and she often fought for him on the playground—his enemies were fortunately a year younger, and she was tall for her age. She had an old-fashioned leather schoolbag—it wasn't stylish at all and she hated it, but at these moments it stood her in good stead. Remembering, she can almost feel the coarse grain of its leather against her palm. The seams made a good sharp edge for clobbering people on the back or on the head, or if she was outnumbered she let them roll on top of her. Being boys, they inevitably thought this meant she had surrendered, and reflexively they would ease up, and she would pinch them, very, very hard . . . Seeing him as an adult, you would never have guessed at his earlier frailties. Physiotherapy experienced a real triumph, in Micky. But Julia knows that in his mind's eye he always remained smaller than everybody else, and weaker; she knows that their mocking laughter always rang in his ears.

Julia has gone to stand at Mara's window. Like all Peshawar gardens at this time of the year, hers, too, is dry and dusty. The occasional pink bougainvillea blossom looks less like a flower than a candy wrapper the wind has blown in. Now she turns back to Mara and finally faces the fact that this woman's behavior is not normal. She seems neither interested nor bored by this story; instead, she seems extremely nervous and agitated.

Well, this is simply the last straw. Faced with this cold, enigmatic stranger, this American woman who was her poor brother's last contact with any sort of home, Julia finally succumbs to the breakdown that has been running after her since she first got the bad news in Zagreb. She succumbs to the tears that have clouded her eyes since the grueling visit to the police station. She succumbs, but not without a struggle. She fights it with deep breaths and energetic blinking, and she almost gets a grip on herself once more, only to lose control completely.

Collapsing on Mara's sofa, Julia cries and cries. Catching her breath, she yaps out a few pitiful observations, only to start sobbing anew. Why, why did such a thing happen! To poor Micky! The best brother, the best human being in the world! The most harmless, the most good-natured! Murdered over some stupid container deal, a job that he was much too good for anyway! Just as he was too good for her! Such a nice person, and she had never given him his due . . . etc., etc., sob sob. Julia cries and sobs and chokes on her tears and coughs, then cries some more, until finally the storm subsides and she is all cried out.

She shakes her head hard to clear it, takes a few deep breaths, wipes her face on her shirt, and tells Mara that she will be leaving now. There is no point in staying in Pakistan. She needs to make her peace with what has happened, somehow. People do, don't they. Somehow. Julia thanks Mara politely for her time and tells her that she will not be seeing her again, since she plans to take the first flight to Islamabad tomorrow and continue on home from there. Wiping around on her smeared-up face some more and giving a few concluding sniffles, she hears Mara say in an oddly panicked voice that well, perhaps she should not leave just yet. "I think you should stay a while longer, honestly," she says. "I think you should definitely stay for at least another week." Julia stares at Mara in confusion and notices that her face is flushed.

"All I mean to say is, maybe he isn't really dead," Mara says. Then she adds nervously, "All I mean is, one should never give up hope."

Julia is instantly alert again; all her confusion and sadness stunned right out of her as her professional instincts take over. There is information here, being covered up. Here is someone who knows something, something definite, a secret. Julia takes a discreet deep breath. This is what she knows how to do. Cannily, carefully, she remarks, "That's so interesting, Mara. Please go on."

Mara has turned very pale now, and looks frightened; Julia tries to sound calming and seductive.

"It's perfectly all right to tell me, Mara, really. You can tell me anything."

Mara hesitates and even opens her mouth a bit to speak, but then she turns on her heel very abruptly and rushes out of the room; Julia runs after her, but there are several doors to choose from, and by the time she identifies the correct one Mara is already in her car with the key in the ignition, and by the time Julia gets to the street Mara is sputtering off in a cloud of dust.

Julia torments herself for a few moments—what might she have said instead that wouldn't have spooked the other woman? Damn! She had been about to say something, so close, so close . . . but then a scooter cab comes puttering around the bend and Julia waves it over and jumps in.

There is no sign of Mara anywhere, so she abandons any hope of pursuit and gives the driver Sonia's address instead. Julia knows the fares by now. She throws some rupees at the driver without haggling, rushes past the drowsy chowkidar into the house without waiting to be announced, and bursts onto the porch, where the assembled company is having its usual long lunch.

"My brother is alive," she announces, surprising herself almost as much as the others. That's what happens when you control yourself too well for too long.

Iqbal looks stunned. He even twists to look behind Julia, expecting from her tone of voice that she quite literally has her living brother in tow. Then he focuses on the American woman, clearly trying to think this through. First he looks astonished, then puzzled; finally, his features settle into a look of profound sympathy. Julia curses herself anew. Why has she come storming over here like this? Why didn't she stop at the hotel to wash her face and put on a shirt that has not been used as a towel for weepy mascara? She must look certifiable.

Iqbal, having reached his conclusion, jumps up and puts his arm around her.

"I am an idiot!" he proclaims. "I have treated you like a machine, just because you are so sensible and so competent. I forget that you are also a sister, a sister and a woman! I forget your heart! But what you are feeling now, my dear, is completely normal. It is completely healthy. Denial is one of the stages of grief, showing that you are on the road to recovery. First comes denial, then soon you will move on to—"

"You really are an idiot!" Lilly interrupts, rudely pushing him away. "Why don't you keep your amateur psychobabble stupidities to yourself and go do some work," she snaps. Then she turns to Julia.

"Why do you say that?" she asks gently. "Have you found something out?"

Julia describes the scene with Mara. Even as she speaks, she can feel that she is not sounding persuasive. It had been absolutely clear to her, she had been absolutely certain, that Mara knew something very important concerning her brother. But now, when she relates what was actually said, it doesn't sound very substantial.

Lilly is encouraging; she asks hopeful questions. *What*

has Mara said *exactly*? Well, Julia is obliged to admit, she just said something vague about not losing hope, but it wasn't just *what* she said, it was *how* she'd said it. It was the expression on her face! It had been obvious, absolutely obvious, that she was hiding something, and that she had almost revealed it, only to become frightened in the end. Lilly nods, but there is doubt in her eyes and, as with Iqbal, pity.

"You don't believe me," Julia says, quite calmly. "I don't blame you, I know I haven't done a good job of explaining what happened." And then, for the second time that day, she bursts into tears.

Iqbal paces up and down in front of her in great agitation, he is even wringing his hands; he would like to put his arm around his distraught visitor but he doesn't dare to, remembering Lilly's rebuke. Lilly is watching her friend with concern but isn't sure what to do, either.

It is Gul, uncharacteristically, who seizes the initiative. She approaches silently, pulls Julia to the sofa, and takes hold of her hand. Then she says, "You can't always tell from the sound of things whether they are true or not, isn't that so? Sometimes you just have a feeling. Especially when it's about someone very close to you. Today you felt something, but now you find you can't express it in words, am I right?"

Julia is so touched at this gentle aid from an unexpected quarter that she can only nod.

"And," Gul continues softly, addressing her husband, "we have to admit that this case is a strange one, don't we, particularly as concerns the brother of Miss Malone. After all, you never found the"—"body," I suppose she intended to say, but she stops herself tactfully and gropes for another term, coming up with the inaccurate but friendlier "the, the . . . corpus delicti. All the other, umm, corpus delictis were found, as I recall. So, where is Mr. Malone? We don't give him up, your brother," she assures Julia, patting her hand. "If you have a feeling, then we must search for him. Isn't that right, Iqbal?"

Iqbal is as surprised as everyone else to hear such a long deposition from his quiet Rose. "Well," he says, "a feeling, well . . . just as you say, my dear. Yes, well, you may be right."

He's a little bit miffed at this implied criticism of his work—isn't everybody saying that he has been hasty and neglectful in writing the American man off? But he is far too much a stranger to his wife to be anything but polite to her—to all of these excited women, for that matter.

Wiping her eyes with a handkerchief proffered by the thoughtful Gul, Julia feels profoundly disheartened. Will Iqbal pursue this matter, vigorously, has she gotten through to him, has she shaken his certainty in her brother's death at least a little bit? She looks at him; he is smiling at her encouragingly and, or so she believes, dishonestly. He is humoring her. He thinks she is nuts. And maybe she is.

Meanwhile, back in her office again, Mara is very, very unhappy about her role in all of this. This is starting to go way, way beyond what even a white-collar anarchist such as herself can condone. Besides possibly putting people at risk, herself included, Mara suspects that she is going to get into major trouble. She hasn't told Malone that he is presumed to be dead; she has let him believe that she has phoned his company. She hasn't told him that his sister is here. She has misled the poor sister. She may even be committing a crime with all of this. Harboring a fugitive . . . no, Micky hasn't done anything bad, so he can't be a fugitive. But impeding an official investigation is bad enough. Deceiving the police, sneaking around, meddling in something the dimensions of which she can't even guess at . . . this is bad, very bad.

Timing is so important. Regrettably, Farid's timing is way off. Mara is sitting behind her desk, feeling guilty about Julia and glumly pondering the possible consequences of actively sabotaging an international police effort, when Farid comes in, weaving his way uncertainly around the filing cabinets, boxes, and bookcases that partition the office, finding her work space at last, and taking a seat on the folding chair beside her desk. "Mara," he says. He is uneasy. He hasn't seen her or spoken to her for months; he has never been to her office. The look on her face, as she registers his arrival, is not reassuring. Actually, she looks scared, but, squinting at her nervously, he takes it to be a look of irritation.

Quickly he launches into his prepared speech. He has respected her decision to be on her own, to have a trial separation, because things had been going so badly and there had been so much tension between them. But the time has come to review this decision. He wants her to know that he misses her. Both of them needed to acclimatize, he thinks. That, he thinks, was the root of their problem. Both of them were in culture shock! Both of them needed to make that giant leap from life in America to life in the North-West Frontier Province. Surely this has happened by now, thanks in part to her wisdom, to her instinctive grasp of the right thing to do. By working here, by getting a job, she has put down roots of her own. She is not just an appendage, not an outsider any longer. She has her own friends, her own sense of purpose, her own turf. This, he has come to realize, is a good thing. He has been wrong to denigrate her work, and he is sorry. He is here today to demonstrate his earnestness. He wants to accompany her to the camps and see for himself the important accomplishments of her labor. He is not here to pressure or to rush her. He wants her back, yes, he's ready to put his cards on the table, he's ready to admit it straight out, but first they must get to know each other all over again. And also, he would like to mention that his views concerning the refugees are undergoing a fundamental change. As it turns out, she has been prophetic on that account. He doesn't want to bore her with local politics, but he will say that his party's views about the refugees, as well as his personal ones, have shifted. So. If she is not too busy, why don't they just swing by the camps to view one of her projects, and the drive will give them the opportunity to chat.

Farid stops talking and looks at her expectantly. This is quite something, what he has done. He has come for her. He has humbled himself. He has given in on several points of principle.

Mara sits opposite him, as pale as a sheet. In the grip of emotion, Farid hopefully supposes, and he is right. In other circumstances, with better timing, this might have worked. Right now, though, his wish to accompany her to the camps sets off panic and paranoia. Now? Why is he showing up now, of all times? Does he know something? Are they after her already, and using him as the decoy?

Mara gets a grip. That's crazy. If they were on to her, they wouldn't need a decoy. An officer armed with handcuffs and extradition papers would be more likely.

Mara allows her eyes to linger on the face of this man

who was, and technically speaking still is, her husband. But almost immediately panic washes over her once again. The camps? Take her estranged husband to the camps? Where she is hiding the man two nations and, just possibly, a posse of Peshawari mafiosi are searching for? The man she—technically speaking—committed adultery with?

"That's not a good idea," she says.

Farid takes heart. Very good, she isn't brushing him off, she is engaging. He didn't expect her to give in right away, of course not. There has to be some pursuit, that's how the man–woman thing works.

"I know," he insists, beaming sincerity her way. "I have been closed-minded about the refugees, I see that now. But I am ready to learn. We'll drive there, we'll talk, that's all. It's all I can expect, it's all I do expect. Really."

"You . . . don't understand," Mara replies. "It's complicated. I appreciate your coming here. We'll talk, later maybe. This is not the right time."

Mara is disgusted to hear herself blathering on like this. She tries to think clearly. She could take him to a camp, why not? There are many camps, she doesn't have to take him to the one where Malone is. But even just thinking about it, she realizes that it is beyond her. She cannot, simply cannot take Farid, of all people, now, of all times, on a fact-finding mission and soul-searching journey to a camp, not to any camp. She can't do it. She has to get him out, out, out of here, and out of her thoughts, until she has the Malone thing resolved and behind her. So, how to get rid of Farid? She reaches out for anger, her usual recourse in difficult situations, but anger eludes her. It would be so pleasant to yell at Farid, to tell him that his pathetic opportunistic show of interest is too little, too late, but she simply cannot summon up the necessary rage. She's too tired. And then there is his face, almost that of a stranger by now, and yet so familiar, and it's not wrong what he's saying, about culture shock. She simply is not angry with him.

"Farid," she says, as calmly as she can, "this is not a good time. I'm glad you came, I will think about what you said, and I will call you, and we will go to a camp. But now is not a good time."

Farid hesitates. Should he push for more? Should he feel insulted? Then something in her nervousness communicates itself. Of course, he knows that the police have questioned her. He doesn't find this upsetting. An American has disappeared, other Americans are asked about him, that's logical. But now, sensing her nervousness, he studies her more closely and sees how pale she is, how hard she has to work to keep her composure.

"If you have a problem, I could help you," he offers.

Mara is not tempted, not even briefly, to confide in him. The only quarter she expects help from is the calendar, mercifully eliminating one day after the other to bring her closer to the consul's return.

"I just need time," Mara responds, truthfully. "I think you're right. We should talk, and we will, but not right now. I will call you, I swear it, and it will be soon, I promise."

Farid hesitates. Should he be forceful and determined, or should he appear considerate and low-key? What will work better here?

"Please," she says.

Farid gets up. "Khadija married a millowner in Lahore," he throws out, in parting. "He's rich, and they have two sons, and he buys her diamonds and takes her to London several times a year. And I've known about it for three months," he adds, because otherwise she would be crazy enough to think he's come by on some kind of a rebound. As he's walking out, he sticks his head back around the edge of the bookcase and, smiling his famous killer smile, observes, "Oh yes, and I figured out what love is. Tell you next time!"

Then he's gone, leaving Mara behind with an involuntary little smile on her face and a droning headache behind her temples.

E leven a.m., and work is well under way in the Pakistani desert. The soreness in his muscles from days of digging has worn off, leaving a dull, not entirely unpleasant ache. Malone has gotten used to the dry, hard soil, has found the rhythm of foot-on-shovel, fling-the-earth-back, that works best on this terrain. The rest of today should suffice for digging, then tomorrow he should be ready to construct something like an outhouse out of those loose planks behind the shed.

Busy with his monotonous task, digging, digging, digging away, Malone does not register the approach of strangers. Malone is awake, wide awake, and yet he is about to have a nightmare. His nightmare has left the realm of sleep and is coming to visit him. Here he is, right in the middle of the open landscape, exposed, far from shelter. He is digging, and Hamid is assisting him. Digging, digging, digging. It is hot. The shovel makes scraping noises, and sweat forms on his forehead and his arms and dribbles down the front of his chest. Absorbed in his task, Malone does not immediately notice the arrival of his nightmare. Suddenly, it is there, all around him. A crowd of tall, young, humorless men, closing in on him from all sides.

Well, not really a crowd, except to Malone's horrified mind. There are only seven of them. Not really totally humorless. One of them, but Malone is too stunned to notice, ruffles Hamid's hair in a playful manner. Then they speak. They speak to Malone, and Hamid answers. It is a long conversation. One of them shakes his head angrily, then grabs the shovel out of Malone's hands, gives his shoulder a shove, and laughs contemptuously. Hamid steps protectively in front of Malone and responds angrily. All the men laugh. One of the men extends his arm, grabs Malone's hand, and shakes it and claps him on the shoulder. Everyone is laughing, except Hamid, who still looks annoyed. And then, as suddenly as they came, they leave.

Hamid tries to explain the visitation. He is a smart boy. He can explain it in English, sort of. "Engineer," he says, "engineer," and gestures after the departed group. "Not good," he says, "not good," and gestures at the hole they have dug. Tugging at Malone's shirt, he pulls him back to the shack. Malone is miffed, relieved, confused. Hamid, on the other hand, appears to have overcome his annoyance and to be quite happy. With an encouraging smile, he tugs Malone to the door of the shed, waves, and is gone.

Not for long. In the afternoon, the boy is back, and so is the nightmare. The nightmare has increased in number and is bearing implements. Hamid, jumpy, excited, insists on dragging Malone over to see. The tallest young man, the one who laughed, has taken command. He is parading across the plain, squinting competently in different directions and shouting orders. The others are digging, measuring, pacing outlines, and marking them with stones. No one appears surprised to see Malone, or anxious to kill him. With gestures, he is instructed where to dig. A lot of activity is unfolding, right here in the middle of the scrub. A rickety truck arrives, with bricks and further implements. In midafternoon, a delegation of children comes from the camp, bearing trays of tea and bread. When everyone squats down to consume this, the tall man signals imperiously for Malone to join them. From the penetrating gaze he fixes on him, and his gestures, it is obvious that he is quizzing Hamid quite thoroughly about the American. Hamid answers happily, fluently.

Malone, choking down the offered bread and trying not to see the flies that land on his sugary teacup whenever he sets it down, would give a lot to understand the questions, the answers, and calculate by them his expected life span. After tea break, the work continues. In a surprisingly short amount of time, the digging is done, and a brick enclosure has been put up. Large numbers of dusty children have collected to watch; Hamid, visibly puffed up with pride at his pivotal role in this endeavor, is pointing out the features of the construction to them and explaining something in an authoritative tone of voice.

By early evening, the project is completed. The young men pack up their tools and leave, some by rickety truck, some on foot. But this is not all, and Hamid and the children seem to know it, for they remain expectantly in place. A while later, a dust cloud in the distance heralds the arrival of another vehicle. It is another rickety truck, and from it emerge a number of black-clad figures that Malone identifies as female. They leap from the truck, revealing themselves to be wearing blue jeans under their voluminous black covers. Long scarves cover their heads tightly, but their faces are free. This female invading force strides energetically toward the newly built sanitary facilities, inspects them briefly, and then marches into the camp. Before leaving, they stand for a moment very sternly regarding Malone, who, even without words, even without too much social sensibility, understands that it is time for him to withdraw. The children scatter, too, and a little while later, when the new facilities are officially inaugurated by a large group of enthusiastic female camp residents under the auspices of their grimly respectable young fundamentalist women duennas, nothing masculine is about.

Malone is in his shed, feeling happy. He cannot wait for Mara's next visit. What will she say when she glimpses the ambitious structure that has been so quickly put in place? Not by him alone, of course, but through his inspiration! His idea, come to life! Tired and content, Malone feels some of the pride of the artist, the builder, the architect. From his window, he can just barely glimpse the fabulous edifice. Hasn't the surface of the earth changed just a little bit because Malone was here? Hasn't he left it just a little better than he found it? Sighing with satisfaction, he reluctantly turns away from this, his little piece of immortality.

The idea that the killer was a woman gives way, in the end, to another and even more disconcerting idea. What if the killer was not a woman in a burqa but a man in a burqa?

The idea takes somewhat longer to emerge than it should, only because the notion of a man dressing himself like a woman seems so unthinkably humiliating to our local chauvinists.

It's a disquieting thought all right, no doubt about it. The fact that no criminal has done it before attests more than anything I could say to the strength of chauvinism in the North-West Frontier Province; otherwise, who would be able to resist this temptation? A burqa—the perfect disguise, the perfect getaway outfit. You cannot be searched in a burqa, except by female police, and since there are hardly any of them, they are unlikely to be at the scene of the crime. You cannot be described by witnesses, except maybe regarding the color of your chaddri or burqa—and what use is that, when there are only a few standard colors? Height, weight, age, none of this can be determined. There is no way to distinguish a man from a woman. You cannot see anything about the face, not even a mustache, through the tight grid. The chaddri, the burqa are, while unpleasant garments for women, perfect for bank robbers, thieves . . . and murderers.

Now that the stigma had been overcome—if it had been overcome—would a rash of crimes be committed in Pakistan by men concealed under the all-concealing folds of a veil?

"It would serve them right," Lilly says, with deep and heartfelt pleasure, to which Iqbal can only chirp out a stricken "Hey, wait a minute! Who's this 'them'?"

"Maybe the detective in charge of the investigation would have a better chance of solving the case if he wore a burqa, too," she muses, merciless.

13

T hree things must be banned, if this country is to return to the path of God!" the Maulana shouts, that evening, eyes flashing and rhetoric flowing with particular brilliance. "Three things are corrupting our hearts and leading us along the path of evil and foreign domination! Three things must be removed! Three things must be eliminated! Soccer! Music and dancing! And women!"

If any in the viewing audience notice that this speech is identical to the one broadcast five weeks ago, they will probably conclude that the topic is so important to the Maulana that he is returning to it once again. They will not realize that the Maulana has, for the first time, not shown up for the prebroadcast taping, forcing the staff to pull out one of the older cassettes for rebroadcasting.

Even with that, today's show is jinxed. Right in dramatic mid-sentence there is a hiss, and the Maulana's image on the screen flickers and spits before giving way to total darkness.

"What?" says Aunt Sonia. "A power cut now? They usually don't come before nine."

For that is all it is, though for a moment it had seemed apocalyptic. No, it's just Pakistan's way of holding to its energy quota. If too much is being used, why, the official in charge simply flicks a switch and turns everybody off. Then people flick on their private generators, and life goes on as before. Click, the lights go out. A few seconds later they flicker on again, a bit more dimly, more shakily than before. That's normal. It happens several times a day. What doesn't happen every day, fortunately, is that someone gets killed, during those brief moments of darkness.

A bit earlier, the same evening. In her neon-green chaddri, Fatima hurries down the alleyway to meet Mushahed. She passes two children, two dogs, a bony cat. Two men walk in front of her, carrying hubcaps. A woman walks behind her, wearing a green chaddri like her own. The Maulana watches Fatima leave the house; his mind is agitated, rage and disappointment fill his heart. Where is she going, at night, alone? She has lovers, he knew it all along; he sensed it in her, that promiscuous need for sex, he felt it, even the very first time, when she was a virgin, when she fought him with all that pretended innocence. A lascivious little bitch, just like the others, trying to fool him with those downcast eyes, that little voice. Pretending to push him away, only to incite him further. Tricks, the tricks of a lascivious little bitch.

Mumbling to himself, the Maulana throws on his coat and slips into the alley behind Fatima. He will catch them in the act, her and her lover, and he will have them killed; fornicators, depraved, godless animals.

The Maulana is upset, very upset. For the first time,

finding his bleak view of women confirmed by reality gives him no pleasure. Fatima, sweet, pleasurable Fatima, why did she have to be like all the others? Distracted by his thoughts, the Maulana does not notice that the distance between himself and the green figure he is pursuing has decreased. Suddenly the woman looks over her shoulder at him—as nearly as he can make out, since the figure has no face.

"Fatima!" he exclaims, and launches into a tirade of abuse and recrimination, followed by a hiss of threats. But instead of recoiling in fear and guilt, she takes his arm and pulls him through the doorway of the small neighborhood mosque they are just passing. Can there be some innocent excuse for her behavior, after all? Does she have something to tell him? Just as he is scrutinizing the impenetrable grid, trying to see her eyes, there is a grinding, sputtering sound, and all the lights go out. She pulls him into the mosque, just a small room really, piled with carpets; she pulls him into the darkest corner and—imploringly?—extends batlike, green-webbed arms to him. A wave of desire overcomes the Maulana —the carpets, soft under his feet, the dark, and Fatima: terrified with guilt? feverish with desire? or perhaps in some kind of innocent trouble, and desperate for comfort?

"Don't try to lie to me, girl," the Maulana says sternly, reaching toward the folds of her chaddri, taking command of an initially distressing situation, and pushing her farther into the dark corner of the mosque.

The Maulana's last thought is out of character; it is a gentle, a redeeming thought. Places can have auras, I believe that; maybe the good thoughts of pious people have given this small mosque, tucked away in a little alley, an aura of spirituality and forgivingness. As he reaches for the woman, there in the darkest corner of the dark room, he wonders briefly whether this act will be a sin that will anger his God more than any of his previous lapses. And then he thinks that no, it is not, because Fatima will soon be his wife, is in a sense his wife already. And when a husband and a wife clasp hands, the Prophet has said, then it is pleasing to God, and their sins shall run out through their fingers like water. With this thought, the Maulana reaches for Fatima, or at any rate, for the green formless shape he takes to be Fatima.

The time between murders seems to be getting shorter; that's a bad sign, in the eyes of the responsible detective. Four of them—by his count—committed right under the nose of Iqbal. And the Americans are still inquiring and sending diplomatic notes, they want their citizen back, even if only in a box, they want to close the file, the insurance company needs to know for sure what happened, they want a body . . . All sorts of senators are writing notes to Pakistani counterparts, and Iqbal knows why, it's that sister, stirring things up. Not that he blames her, not a bit. No, if anything, he's worried about her, roaming all over the place, making phone calls, reading files, asking questions. He wishes she would go home. What if she gets killed, too? How will he ever face himself again, if that happens?

So, when news of the sixth murder reaches him, for one awful moment he thinks that his worst fears have come true, and the Malone sister has gotten herself killed. Thankfully, this is not the case. But that's about the only reassuring thing about this most recent murder. It spells trouble, trouble, trouble. Iqbal knows that, and conceals his apprehension beneath the flip tone in which he communicates it to his household.

"Well, girls," he says, strolling in the door, "we can all bring out our cleats, we can drool over those naked thighs: the conscience of Pakistan has bitten the dust."

Untangling his metaphors distracts everyone just for a moment from the substance of his communication and makes Lilly frown an irritated "What?"

"His illuminated saintliness the Maulana is with us no longer. The last bulwark between us and our base animal instincts has fallen. Nothing now stands between us and utter depravity," Iqbal goes on, ending with a mock lunge at his wife. "I can't understand what you are talking about," Gul says, half-annoyed, swatting him away. "Murder, my dear. The Maulana has been stabbed to death, may-peace-be-upon-him, and is at this very moment being indecently caressed by virginal houris while his pudgy little lips sip the nectar of paradise and—"

"You're making this up," says Lilly.

"The virgin stuff is a little retro, I agree," Iqbal replies.

Once she gets used to the idea, Lilly finds the Maulana's demise positively inspiring. She and Iqbal start inventing titles for a series of detective books they could write that would star the Maulana in fictionalized form: *On Friday the Maulana Ate Pork, On Saturday the Maulana Drank Bloody Marys,* etc.

Still. Two fundamentalists in a row, it's not really all that funny, and Iqbal knows it.

Julia finds out about this latest murder from the newspaper that arrives with her breakfast tray. So. A new item to occupy the busy detective, while her poor Micky drops down yet another slot on the list of Iqbal's priorities. She has adjusted to the jet lag. Croatia's horrors have started to recede into geographic and mental distance. Julia is feeling better, her energy is back. If anything is going to happen here concerning her brother, then, obviously, it's up to her.

Journalism, Julia tells herself not for the first time, isn't that different from detective work. You try to discover the truth. You try to identify the guilty. You get people to confess. You search for evidence. She calls Mara's office. They say just a moment please, they will get her. Then they come back and say oh, sorry, she's out. They sound too glib, engaging in a routine office lie. In the evening Julia takes a cab to Mara's house and knocks on the door. Nobody answers, but lights are on upstairs. Julia tries to imagine what secret Mara might be concealing.

She reviews all the possibilities, trying to leave out none. Could Mara be the killer? That doesn't make any sense. Maybe she is covering up for the killer, and Julia's breakdown made her feel guilty? But no, that doesn't explain why she would hint that Julia should stay, should not leave Pakistan. And why did she refer to time in such a specific way? A week, she said. Why would she want her to stay in Pakistan for another week? And why did she change her mind? Of course, it could be projection, just wishful thinking, but Julia got the sense from Mara's fragmentary remarks that her brother is still alive. But if he is, and needs help, why had she run away, and why is she avoiding Julia now? Why doesn't she just go to the police? Something illegal must be involved. But that doesn't sound at all like Micky. Or is he being held for ransom, and have they threatened to kill him if the police are told? That would explain a lot of things about Mara's peculiar behavior. But still, why wouldn't she enlist his own sister's help in raising the money or whatever else it is that the kidnappers want? It just does not make sense.

No matter how often she tots up the available facts, there seems to be only one possible conclusion: her brother is alive, but he is in grave danger. He is involved in something extremely illegal, which is why the police must not be brought in. Or he is being held hostage, and Mara is afraid of spooking his captors. It is obvious, too, that some sort of crisis is approaching, which will determine things one way or the other within a week. This chain of thought makes Julia absolutely frantic. She just doesn't know enough to help her brother; she can't bear to do nothing; but what if she does the wrong thing? A rash gesture could make things even worse.

She has to talk to somebody, but she doesn't entirely trust Iqbal. Her instincts tell her that Lilly and Gul would be good filters: a direct conduit to the police, but not a blindly loyal one. And indeed, the two women are flattered to be consulted and eager to help. Gul immediately gets her Aunt Sonia to lend Julia her driver and her car. Together, they decide that Mara is their best starting point for a supplemental investigation. They decide that Julia should shadow Mara.

Sonia's driver, Hakim, leads a pretty boring life. The most excitement he ever gets is to drive the old lady to the house of another old lady, or maybe to pick up alterations from the tailor, or a very occasional guest from the airport. He enthusiastically throws himself into the espionage mission. Parking the car at an oblique angle, not too obviously in view but with clear sight of the front door, he fastens his eyes firmly on Mara's house and encourages Julia to relax and read her book in the backseat.

The first day is very boring. Julia and the driver wait for over an hour until Mara finally appears at her front door. She gets in her car and drives directly to her office. She stays there all day. In the afternoon she drives directly home. No one comes to see her, and she doesn't go out. Julia isn't really disappointed. She more or less expects that if anything happens, it will be closer to the end of the week, the week Mara had mentioned. She sits in the back of the car, reads a novel, chats with Hakim, and halfheartedly keeps Mara under observation, just in case.

On the second day, Mara drives to the UNICEF office. A lot of other cars are there; it looks like a big meeting. She stays there until one. Then everybody drives to a restaurant together for lunch. After that she spends a few hours at her office. Then she goes home.

It's pretty tedious, but Julia is just marking time. Meanwhile she has learned all about Hakim's three sisters and two brothers and has familiarized herself with his opinions on all issues of Pakistani domestic politics. She can sing along with two of his three favorite cassettes.

On the third day, Mara drives to her office. Hakim has just started telling Julia the plot of the Indian movie he saw on video the night before when their drowsy automotive domesticity comes to a sudden halt. Mara comes running out of the office building; she seems excited. A second woman comes running after her, but Mara just yells something at her over her shoulder and races across the parking lot. She jumps into her car and off she goes, with Aunt Sonia's driver racing ecstatically behind her. She heads directly out of the city; Hakim has a few guesses as to where she might be heading, but Julia has never heard of any of these small towns before.

After twenty minutes Mara turns off onto a smaller side road; Hakim now supposes that she might be heading for one of the refugee camps. When he says that, Julia feels a stab of disappointment and forces herself to calm down again. Of course, that is probably all this is; some sort of an office-related crisis in one of Mara's clinics. They drive behind her for another ten minutes or so until the road forks. But Mara takes neither a left nor a right turn; instead, she veers suddenly and goes thundering off into the landscape. From the cloud of dust she throws up behind her, they assume she has driven straight into the wilderness, but as they get closer, they see a road, a rough, unpaved road.

Hakim slows down to ease them more gently onto that rough terrain; the car shakes, then suddenly jerks to the left. They hear a thud. The car shudders. There is another thud, and Hakim yells, "Down, missis! Get down!" as his head disappears behind his seat back. Julia is still thinking that they are having engine trouble. Not until the car window splinters next to her face does she decide to heed his warning and throw herself down on the seat. The car shakes some more, then crashes down abruptly to the left side. They hear another car accelerating, then a shower of rocks crashing down on their hood, and then it is quiet.

After a few moments they cautiously lift their heads. Finally they get out of the car and carefully look around. In the distance, they can just make out a dust cloud, pursuing another dust cloud.

"Mara! Stop! Wait!" Julia screams, trying to commune with the first of the clouds. Then she screams, "No! No!"

Hakim, meanwhile, is walking sadly around the car, studying it and clucking. Three of the tires have been shot flat and gasoline is dripping from a hole in the tank.

Still shaking his head in dismay, he marches resolutely to the crossing in the hope that someone will pass and stop for them. Julia stands looking after the two dust clouds. Is Mara on her way to see Micky? Has Julia, with her stupid, ill-advised, amateurish sleuthing, led his pursuers right to his hiding place? Had he been safe until his idiot sister came lumbering into his life?

Mara, unaware of all the excitement behind her, continues rocketing down the dirt road in great urgency. The consul was supposed to be back on Monday, but today, when she placed her strictly routine, just-checking call, the operator offered to put her right through to Jim. So they're back! They're finally back!

"James Taylor, Political Desk," the Southern voice had said, before Mara could demur. Hanging up the receiver ever so gently, Mara breathed a huge sigh of relief. And now her worries are over, almost over. It's time to get Malone, time to hand him over to his friendly neighborhood diplomats. She knows exactly what to do. She will get him. She will make him lie down flat on the backseat of the car. She will drive him right smack to the consulate.

Yes, and as soon as she has delivered him to the consulate, she will go and fetch his sister. The consulate, she hopes, will ship both of them out on the next available plane, back to Maryland with them, ASAP. And the headache will finally end. Mara is surprised to discover that this thought is not quite so unequivocally a relief as she would have expected. She can't have grown somehow sentimentally attached to Malone, can she, for God's sake? Or is it the idea of going home that is making her so nervous? Is her subconscious trying to tell her that she wants to go home, too? All of these confusing thoughts keep her so busy that she does not pay as much attention as she otherwise might to events transpiring on the road behind her. Not that she could see much, even if she were paying attention. It's a lot easier to follow someone else's dust cloud than to see behind your own.

S trangely, the death of the Maulana had provided an impetus to several people who did not otherwise have cause to mourn his passing. It had upset Julia, because she figured that with such a high-profile new victim, nobody would bother about her brother at all anymore.

And Walid Khan, though the elimination of his archrival was politically opportune, found himself disconcerted. Fatima. It can no longer be overlooked that each victim has some kind of a link to Fatima. Can this be pure coincidence? Isn't that very, very unlikely?

Khan studies her closely, the next time she comes. He sits in his chair and lets her stand before his desk, and studies her coldly. There is something strange, something very strange about this woman. It isn't apparent, as she stands there, slowly growing flustered under his stare, but it's got to be there. She must be some kind of jinx, a raven bringing death . . . except that Khan does not believe in jinxes or jinn. Nor does he believe in coincidence. Sitting behind his desk, with Fatima at uneasy attention before him, he instructs her to review for him once again her last visits to the murdered men. Malone. She did exactly as she was told, Fatima says, stammering. She went to the room, said the odd English sentence as well as she could, took off her clothes, and did a small dance. She did exactly as she was told, really; only Malone seemed not to like it, and she is so sorry. He spoke a lot, but Fatima could not understand what he said. But she understood that he was urging her to put her clothes back on. He seemed flustered and upset and rushed her out of the room. "Maybe he's in love with his wife?" Fatima offers shyly, eyes misting a little with her fantasy of America, where people marry for love and women are always happy. Khan snorts in exasperation at this silliness. Never mind all of that; what about the others?

Standing before him like a schoolgirl in an examination, Fatima gives her report. She went to them, she did what they told her, she left again . . . except for the famous Indian, but he knows that already. His nephew wouldn't let her go to the famous Indian.

Khan finds her upsetting; finds himself angry with her, as she stands there so obediently. Almost stupid in her obedience, and yet it must all be an act, an elaborate act. But can that be true? Though he has spent quite some time with her, he has not paid her much attention. Just another simple village girl, biddable, pathetic—isn't she? Can he have been totally wrong about her? Could she be involved with political extremists and killers? "Less than the dust," well, that applies to her, certainly; to whom better? In a country where no girl is worth very much, and where a girl who has erred but once is worth nothing at all anymore, what can Fatima's value be?

Absurdly, Khan begins to feel himself becoming stimulated by these thoughts. Fatima, standing meek before him, flushing under his displeasure, what is she? A creature less than the dust, beneath the insects, entirely at his mercy? Or the avenging angel of some fanatical group, infiltrating Pakistan's elite, draining them of their masculine strength, and then leaving them to be slaughtered naked in their beds by her comrades? And why do these thoughts excite him? Khan studies Fatima, who looks at him, cheeks flushed, frozen into paralysis by the cold gleam in his eyes. Power, as the old cliché has it, is an aphrodisiac; what about its absence? Frozen between power and powerlessness, between victimization and murderous guilt, between servitude and seductiveness, Fatima stands before Khan with a dazzling multiplicity of erotic possibilities along the axis of fear and danger, intellect and instinct, pleasure and defeat.

I sn't it strange, the kinds of things that can change your life? It can even be something as trivial as a latrine. Were we to examine Malone's Lifeline, we could see a distinct, sharp turn, and trace that turn back to the moment when he chose to shoulder a spade and make life just a little bit better for Mara's Afghan sisters. Are good deeds rewarded? It's time to find out.

Malone is elated by his experience as a builder, elated by the camaraderie of his construction team. And the feelings are reciprocated! Who could remain unmoved by such an enthusiastic volunteer? Not his new young friends. His friends have lots of plans for the camp, and the lumbering, well-meaning American, who decided to build latrines all by himself and went about it all wrong, hahaha, amuses them. Amusement is scarce in the desert. Malone is a precious commodity.

Here is what would probably happen if Malone knew who his friends are: he would die. The CIA would turn green with envy, the American consul would turn pale with fright, if they knew that Malone was the best buddy of the newest, most rapidly growing, most determined radical Islamic movement in Asia. They are young. They call themselves the Taliban. Most of them have grown up knowing nothing but war. All of them are students of religious colleges, where they live and study in austere but adequate conditions under the guidance of stern but idealistic elderly men. They are healthy and well fed and their bodies, full of life and youth, are taut from too much sitting, too much learning, no sports, little exercise, and not even the dimmest prospect of sex.

Their spirits are still tender; it hurts them to see their compatriots in the wretched camps, the dirty, sick, neglected children, the miserable old people. And the rich, arrogant leaders, living in enormous villas, stockpiling wealth, and struggling for power while their people drift relentlessly into barbarism and stupidity. Their tenderness, coupled with the mercilessness of youth, will make the Taliban into a deadly force. They will arm themselves from the lavish arsenals in the camps. They will receive money, encouragement, and more weapons from their elderly teachers. They will march into Afghanistan, they will advance on Kabul, and as they go, the followers of the fat, corrupt, complacent leaders will rush to join them. Malone's buddies will soon be featured in *Time*, in *Newsweek*, and on CNN. But not just yet. Just now they are engaged in peaceful pursuits, wielding plowshares, not swords.

On the very morning that we are speaking of, as Mara is steering her car toward the camp, as Malone's sister and Aunt Sonia's chauffeur are barreling along behind her as discreetly as they can, as someone far more ominous is following both parties in an expensive car, about to shoot at them, Hamid is excitedly jumping toward the shed. The young men have a new project, they are going to build a classroom, a proper classroom, and they have empowered Hamid to come and get Malone, their funny foreign mascot, to help them dig the foundations.

But there is more! Hamid has a present for Malone, a surprise! He has asked his young friends for it, and they have granted his wish, and now he has this wonderful gift for Malone, wrapped up in brown paper.

When Mara arrives at the shack, there is no sign of Malone. She waits for a little while. Restless, she starts packing his things, throwing them into a box. She carries the box outside and puts it in her trunk, but still he does not come. Where can he be? Mara can't stand waiting around. She decides to drive to the neighboring camp and check out the tuberculosis clinic; a visit to that clinic is overdue, anyway. She leaves a note for Malone, ordering him to stay put and wait for her return. Then she drives away.

As soon as she is gone, a black car comes rolling out from behind a hill and bumps into the shrubbery behind the shack. There are two men in the car. They come to a stop behind the shrubs, open the car doors for ventilation, and wait. They are waiting for Malone. When they see him, a pudgy, pale foreigner who evidently lives in this shack, they will lift the pistols from their laps and shoot him. They will throw the body in the backseat. Then they will dump it somewhere in the desert.

An hour goes by. It is hot, the men are tired, and they will shoot him with special pleasure now, to punish him for their discomfort. They wait, they wait. And finally, here comes a man. But damn, it can't be their man, their American. This man is not pudgy. His skin, tanned from the desert sun and filthy with sweat and dust, is not pale.

Well, as a matter of fact it *is* Malone, tired from the day's digging, but he does not look anything like his former self. He is wearing Hamid's gift, a baggy gray trouser outfit. He looks like a refugee. And he is not alone. His little sidekick is with him. The men in the car, squinting at these new arrivals, see what appears to be an Afghan father trudging up with his son. This is the way things would have gone, without the latrines: the assassins, identifying a pale and pasty Western-dressed Malone easily from afar, would have shot him and dumped him in the desert, to be just as dead as most people already think he is.

But wait, even now, Malone is not safe yet. If only he were a little less exhilarated by his desert adventure. If only he would march quietly into the shack, but no. Standing in the doorframe, proud of the little schoolyard they have excavated today, struck as always by the moonlike appearance of his desert home, he lifts his arms expansively and shouts, "A small step for education, a large step for mankind!"

His face, turned directly to his clandestine observers, is clearly Western. His words, booming out toward them, are clearly English. And so his announcement, declaimed into the stillness of the desert, is followed by great sequences of noise.

First comes the laugh of the ever-appreciative, ever-admiring Hamid. Then comes the crack of pistol shots. Next there is a thud, the thud of bodies striking a floor. And one more thud, the shed door slamming shut from the impact. Hamid, who has hit the floor in panic, lifts his head cautiously and skitters across to where his friend has fallen. Sprawled on his back, Malone is motionless. He is limp, his head at an odd angle. Clearly, he is dead.

A wail of pain escapes Hamid's throat.

Such a brave little child. He has endured so much. His father has died, his mother is an outcast, he has no home, all of this he has endured, sobbing quietly into his blankets at night, almost every night, but acting like a man all day, always, as is expected. But this, isn't this just too much? His friend, the second father he found all for himself, killed right in front of him! And just now, when this man was metamorphosing from the timid, slightly ridiculous person he initially was, let's face it, into a fine figure of a man, properly dressed and accepted by other men. Felled, just when he was becoming the sort of man Hamid could be proud of.

Hamid wails quietly, but it is too much. His whimper turns to tears, then to a scream. Hamid screams with pain and rage, and screams and screams.

He is heard by the assassins, who realize their job is not finished.

He is also heard by the school construction brigade, who have pricked their ears up once already, hearing shots, and are now in full alert, hearing screams.

The assassins approach the shed with caution, pistols drawn, to finish the job. From a more distant point, five young fundamentalists armed with spades and knives rush toward the shed to investigate the source of all this clamor. Hamid still screams. In his sorrow, he pulls at his clothes in the traditional gestures of grief, and falls upon the body of his fallen adoptive father, who grunts at the impact. In his noisy mourning, it takes Hamid a while to register the grunt. And then he screams some more, from relief and pleasure, and hugs Malone and shakes him, while Malone winces from the pain at the back of his head, where it struck the floor, and tries to shake off the effects of shock and the stunning crash to his skull. One of the killers has reached the window and is peering in, but the angle is wrong and he sees nothing. Flattening themselves against the outer wall, he and his partner inch their way toward the door. Meanwhile, the angry fundamentalists are advancing on the intruders, who have spontaneously modified their plan. Someone inside is screaming, so someone inside is obviously alive. They now plan to take that person hostage and get themselves away from this mob, then shoot their hostage later on. They storm into the shack, they see a man lifeless on the floor and a boy kneeling over him, they grab the boy. Yanking him roughly to his feet, they put a pistol to his head. One of the men thinks about putting a bullet through the man's head, just to make absolutely sure he's totally dead, but he is distracted by furious shouting outside the door. The cavalry has arrived.

Malone is not dead, as we know, but he is nearly in a coma, a coma of fright. He can barely breathe. They actually shot at him, at him, for real, someone shot at him. His head still dizzy from the fall, Malone loses his sense of time and feels himself transported back to his boyhood, much of which was spent lying flat on his back, waiting for one group of bullies or another to get tired of punching him and leave. Yes, that is what he will do. He will just remain here, flat on his back, and eventually the bullies will get tired and go away.

Niggling away at his conscience, hindering this familiar solution, is a feeling, a feeling of responsibility, no . . . more than that, really, a feeling of love. He's not a little boy anymore. He hasn't been kicked by bullies, he's been shot by killers. These bad guys have captured his little sidekick, his pal. And they are armed. Struggling to breathe, fear squeezing his lungs and compressing his chest, Malone shakes off his lethargy and slithers gracelessly across the floor, on his back, toward his mattress and the gun.

The two assassins move sideways, crablike, to their car, keeping the group of angry young men at bay by dragging the boy along with them as their shield. On television, this always works, because everyone is afraid of harming the hostage. But our assassins are dealing with men of a different caliber. The young fundamentalists are incensed and combustible, Malone is confused and dizzy, and altogether they haven't got a rational brain cell between them.

On television, in a hostage situation, nobody shoots except the crack swat team, confident of angles, aim, and consequences. Here is how it goes, instead, in the Pakistani desert: Malone comes swaying out of the house. Every fiber in his body is screaming at him to run away; it takes absolutely all of his mental power to make himself, instead, walk right toward the danger. It takes absolutely all of his concentration to remember, from the long-ago days in rural Maryland, shooting at tin cans with a BB gun, how you aim these damn things. Not one brain cell is available to consider the nuances of a hostage situation.

Boom.

Malone fires.

His first shot goes far afield. The second shot gets one of the assassins in the shoulder. Blood comes seeping through the man's shirt. Hamid pulls himself free and runs away. The young fundamentalists converge on the assassins and throw them to the ground under a hail of blows. It looks as if they are going to be torn to pieces, but then someone shouts commandingly. It's the one they call Engineer. He marches over to the two men, who lie whimpering on the ground, and gives each of them a firm kick. He yells at them. They pitifully whimper something back. One can repeatedly make out the word "Khan," as they try to escape responsibility by referring Engineer to their master.

Engineer calls something out to Hamid, who tries, face screwed up in concentration, to translate it for Malone. "Not good," he says, gesturing to the two men. "Dog," he explains, pointing to them. "Khan dog. Engineer say, we make bumm! Finish?" he suggests invitingly, in conclusion, and signals to Malone to hand Engineer his rifle. Malone, appalled, looks at Engineer, who nods affirmatively.

"No!" Malone shouts, then collects himself. He breathes deeply in, out, in, then pulls his shoulders back and strolls over to Engineer, ever so cool, just as on television.

"Hey, thanks a lot, guys," he says. "But I think, you know, maybe we'll just let them go now. You know. I think it'll basically be less trouble that way, in the end."

Engineer seems to get the drift. He claps Malone on the shoulder and indicates to his comrades that they should let the men go. First he yells at both of them again, a long, very angry-sounding sentence, while the two of them nod eagerly and make their servile, terrified way, half creeping, half bowing, back to their car. The unhurt one shoves the injured one onto the backseat, then climbs behind the wheel and tries to start the engine. The mob bashes at their car for good measure, enamel chipping under the blades of their shovels. The battered car spins its wheels frantically in the sand, gains purchase, and drives away.

J ulia was upset and Khan became suspicious when the Maulana died. And Shabnam, who didn't love him either, is made nervous by it, too.

Something strange is happening, something very strange. Has some jinni decided to fulfill her evil wishes? Her enemies are conveniently perishing, one after the other, of unnatural causes.

She doesn't notice it right away. Not as soon as someone else might. Shabnam quite often wishes someone ill, wishes someone dead, and doesn't really mean it. She is an autocratic person, and besides, overstatement is part and parcel of upper-class Pakistani English. What a fiend! she will say, of her enemies. What a blight on the face of this earth! Why doesn't he crawl in a hole and die! Then, too, abrupt deaths are not uncommon in the North-West Frontier Province. It's a violent society, and violent things happen all the time. So it takes a while before Shabnam notices that a helpful jinni appears, unbidden, to be granting her evil wishes. Shabnam has merely to wish that this or that unpleasant individual might disappear from the face of the earth . . . and he does.

"That Nang is a disgusting, sleazy little worm," she had said, for example, when he turned up as one of the sponsors of fundamentalist legislation. "He's going to ruin everything that I've done! Why doesn't he crawl in some hole and die!"

And lo and behold, *alakazam*, he does just that.

"We have to figure out a way to stop that Jamal Abbas!" she had exclaimed, in genuine alarm, when his plans for the North-West Frontier Province's universities became known. Jamal Abbas, that had been someone she genuinely feared, someone with the potential to become a damaging adversary. "Why doesn't he just walk in front of a car bomb," she had wished.

And "Do you know what's wrong with Pakistani culture?" she had often asked, rhetorically, about the Maulana. "We have censorship, but the real garbage is on TV all the time. Just look at this revolting ball of lard lecturing about morality. Just look at his nasty stupid eyes. And thousands upon thousands of Pakistanis listen to him. He's a national enemy!"

And quick as a blink, *simsalabim*, the Maulana is gone forever! It's convenient, but it's a little eerie, too.

Shabnam is used to having her wishes fulfilled. She was born to it. But this is too much. Somewhere, somehow, an overzealous supernatural servant has taken it upon himself to fulfill Shabnam's dark, frivolous commands.

Well, Khan, following a similar train of thought, thinks he knows more. He thinks he knows who the mysterious jinni is, or at least that he knows that jinni's little female helper. First he will discover the details from the misguided little tramp. He will find out who she is operating for, and then he will decide on his course of action.

Fatima's mission, on previous trips to Mr. Khan's weekend retreat, was always straightforward. This trip is different. Neither party knows what it is that the other wants, but both can sense that this will be more than the usual transaction. Mushahed and Fatima don't speak during the drive. Maybe they are remembering the first time they drove this route. Both of them, that time, thought of themselves as jaded and worldly; both of them remember that time, now, as a time of great innocence.

Mushahed, besides, is angry. He wanted Fatima to refuse to go to the weekend house; he cannot understand her stubborn insistence that she will go, she must go. Fatima is preoccupied with her thoughts. Tonight, she must convince Khan to give her money, a lot of money.

Well, it won't be a lot for him, but for her, it is essential, absolutely essential that she succeed. Her life, bad as it was, has fallen to pieces; she must get the means to build another. With the Maulana dead, she will soon be without a roof over her head. Her brothers will come to fetch her, to deliver her to her fiancé and thereby to disaster. She must have the money to get away, to disappear to another town and open her little shop.

As for Mushahed, well, what of him? He knows her situation, and all he can do is stew and steam about the men she goes to see, without offering an alternative. Walid Khan is already in his house; he has had himself driven here, hours earlier. This weekend, he has not come to relax, he has not come to manipulate business deals in an ambience of culinary and erotic gentlemanly camaraderie. In fact, there are no other gentlemen expected this weekend. It will be Fatima and him, just Fatima and him. What a distinction for Fatima, if only she knew it; Khan is afraid of her, puzzled by her, intrigued by her, so much so that he has devoted an entire weekend of his precious time to solving her riddle. Tonight he will discover the truth about this little girl, one way or another.

A lot of things are in motion tonight; a lot of people are swerving from their accustomed paths. Fatima, passively usable little Fatima, is calculating, plotting, strategizing how best to seduce her way into lots of money. Khan is thinking, for the first time in his life, about the possible contents of a female brain. Isa is pacing the streets, with worry and suspicion in his heart. Then we have Mushahed. The chauffeur, but so much more than the chauffeur. He lets Fatima out at the door and waits for her to go inside. He is to go back to Peshawar tonight, and return the next afternoon. He turns the car around, heading back toward Peshawar. Then he parks it in a deserted orchard and sits for a few moments, listening to the grasshoppers and to the discordant humming in his own head. Mushahed has always preferred, in the past, not to think of Fatima with other men. He has thought of her, instead, as a kind of valuable but inert mineral stuff, like oil or uranium, mined against its will—no, as a material substance possessed of no will and therefore beyond guilt and innocence. But now, he turns the car around and heads back to his uncle's house. What are his intentions? Does he plan to intervene? To watch? Not wishing to be heard, he stops at some distance from the house, and trudges the rest of the way through the darkness, on foot.

Fatima, meanwhile, enters the lodge. She takes off her shoes and puts on slippers. She enters the main room. She drapes her chaddri over a chair; underneath she is wearing her best embroidered dress. Khan is already there, sipping scotch, slitting open envelopes with a silver knife, scrawling notes on the margins of each letter. He hears her, but pays her no attention. After a few minutes he leans back in his chair, and for a Strindbergian moment the two face each other. Khan's expression is decidedly unfriendly, cold. It freezes Fatima in place, but only for a moment. Then she comes to life, jerkily, like a puppet. She smiles tentatively and takes a step toward him. Her plan is simple. She will seduce him and then, when he isn't angry with her anymore, she will beg him to give her the money she needs for her tobacco shop. The thing is, though, Fatima has never taken the initiative before. So now, when she looks at this intimidating man with an expression of seductive intent, he finds her oddly menacing. Clearly, he has been wrong all along about this girl; he thought she was a helpless village girl, but now he suspects that she is the agent of a very dangerous and very well organized political group.

Khan leans back in his chair, fixing Fatima with a cool, thoughtful gaze. Fatima decides to take a more gradual approach, since he is so tense; she turns to step behind him, intending to massage his shoulders. He likes that; it will relax him, she thinks. Instead, Khan leaps to his feet as though stuck by a pin, and shoves her away.

"Don't touch me!" he yells.

In other circumstances, this could be very funny: our Khan, primly defending his virtue. "Don't touch me!" I'll bet he's never said that before to a young woman.

Then he grabs Fatima, who is totally perplexed, by the arm and shakes her.

"Don't think you can outsmart me, you stupid, conniving little bitch!" he screams. Fatima turns pale with fright. "Did you really think you could deceive me, *me*?" Khan snarls.

Fatima is afraid now. It does not occur to her that this might be rather harsh treatment for a woman who is trying to seduce a wealthy and powerful benefactor out of the pittance she needs to open a tobacco shop; it seems to her instead that he has somehow anticipated her plan and is appropriately angry. He's right, she is stupid. How could she ever have hoped to manipulate such a man?

In a rush of nearly incomprehensible sobbing, she tries to explain herself. Homeless, now that the Maulana is dead; can't go back to her family; just a little money still missing. No one could understand a word underneath that gush of tears and apologies. Hearing this delirious mess, Khan concludes only that she is guilty. "All right," he says, shoving her roughly into an armchair. "And now you will tell me who you really are."

Fatima searches for meaning in this sentence, but he is already continuing.

"I am going to listen to what you have to say, and be assured that I will listen carefully, and then I will decide what is to be done with you. You will tell me the names, all the names of the people in your organization. You will tell me where they live, and exactly what they are planning. You will tell me how they recruited you for this. And then I will decide what to do with you. Right now, I intend to have you killed. So you have nothing to lose by telling me the truth, and you may, you just possibly may, be able to persuade me to let you live."

There is more. Khan goes on to say that if she doesn't confess all, right now, then fine, he will just leave her here, tied to a chair, and send his goons. If she doesn't talk now, well, he can assure her that she will very definitely talk to them. One way or the other. Walid Khan is not by nature a violent man; nor would he ever stoop to the actual work of the blackmailing, the threats, the beatings, etc., that are part of the political process, and part of commerce, in his world. You hire people for those kinds of things. He would not actually lay a finger on Fatima himself, and it gives him no pleasure to think of others torturing her. He is a man of words and intellect, and would much prefer to deal with Fatima on that level, overcoming her by the force of his personality and his power. When he idly picks up his paper knife and waves it in Fatima's face, he is only underscoring his words; he might as well be holding a pencil.

Fatima is terrified, disoriented. Organization? Members? Plan? What is he talking about? Why is he so dreadfully angry? What does he want from her? What should she do? It occurs to Fatima briefly that perhaps this is a game, one of those incomprehensible games that rich men like to play. Is this, maybe, something like that Belly-Gram thing he wanted? If yes, what is she supposed to do? What does he want her to do?

As they silently face each other, Khan waiting for Fatima to confess, Fatima waiting for an erotic inspiration, there is a noise. Khan looks to the door, startled, alarmed. His heart starts pounding. Has he made a terrible mistake? Are the little whore's terrorist friends arriving? Has he misjudged, miscalculated? Fatima hears the noise, too. She sobs. It must be the goons, the bullies, coming to torture and kill her. Khan rushes to the window and peers out into the darkness. His rifle! He must get his hunting rifle! "You'll pay for this!" he shouts, in the direction of Fatima. "That's it! You've abused my patience long enough!"

Fatima decides to flee. She makes for the door, but Khan intercepts her. He grabs her arm, yelling threats. He drags her toward the back of the house, where he keeps his rifles. Fatima resists. She tries to grab on to things, to slow his progress. She grabs a chair, which topples. She grabs a table. Through her tears, she sees something glinting silver on the surface of the table, the letter opener. If she stabs at his fingers with it, will he let her go? Long enough for her to make it out the door? Stab at Khan's fingers? A dizzy shudder runs through Fatima, turning her mind into a blank. Mindlessly, her hand closes on the letter opener, but the combination of stretching and being shoved by Khan makes her lose her balance, and with a desperate little cry, she falls.

Meanwhile, Mushahed is making his way up the driveway, crunch, crunch, across the gravel. It is a cloudy night, very dark. In the dark he stumbles over something, a log, and kicks it out of the way. He stops for a moment, trying to decide on his approach. Should he go around the back, where the bedrooms are? Should he check out the living room first, where he sees light? Before he can decide, the door flies open and someone comes running out. It's Fatima! He calls out her name; she stops, bewildered, sees him, and throws herself into his arms. "Heaven has sent you!" she exclaims. "Mushahed, it's you! It's you! You are sent by heaven!"

This doesn't feel bad at all, Fatima in his arms, clinging to him, calling him a hero, but all too soon it is over. She pulls back and pleads, "Take me away from here. Let's get away!" Together they run down the driveway to the car. Fatima throws herself into the passenger seat and commences sobbing. Mushahed wants to know what happened, but obviously she can't speak. But he can guess what she would say! She loves him! She ran away from Khan because she loves him! That thought, combined with the tactile memory of her embrace, is more than Mushahed can bear, and so the evening culminates in yet another violent misunderstanding.

Mushahed stops the car. He only wants to calm Fatima down, and to talk to her; at least, that's what he tells himself. He reaches for her, but she pushes him away; he decides that some fresh air will do her good and comes around the car to help her out, she doesn't want to get out, and in the subsequent tangle of holding and pushing and crying and hugging, it's hard to say what is going on, exactly, until finally they are both lying on the ground beside the car, in a field.

Fatima doesn't care what happens, anymore; through a muddy eyewash of tears and kohl, she regards Mushahed as part of the dark karma of this awful night. She does not notice the rocks and twigs that scrape her back, her arms, her thighs; Mushahed, similarly in the grip of darkness, does not feel the stones that cut the palms of his hands, his knees, his legs, he feels nothing at all, really, certainly not pleasure.

Afterward, it is clear that Fatima cannot return to face Jamila in her state of distress; nor can she go where her relatives might at any moment appear to collect her. Given the limited choices, only one person comes to mind who is unconventional and benign enough to help them. Mushahed drives to Shabnam's house, hands over his disheveled girlfriend, and drives away again before he has to answer too many questions.

14

People are helpful to travelers in distress, in the Pakistani desert. So it isn't too long before a car comes by and stops for Sonia's distraught but clearly respectable, middle-aged driver. Julia races over to their savior, hoping for a chance to catch up with Mara somehow. But after that, events slow to an exasperating crawl.

The rescuer insists on examining the damaged car and spends some time clucking over their shocking experience. Someone shot at them! Can you imagine! What lawlessness. What are things coming to! Julia tries to talk him into following Mara's trail, but he studiously avoids looking at the hysterical foreign woman, especially after she has the terrible bad manners to try to offer him money. Ultimately, Julia has no choice but to meekly climb into his car and let him ferry them to the nearest village. Once there, it is quite a job to find a functioning telephone. At last they have Iqbal's office on the line, and are told that he is busy.

Julia grabs the receiver and throws a tantrum. She is threatening to call the embassy and *Newsweek* and is just about to mention CNN when the hapless assistant gives in and rushes away to get Iqbal. Who says he will come immediately, of course, is as good as on his way, if Julia will just tell him where she is. For that, she hands the phone to the driver. Then there is nothing to do but wait.

Iqbal has to summon a car and some backup and he has to come. He has to talk to the driver. He has to be elaborately and politely greeted by the owner of the telephone and by the person who gave them the lift. Then they all have to track back to where the smashed car waits. And then they have to set off into the desert, following the treadmarks of the earlier vehicles.

So it is about an hour later when Julia and Iqbal finally roar into the refugee camp accompanied by two Pakistani police cars. The crowd is still assembled, it is obvious that something of great magnitude has transpired, and Julia is so frantic by now that she doesn't even recognize Micky in that dusty brown mass of humanity. Well, just like his assassins, she, too, wasn't expecting him to look like one of the natives.

Their reunion causes some murmurs of alarm, until Iqbal shouts to the mob that these two foreigners are brother and sister. Well, that's okay, then. You're allowed to hug your sister. The crowd murmurs sympathetically and benign smiles approve of all subsequent embracing and carrying-on.

Meanwhile, Iqbal receives a muddled briefing on recent events from Engineer and the other young Talibanis. They describe the two assassins, and summarize the results of their interrogation. Iqbal is very upset to learn that he has only narrowly missed the fleeing assassins. Finally Mara comes driving up, confused and

alarmed at the sight of so many people, and all the ex-
planations have to be repeated, but finally they are on
their way back to town. Iqbal assigns both police vehicles as Micky's personal bodyguards and orders them
to deliver him directly into the American consulate compound and not come back until the Marine guards are
in physical possession of him. Then he starts organizing.
He orders the arrest of Khan, for sending out assassins.
He places an urgent call to the U.S. consul, to let him
know his citizen is on the way. Finally, in response to
Hakim's incessant pleading, he summons a tow truck to
haul Sonia's car back home.

If he weren't planning to arrest him, Iqbal wouldn't
find Khan so quickly. His office says he has gone to
the weekend house, driven there by his nephew. A couple of officers are dispatched to arrest him, but this
proves impossible. By the time they find him, he is thoroughly dead, his artery severed by an embossed, very
beautiful silver knife. And beside him, scrawled on an
envelope, it says: WHO CAN STOP DEATH?

Despite this additional murder and the philosophical
question it poses, Iqbal feels very hopeful. First of all,
the killer is down to the last verse of his song—that
seems like good news, right there. Better still, he knows
who has driven Khan to this isolated spot: the nephew.
Talking to Khan's assistant, who has no further cause to
be discreet or loyal to a dead employer, also brings to
light the existence of a shared woman, Fatima. Everything he hears about this young man is perfect, just perfect; perfect for a killer. He is a radical. He's in love with
his uncle's playmate. He is young and idealistic, just the

sort of person who would leave sentimental, meaningful little notes by his victims. And once he started killing, it was no big deal, in the heat of an argument, to kill his own uncle, too, for love or politics or both. Perfect, just perfect.

The following morning. Mushahed is still in bed, unaware of the noose that is forming itself around his neck. He has enough worries, even so. He is trying to decide what to do about Fatima. He should go and see her, he should make a plan for her, but he doesn't know what to do. How can he face her, after what happened by the roadside? How can he face Shabnam, if Fatima told her what happened by the roadside?

His sister knocks on the door. "Someone to see you," she calls.

Mushahed groans. "Who is it?" he wants to know. It can't be one of his friends, they would just come right in. He gets up reluctantly, slips into clothes, runs his fingers through his hair, and emerges from his room.

A slender, good-looking man is waiting for him in the living room. He studies Mushahed coolly before introducing himself.

"Detective Iqbal, Special Investigations, Islamabad," the man says. "I'm here to ask you why you killed your uncle."

Well, how's that for an opener? Shock and surprise drive the color right out of Mushahed's face and take his breath away. Iqbal nearly concludes that this fellow must be innocent, worse luck, but then the young man suddenly makes a dash for the door. This has been anticipated; two officers are right outside, waiting for just this eventuality. Nonetheless, it's a reflex, Iqbal moves quickly to intercept Mushahed, managing to seize his arm. As they struggle, the loose sleeves of Mushahed's shirt slide up above his elbows, revealing welts and scratches from his recent roadside tryst. The two officers hear the scuffle and rush inside. They pin Mushahed to the ground, calling "Sir! Sir!" to draw Iqbal's attention to these wounded arms. Iqbal does what he has to do. "Arrest him!" he says.

Under arrest, in a jail cell. Actually, this is a situation Mushahed has often dreamed of. You might say it is one of his favorite fantasies. In his fantasies, he is a political prisoner in a grim cell block. Abused, mocked, and threatened, he remains steadfast, until even the guards are impressed with his stoic courage. His fellow prisoners admire him and turn to him for teaching. As he enlightens them on the tenets of Marxism, they begin to organize themselves into discussion groups. In some of his daydreams, this political education culminates in a prison uprising, led by him . . .

Reality is a little different. Nobody tortures him, but the food is really bad, the bed is hard, and they wake you up at five. His fellow prisoners are smelly ruffians; they address him as "rich boy" and spit on the ground when he comes near them. There is very little romance in the situation. Nor is there much romance for Mushahed, anymore, in thinking about Fatima. Isn't it her fault, basically, that he's in this fix? A "fix," that's how Mushahed prefers to think of it—as an essentially minor matter that will eventually be cleared up. He prefers to suppress other thoughts: that the police are probably not even looking for the real killer anymore, since they think he is it. That under some political circumstances, in a country as corrupt as Mushahed has always made Pakistan out to be, when you're looking for a fall guy, almost anybody will do. Who killed his uncle? Well, no lack of candidates there. Dozens of enemies, of cheated business partners, of ruined opponents quickly come to mind. But nobody is looking into that anymore, because they have him—him with his scratched-up arms and legs. Of course, they asked him to explain his injuries. In mortal embarrassment, stammering and flushing, he finally had to tell Iqbal about the roadside interlude. "Doesn't look much like fun to me," the detective commented. "Looks more like rape, I would say. Looks like your so-called girlfriend put up quite a fight. Well, as soon as we find her she can tell us her version of the story. Or can she? You didn't kill her, as well, did you?"

Because Iqbal, hard as he has tried, has not been able to find Fatima. Well, he doesn't know where to look. There is no reason, no reason on earth, why he should ever think to look for her in Shabnam's house. There is absolutely no reason to think that Shabnam, a feudal progressive emancipated lady politician, should even know that Fatima, a downtrodden anonymous prostitute, exists. Much less that they might be acquaintances and, at the moment, flatmates.

Mushahed knows, obviously, but he isn't telling. Not yet, anyway. That much of his fantasy is still alive. "Even under torture, the brave young revolutionary steadfastly refuses to divulge the names of his comrades. His heroism inspires even his tormentors. One of the guards helps him escape. In thanks, the young revolutionary presses a tattered volume of Trotsky into his hands . . ."

It's surprisingly hard not to tell, though nobody is torturing him. It's surprisingly hard to hold on to his feelings for Fatima. It's hard even to conjure up an image of her; all he seems to be able to remember is the way they rolled around together in the dirt, like animals. And when he remembers that, it makes him think that she really is a whore, deep down inside. Through no fault of her own, of course, tragically, due to socioeconomic circumstance; but a whore nonetheless. He's never done anything like that before, so it had to be her influence, didn't it.

Meanwhile, Iqbal has caught yet another fish. He had posted an officer outside the Maulana's house, in case Fatima were to show up there. No Fatima, but the officer couldn't help but notice a suspicious individual, a young man, loitering all day outside the premises. He decided to take him in, only to discover that the young man was the missing Fatima's brother. Iqbal arrested him right away, of course. A jealous brother, that certainly was another promising candidate. First he had none, and now, in just one day, he has two very strong suspects! That's one too many, but it'll sort itself out. Until it does, he figures that the tersely dramatic announcement that "arrests have been made" should be enough for the press, and sends out a corresponding bulletin.

As with most Peshawar news bulletins, everyone knows all about it anyway, long before it's in print. Certainly Shabnam does, since, in Lilly, she has her own private source in the detective's household.

M icky and Julia are cosseted and gently debriefed at the consulate. Calls are made to their mother, who sobs in relief and screams for her sister, to Julia's newspaper, and to an exultant George at West-Fab. Micky is led away to the guest apartments for a bath and a change of clothes and a good night's sleep. Arrangements will be made for their journey home. As soon as possible, a small embassy plane will take them to Islamabad, where they will board a flight to London and connect with a flight to Washington.

Before this happens, though, Julia wants to say good-bye to Lilly. So, while Micky reacquaints himself with the amenities of modern life, takes showers, drinks beer, and watches CNN, Julia ducks out of the compound to visit her friend.

The servant lets her in and goes off to announce her arrival, but then he doesn't return for quite a while. She is beginning to think no one is home when he finally returns and ushers her in. Lilly and Gul are sitting on the couch, a little stiffly, it seems to Julia. Opposite them, an elegant young woman with a perfectly made-up, expressionless face is sitting in an armchair. She studies Julia coolly and nods unsmilingly in greeting when Lilly introduces them. So, Julia thinks, this is the famous Shabnam.

"There's been a new . . . development," Lilly says. "And I was just explaining to Shabnam that you are a good friend and that we can trust you." That's the kind of sentence that piques your curiosity. It works on Julia. She takes a seat and tries to look not too interested, to look nonchalantly trustworthy.

"Besides, it doesn't really affect you," Lilly continues. "There's no reason why you shouldn't be neutral in this matter. I think we can discuss it with you. You'll keep this confidential, won't you?"

Julia assures them that they can rely on her, absolutely. Shabnam does not look convinced, but she shrugs her shoulders and nods to Lilly to go on. Lilly picks up a yellow piece of paper and a white card and holds them out briefly for Julia's perusal.

"There's this girl, Fatima," she says. "She's only six-teen. The Maulana, that one on television? The one that got killed? He basically forced her to be a prostitute. She's a simple little girl from the country, she never went to school, but Shabnam says she's very bright. Shabnam has been trying to help her. Some of the guys that were killed, they were customers of Fatima. So sus-picion has fallen on her fiancé, and on her brother, for the murders. Fatima is at Shabnam's house, she's hiding there. But she found out that Iqbal arrested her brother and the fiancé, Mushahed. So she wanted to save them. Because she . . . because, she knows who the murderer is. Yes, that's right, she's a witness."

Lilly glances quickly at Shabnam, who nods slightly. Julia takes note of this interchange. Well, at least she knows now why the servant didn't admit her right away. First, they had to rehearse their story. But why are they lying to her? What's going on?

Lilly is speaking again. As she talks, her eyes keep sliding toward Shabnam, searching for reassurance.

"Yes, Fatima was a witness, but she was terrified. She couldn't possibly testify. She would have had to admit that she's a prostitute. You go to jail for that in Pakistan and you stay there forever. They never let you out again. She decided to commit suicide. She decided to write a note, in which she confessed to committing the murders herself, and then to kill herself. So she wrote this letter, a confession. She gave it to the chowkidar, and asked him to deliver it to the police. Well, Shabnam's chow-kidar certainly wasn't going to deliver a letter to the police without showing it to her first! So she was able to stop Fatima from committing suicide. She's going to get her out of the country. Shabnam's cousin works in the Pakistani embassy in London, so Fatima can travel there as part of his domestic staff. When she gets there, she can live with her brother. As soon as he gets released from jail, he can go back to England, and they can live together there!" Lilly explains brightly, perking up now that she has nearly finished her presentation.

"There's just one little problem, and we were just discussing it when you arrived," she goes on. "You see, we're not sure how to explain all of this to Iqbal. If Fatima is still in Pakistan when he finds all of this out, he'll surely want her to testify . . . but if she's gone already, and we explain it all to him very carefully the way we've explained it to you, will he really let Mushahed and her brother go?"

Not, Julia thinks to herself sardonically, unless he is highly gullible and a lot less bright than he seems. She is annoyed to be served up such a shoddy fabrication, insulted that they don't trust her, offended in her professional pride that they think she will swallow this. But she's confused, too.

It is like listening to one of those radio stations that get poor reception, where you hear a second station at the same time. Julia tries to follow Lilly's story, while at the same time trying to tune in to the second story, the one they don't want her to hear.

"I don't understand," she says, finally. "Why don't you just give Iqbal her letter of confession and persuade him to take her statement discreetly. He'll let her leave the country then, why shouldn't he? If she tells him who the real killer is, he should be able to nail him even without her official testimony. Anyway, who is the killer? Did she tell you?"

"Actually"—Shabnam takes over—"the person responsible for all the murders was Khan. Fatima heard him giving the orders for each of those killings. He was one of her customers. And the notes, mmm, the notes were just a distraction, to cloud the issue. And then, at some point, Khan realized that Fatima was dangerous, because she knew all of this about him. So he decided to get rid of her. He was planning to kill her at his week-end house, but he was clumsy about it and she was able to defend herself. She killed him, in self-defense. Yes. It was an accident, you could say. But we feel she must not go to trial for it. Just imagine, a young prostitute kills somebody as important as Khan. She will never get justice. She will surely be hanged. So, we have to get her out of the country, and we have to keep her out of this story completely."

Uh-huh. Julia spends a few moments thinking about this. Does it make sense? Not really. Would Khan kill the Maulana? Maybe. But why would he want to kill an Indian movie star?

"So our problem, you see . . ." Lilly begins, while Julia is still pondering, "our problem is how to let Iqbal know that Khan killed all the others, without telling him that Fatima killed Khan."

In her nervousness, Lilly is nearly wringing her hands. In the process, she drops the second piece of paper. Julia picks it up for her, a reflex. It is a greeting card, with garish golden letters and a green flag on it.

"Isn't this a holiday card?" Julia blurts out. "Hey, this looks just like that African card that one of the murder messages was on."

She doesn't even think about what she is saying, really, she is just sort of stream-of-consciousness commenting on what is in front of her.

"Oh, Fatima was just trying to make her confession more credible by sending that along. Who knows where she got that from, maybe from Khan's office . . ."

Shabnam interrupts Lilly's stammering to say, with some irritation, "Look. It's just a lot simpler if Iqbal doesn't find out that Fatima knows how to write. He would never expect someone like her to be literate, and it's best to leave it that way. Then he won't ask himself if she committed the other murders, because he'll assume she couldn't have written the notes. And she didn't! So you see, this way it's just simpler for everybody, including Iqbal."

This does not immediately make sense, if indeed Fatima only committed one of the murders and only in self-defense, but before Julia has a chance to react to yet another twist of logic, Shabnam is addressing her.

"Julia," she says, "I didn't want you to hear this story, because I didn't think you would understand. Things are different here. You can't always do things directly, here, because there are too many factors to consider. You have to consider the family, its honor, you have to respect people's obligations and their political ties . . . That doesn't mean justice is not served, in the end. Take your own case, for example. Khan wanted to have your brother killed. But as things turned out, your brother is just fine, while Khan is dead—that's justice right there, isn't it? Was any one of those perverts that got murdered worth shedding a tear over? Would justice be served if that poor little girl gets hanged? Of course not. But we have to be mindful of Iqbal, too. He has a job, he has his responsibilities, we can't expect too much of him. In the end, he would agree that our way is best."

"What can't we expect of Iqbal?" a male voice asks. The smell of conspiracy is so thick in the room that even Julia jumps at the sound, though she is surely the least guilty party present.

In the utter silence that greets Iqbal's unexpected arrival, there is only one sound to be heard: the hasty slap-ping sound of Gul stuffing two pieces of paper under a stack of magazines.

Iqbal walks directly to his wife and gestures com-mandingly for them to be handed over; instead, Gul gets up and stands by the window, hands clasped defiantly before her.

Iqbal watches her with some surprise; then he stalks over to the magazine stack and starts rummaging through it on his own for the contraband. He is studying the two pieces of paper when Shabnam starts talking.

"Actually, it's just as well that you're here," she says calmly. "We wanted to spare you, that's true, but in the end it's probably better this way. It's better if we work this out together." And then she tells Iqbal that Mu-shahed and Isa are innocent, that they have an airtight alibi. They were at her house the night Khan was killed. All three of them were there, Mushahed, Fatima, and her brother. Her chowkidar let them in, her servant ad-mitted them to the living room, her other servant brought them tea—all of which, of course, these many witnesses will be happy to testify to. "I'm sure," Iqbal murmurs. "To that, and to anything else." Shabnam ig-nores his sarcasm, except to allow herself a tiny smile. Julia listens with interest. So, here comes still another version! The third one within one hour. No suicidal self-sacrifice this time, and no courageous self-defense. At least she knows, now, why they lied to her. Apparently she was the dress rehearsal, and they were not satisfied with their performance. To her own surprise, Julia finds herself rooting for Shabnam, for the success of her improvisation.

In this new, improved version, Shabnam claims that Isa, Mushahed, and Fatima came to tell her about a se-rious disagreement that had taken place between Fatima and Khan. Fatima wanted to quit being a prostitute, and Khan thought that was disloyal. Fearing his anger, they came to ask Shabnam for help. Because she knew Khan quite well, of course; her father did a great deal of business with him. She had immediately phoned Khan in his weekend house and commiserated with him. So annoying, these troubles with servants! Then she had put in a good word on Fatima's behalf, had explained that her brother was shocked at her immoral life and wanted her to mend her ways, that this was the only reason she was seeking to leave his employment. This conversation, Shabnam says, took place at about 10 p.m., and when she spoke to him, Khan was absolutely healthy and hale. Since Fatima and her brother had no suitable accommodation for the night, she then put up all three of them, the brother and sister and Mushahed, too, in her guest rooms; a fact to which, of course, her employees can and will attest. So as Iqbal can plainly see, there was no way that any one of them could have committed a murder in Khan's country house, miles away, that evening. All present and accounted for! So, as Iqbal will surely agree, there is no reason to keep two innocent young men in prison! Especially not since her father needs Mushahed urgently for one of his offices in Saudi Arabia, and is taking a particular interest in Isa's studies, which require him to return to London ASAP for the start of the new term. Not every case can be solved, Shabnam philosophically concludes. In fact, statistically speaking, the majority remain unsolved, don't they? No disgrace there, then. Iqbal certainly gave it his all, a fact which she intends to point out to her father. He likes to hear about intelligent and diligent officials so that he can help the Minister of Justice promote the right individuals.

It's pretty crude, but Shabnam tempers it with a slight

CHERYL BENARD

smile, inviting Iqbal to be her collaborator in this little feudal game.

When he finally answers, though, he doesn't address Shabnam at all. He speaks to his wife. "Gul," he says. "I want to know what went on here, before I walked in."

His tone is cold, bare of the politeness with which he usually addresses his wife.

What will she do? The three other women find the moment quite suspenseful. If there is a weak link in this chain, they know, then Gul is it. Will this quiet, withdrawn little person have the nerve to lie to her police-official husband? Or will she blabber everything out? Actually, she does neither.

"You must let the girl leave the country," she says to Iqbal, very gently. "After what the child has gone through, you must let her leave the country and have a chance at a new life."

"Thank you for your opinion on that," Iqbal replies frostily. "But that is not what I asked you. I want to know what was being discussed here, when I walked in."

Gul looks straight at him. "We were discussing justice," she says.

Her voice is as quiet as ever, but there is steel in it. If anything, she sounds harsher than the arrogantly commanding Shabnam. Iqbal looks about him in some amazement. His eyes move around the room as he takes the other occupants in, one by one. He surveys them thoughtfully: his friend and verbal sparring partner Lilly; his pretty, compliant little wife; the bossy rich girl; and the American journalist. There they are, four women who have just attempted to derail his murder investigation by concealing crucial evidence under a pile

260

of old *Vogue* magazines and who meet his eye even now, unblinking and unrepentant. None of them looks the least bit sorry, though, if anything, the American looks slightly more distressed than the others.

"I can only conclude that you have all lost your minds," he says, finally. "Accessory after the fact, perjury, conspiracy to commit perjury, concealing evidence in a felony murder investigation . . . I guess you have all gone crazy."

"Some things can make you crazy," Gul replies.

They stare at each other. After what seems like a very long time, Iqbal glances once more at the two pieces of paper in his hand, nods curtly, and hands them back to Gul. Then he leaves the house.

The airplane ascends, rushing up and away from the streets and houses, which get ever smaller, smaller. Fatima peers down intently, she can see the dome of a mosque, she can see streets, she can see the flat tops of houses, she tries to think which way her village is. Will she fly over her village? If she looks very, very hard, will she see her old home? The airplane rises higher, higher, and soon she sees only drab yellow dust, no, not even yellow, just a monotonous, dreary tan. Fatima discovers that she has been clutching the armrests of her chair and sitting tautly forward; she leans back in her seat now, and closes her eyes. Her village. Her home. Herself, still a child. Perhaps she will just never think about it again, perhaps she will forget it, let it grow dusty and drab in her memory. As it is, eyes closed, vents blowing cold air over her, unfamiliar engine noises whining in her ears, thinking about her childhood evokes two memories only.

One picture, and two memories. In her memory, Fatima sees the barn. In the barn she sees herself. It is her job to kill the rabbits, behind the barn. How she has begged to be excused from this job, and earned only slaps and curses for her disobedience. So little Fatima kills the rabbits; skins them, too. She can just manage to do it if she is quick, and with time, she becomes very quick. A knife, a slash, then blood.

Fatima learns, over time, to blot those minutes right out of her head, to deliver the rabbits to her mother for cooking, shake her hair, and repress the bloody memory. She can make herself feel as if it never happened. Until the next time they send her out.

The barn holds a happier memory, too. She sees herself sitting behind it, with her brother. It is summer, a summer five years ago. Her brother is nineteen and sorry that he hit her, sorry that he bossed her around, sorry that her life is so much worse than his. He is spending the summer at home. Making things up to Fatima is one of his summer tasks. They sit behind the chicken coop, in the sunshine, out of everybody's sight, and what are their heads bent over? Fatima smiles, remembering the reading primer, remembering her brother teaching her the alphabet. Making her a present of the words of God and Marx, as he says dramatically. Whichever she should choose one day, he says, looking at her fondly with tears of emotion shimmering in his eyes, her sweet brother.

But never mind God or Marx, Fatima has more profane things to read right now, such as the menu card for her in-flight meal. Not the chicken, she thinks, no. Not with the memory of blood still on her mind. The vegetable curry, she decides, is what she will ask for.

———

Sweet brother Isa returns to his studies in London. He has no regrets. Those days in jail were scary, he had bad dreams there, dreams of choking inside a green chaddri, but he hasn't dreamed it once, now that he's back in London. In the dream, the Indian film star pulls up the chador, but instead of coming off, it wraps itself around Isa's face and neck tighter, tighter, until he can't breathe . . . But the dream is gone now, and after all the Indian had assaulted him, and was a pervert . . . and exams are in a month, and Peshawar is as far away as a bad dream.

Iqbal smarts under his failure, but his superiors see things differently. They are very pleased with him, actually. Didn't he miraculously bring an American citizen back to life? That alone should be worth two fighter jets, in the next aid deal. The warm praise he received from local notable Mansuri doesn't hurt, either. His boss tells him more or less directly that with sponsorship like that, he should make the next grade within the year.

Through Mara's good agencies, Hamid's mother is placed in a training program for midwives, job guaranteed upon graduation. She leaves the camp and receives a room for herself and Hamid in the nurses' home. Hamid starts school in Peshawar. Malone sends them money every month; Mara was very insistent that twenty dollars would be absolutely adequate, but he chooses to make them affluent at double that amount, and is already plotting to bring Hamid to America for college.

Mara escorts Farid on a tour of her refugee projects. She is extremely frosty, but he is extremely charming, and by the end of the day is making excellent headway.

Micky gets quite a bit of mileage out of his adventure. State Department officials come to debrief him; the secretaries at West-Fab swoon over his incredible weight loss and consult him about their diet and exercise plans; his boss, who turns out to be completely innocent of any planned wrongdoing, trots him out at board meetings and takes him to his snazzy golf club every other weekend to tell his Heroic American Businessman story to all his rich friends, who in turn invite him as the keynote speaker to seminars and gala events. Julia goes home to her goldfish and knocks off a proposal for a PBS special on the women's movement in the Islamic world, which is accepted.

So if nothing else, the whole episode at least was good for everybody's career.

And Fatima? I think she will be happy; I think she will do well. She really is exceptionally beautiful; heads turn and hearts break even on the airplane when Fatima passes through the aisles. Withdrawn and exotic, stunning and aloof, Islamic but accustomed to taking off her clothes, perhaps Fatima will become a model. Perhaps we will find her, one day, in the pages of *Vogue*, looking arrogant in a little two-string bikini, pleated green silk chaddri flung onto a beach chair for color and effect. Just think what Helmut Newton could do with Fatima and her chador.